The Last Thing He Told Me

A Novel

Laura Dave

Simon & Schuster

NEW YORK · LONDON · TORONTO
SYDNEY · NEW DELHI

To Josh and Jacob, my sweetest miracles
and
Rochelle and Andrew Dave,
for every single thing

CONTENTS

Prologue

Owen used to like to tease me about how I lose everything, about how, in my own way, I have raised losing things to an art form. Sunglasses, keys, mittens, baseball hats, stamps, cameras, cell phones, Coke bottles, pens, shoelaces. Socks. Lightbulbs. Ice trays. He isn't exactly wrong. I did used to have a tendency to misplace things. To get distracted. To forget.

On our second date, I lost the ticket stub for the parking garage where we'd left the cars during dinner. We'd each taken our own car. Owen would later joke about this—would love joking about how I insisted on driving myself to that second date. Even on our wedding night he joked about it. And I joked about how he'd grilled me that night, asking endless questions about my past—about the men I'd left behind, the men who had left me.

He'd called them the could-have-been boys. He raised a glass to them and said, wherever they were, he was grateful to them for not being what I needed, so he got to be the one sitting across from me.

You barely know me, I'd said.

He smiled. *It doesn't feel that way, does it?*

He wasn't wrong. It was overwhelming, what seemed to live between us, right from the start. I like to think that's why I was distracted. Why I lost the parking ticket.

We parked in the Ritz-Carlton parking garage in downtown San Francisco. And the parking attendant shouted that it didn't matter if I claimed I'd only been there for dinner.

The fee for a lost parking ticket was a hundred dollars. "You could have kept the car here for weeks," the parking attendant said. "How do I know you're not trying to pull a fast one? A hundred dollars plus tax for every lost stub. Read the sign." A hundred dollars plus tax to go home.

"Are you sure that it's lost?" Owen asked me. But he was smiling as he said it, as if this were the best piece of news about me that he'd gotten all night.

I was sure. I searched every inch of my rented Volvo anyway and of Owen's fancy sports car (even though I'd never been in it) and of that gray, impossible parking garage floor. No stub. Not anywhere.

The week after Owen disappeared, I had a dream of him standing in that parking lot. He was wearing the same suit—the same charmed smile. In the dream he was taking off his wedding ring.

Look, Hannah, he said. *Now you've lost me too.*

Part 1

I have little patience with scientists who take a board of wood, look for its thinnest part, and drill a great number of holes where drilling is easy.

—Albert Einstein

If You Answer the Door for Strangers...

You see it all the time on television. There's a knock at the front door. And, on the other side, someone is waiting to tell you the news that changes everything. On television, it's usually a police chaplain or a firefighter, maybe a uniformed officer from the armed forces. But when I open the door—when I learn that everything is about to change for me—the messenger isn't a cop or a federal investigator in starched pants. It's a twelve-year-old girl, in a soccer uniform. Shin guards and all.

"Mrs. Michaels?" she says.

I hesitate before answering—the way I often do when someone asks me if that is who I am. I am and I'm not. I haven't changed my name. I was Hannah Hall for the thirty-eight years before I met Owen, and I didn't see a reason to become someone else after. But Owen and I have been married for a little over a year. And, in that time, I've learned not to correct people either way. Because what they really want to know is whether I'm Owen's wife.

It's certainly what the twelve-year-old wants to know, which leads me to explain how I can be so certain that she is twelve, having spent most of my life seeing people in two broad categories: child and adult. This change is a result of the last year and a half, a result of my husband's daughter, Bailey, being the stunningly disinviting age of sixteen. It's a result of my mistake, upon first meeting the guarded Bailey, of telling her that she looked younger than she was. It was the worst thing I could have done.

Maybe it was the second worst. The worst thing was probably my attempt to make it better by cracking a joke about how I wished someone would age me down. Bailey has barely stomached me since, despite the fact that I now know better than to try to crack a joke of any kind with a sixteen-year-old. Or, really, to try and talk too much at all.

But back to my twelve-year-old friend standing in the doorway, shifting from dirty cleat to dirty cleat.

"Mr. Michaels wanted me to give you this," she says.

Then she thrusts out her hand, a folded piece of yellow legal paper inside her palm. HANNAH is written on the front in Owen's writing.

I take the folded note, hold her eyes. "I'm sorry," I say. "I'm missing something. Are you a friend of Bailey's?"

"Who's Bailey?"

I didn't expect the answer to be yes. There is an ocean between twelve and sixteen. But I can't piece this together. Why hasn't Owen just called me? Why is he involving this girl? My first guess would be that something has happened to Bailey, and Owen couldn't break away. But Bailey is at home, avoiding me as she usually does, her blasting music (today's selection: *Beautiful: The Carole King Musical*) pulsing all the way down the stairs, its own looping reminder that I'm not welcome in her room.

"I'm sorry. I'm a little confused... where did you see him?"

"He ran past me in the hall," she says.

For a minute I think she means our hall, the space right behind us. But that doesn't make sense. We live in a floating home on the bay, a houseboat as they are commonly called, except here in Sausalito, where there's a community of them. Four hundred of them. Here they are floating homes—all glass and views. Our sidewalk is a dock, our hallway is a living room.

"So you saw Mr. Michaels at school?"

"That's what I just said." She gives me a look, like *where else*? "Me and my friend Claire were on our way to practice. And he asked us to drop this off. I said I couldn't come until after practice and he said, fine. He gave us your address."

She holds up a second piece of paper, like proof.

"He also gave us twenty bucks," she adds.

The money she doesn't hold up. Maybe she thinks I'll take it back.

"His phone was broken or something and he couldn't reach you. I don't know. He barely slowed down."

"So... he said his phone was broken?"

"How else would I know?" she says.

Then her phone rings—or I think it's a phone until she picks it off her waist and it looks more like a high-tech beeper. Are beepers back?

Carole King show tunes. High-tech beepers. Another reason Bailey probably doesn't have patience for me. There's a world of teen things I know absolutely nothing about.

The girl taps away on her device, already putting Owen and her twenty-dollar mission behind her. I'm reluctant to let her go, still unsure about what is going on. Maybe this is some kind of weird joke. Maybe Owen thinks this is funny. I don't think it's funny. Not yet, anyway.

"See you," she says.

She starts walking away, heading down the docks. I watch her get smaller and smaller, the sun down over the bay, a handful of early evening stars lighting her way.

Then I step outside myself. I half expect Owen (my lovely and silly Owen) to jump out from the side of the dock, the rest of the soccer team giggling behind him, the lot of them letting me in on the prank I'm apparently not getting. But he isn't there. No one is.

So I close our front door. And I look down at the piece of yellow legal paper still folded in my hand. I haven't opened it yet.

It occurs to me, in the quiet, how much I don't want to open it. I don't want to know what the note says. Part of me still wants to hold on to this one last moment—the moment where you still get to believe this is a joke, an error, a big nothing; the moment before you know for sure that something has started that you can no longer stop.

I unfold the paper.

Owen's note is short. One line, its own puzzle.

Protect her.

Greene Street Before It Was Greene Street

I met Owen a little over two years ago.

I was still living in New York City then. I was living three thousand miles from Sausalito, the small Northern California town that I now call home. Sausalito is on the other side of the Golden Gate from San Francisco, but a world away from city life. Quiet, charming. Sleepy. It's the place that Owen and Bailey have called home for more than a decade. It is also the polar opposite of my previous life, which kept me squarely in Manhattan, in a lofted storefront on Greene Street in SoHo—a small space with an astronomical rent I never quite believed I could afford. I used it as both my workshop and my showroom.

I turn wood. That's what I do for work. People usually make a face when I tell them this is my job (however I try to describe it), images of their high school woodshop class coming to mind. Being a woodturner is a little like that, and nothing like that. I like to describe it as sculpting, but instead of sculpting clay, I sculpt wood.

I come by the profession naturally. My grandfather was a woodturner—an excellent one, at that—and his work was at the center of my life for as far back as I can remember. He was at the center of my life for as far back as I can remember, having raised me mostly on his own.

My father, Jack, and my mother, Carole (who preferred that I refer to her as Carole), were largely uninterested in doing any childrearing. They were largely uninterested in anything except my father's photography career. My grandfather encouraged my mother to make an effort with me when I was young, but I barely knew my father, who traveled for work 280 days a year. When he did have time off, he hunkered down at his family's ranch in Sewanee, Tennessee, as opposed to driving the two hours to my grandfather's house in Franklin to spend time with me. And, shortly after my sixth birthday, when my father left my mother for his assistant—a woman named Gwendolyn who was newly twenty-one—my mother stopped coming home as well. She chased my father down until he took her back. Then she left me with my grandfather full-time.

If it sounds like a sob story, it isn't. Of course, it isn't ideal to have your mother all but disappear. It certainly didn't feel good to be on the receiving end of that choice. But, when I look back now, I think my mother did me a favor exiting the way she did—without apology, without vacillation. At least she made it clear: There was nothing I could have done to make her want to stay.

And, on the other side of her exit, I was happier. My grandfather was stable and kind and he made me dinner every night and waited for me to finish dinner before he announced it was time to get up and read me stories before we went to sleep. And he always let me watch him work.

I loved watching him work. He'd start with an impossibly enormous piece of wood, moving it over a lathe, turning it into something magical. Or, if it was less than magical, he would figure out how to start over again.

That was probably my favorite part of watching him work: when he would throw up his hands and say, "*Well, we've got to do this different, don't we?*" Then he'd go about finding a new way into what he wanted to create. I'm guessing any psychologist worth her salt would say that it must have given me hope—that I must have thought my grandfather would help me do the same thing for myself. To start again.

But, if anything, I think I took comfort in the opposite. Watching my grandfather work taught me that not everything was fluid. There were certain things that you hit from different angles, but you never gave up on. You did the work that was needed, wherever that work took you.

I never expected to be successful at woodturning—or at my foray from there into making furniture. I half expected I wouldn't be able to make a living out of it. My grandfather regularly supplemented his income by picking up construction work. But early on, when one of my more impressive dining room tables was featured in *Architectural Digest*, I developed a niche among a subset of downtown New York City residents. As one of my favorite interior designers explained it, my clients wanted to spend a lot of money decorating their homes in a way that made it look like they weren't spending any money at all. My rustic wood pieces helped with their mission.

Over time, this devoted clientele turned into a somewhat larger clientele in other coastal cities and resort towns: Los Angeles, Aspen, East Hampton, Park City, San Francisco.

This was how Owen and I met. Avett Thompson—the CEO of the tech firm where Owen worked—was a client. Avett and his wife, the ridiculously gorgeous Belle, were among my most loyal clients.

Belle liked to joke that she was Avett's trophy wife, which may have been funnier if it also wasn't so on point. She was a former model, ten years younger than his grown children, born and raised in Australia. My pieces were in every room of her town house in San Francisco (where she and Avett lived together) and her newly constructed country house in St. Helena, a small town on the northern end of Napa

Valley where Belle tended to retreat alone.

I had met Avett only a handful of times before he and Owen showed up at my workshop. They were in New York for an investor meeting and Belle wanted them to stop by to check on a rolled-edge side table she'd asked me to make for their bedroom. Avett wasn't sure what he should be checking for, something about how the table would look with the bed frame—the bed frame that would hold their ten-thousand-dollar organic mattress.

Avett couldn't have cared less, honestly. When he and Owen walked in, he was in a sharp blue suit, his graying hair crunchy with hair gel, the phone glued to his ear. He was in the middle of a phone call. He took one look at the side table and briefly covered the mouthpiece.

"Looks fine to me," he said. "We good here?"

Then, before I answered, he headed outside.

Owen, on the other hand, was mesmerized. He did a slow sweep of the whole workshop, stopping to study each piece.

I watched him as he walked around. He was such a confusing picture: This long-limbed guy with shaggy blond hair and sun-drenched skin, in worn-out Converse sneakers. All of which seemed at odds with his fancy sports jacket. It was almost like he fell off a surfboard into the jacket, the starched shirt beneath it.

I realized I was staring and started to turn away just as Owen stopped in front of my favorite piece—a farm table that I used as a desk.

My computer and newspapers and small tools covered most of it. You could only make out the table beneath if you were really looking. He was. He took in the stiff redwood that I had chiseled down, gently yellowing the corners, welding rough metal to each edge.

Was Owen the first customer to notice the table? No, of course not. But he was the first to bend down, just like I'd often do, running his fingers along the sharp metal and holding the table there.

He turned his head and looked up at me. "Ouch," he said.

"Try bumping up against it in the middle of the night," I said.

Owen stood back up, giving the table a tap goodbye. Then he walked over to me. He walked over to me until somehow we were standing close to each other—too close, really, for me not to wonder how we'd gotten there. I probably should have felt self-conscious about my tank top and paint-splattered jeans, the messy bun on top of my head, my unwashed curls falling out of it. I felt something else though, watching him look at me.

"So," he said, "what's the asking price?"

"Actually, the table is the only piece in the showroom that's not for sale," I said.

"Because it could cause injury?" he said.

"Exactly," I said.

This was when he smiled. When Owen smiled. It was like the title of a bad pop song. To be clear, it wasn't that his smile lit up his face. It wasn't anything as sentimental or explosive as that. It was more that his smile—this generous, childlike smile—made him seem kind. It made him seem kind in a way I wasn't used to running into on Greene Street in downtown Manhattan. It was expansive in a way I'd started to doubt I'd ever run into on Greene Street in downtown Manhattan.

"So, no negotiating on the table then?" he said.

"Afraid not, but I could show you some different pieces?"

"How about a lesson instead? You could show me how to make a similar table for myself, but maybe with slightly kinder edges..." he said. "I'll sign a waiver. Any injuries acquired would be at my own risk."

I was still smiling, but I felt confused. Because all of a sudden I didn't think we were talking about the table. I felt fairly confident that we weren't. I felt as confident as a woman could who had spent the last two years engaged to a man whom she'd realized she couldn't marry. Two weeks before their wedding.

"Look, Ethan..." I said.

"Owen," he corrected.

"Owen. That's nice of you to ask," I said, "but I kind of have a no-dating policy with clients."

"Well, it's a good thing I can't afford to buy anything you're selling then," he said.

But that stopped him. He shrugged, as if to say *some other time,* and headed toward the door and Avett, who was pacing back and forth on the sidewalk, still on his phone call, yelling at the person on the other end.

He was almost out the door. He was almost gone. But I felt instantly—and strongly—the need to reach out and stop him from leaving, to say that I hadn't meant it. I'd meant something else. I'd meant he should stay.

I'm not saying it was love at first sight. What I'm saying is that a part of me wanted to do something to stop him from walking away. I wanted to be around that stretched-out smile a little longer.

"Wait," I said. I looked around, searching for something to hold him there, zeroing in on a textile that belonged to another client, holding it up. "This is for Belle."

It was not my finest moment. And, as my former fiancé would tell you, it was also completely out of character for me to reach out to someone as opposed to pulling away.

"I'll make sure she gets it," he said.

He took it from me, avoiding my eyes.

"For the record, I have one too. A no-dating policy. I'm a single father, and it goes with the territory..." He paused. "But my daughter's a theater junkie. And I'll lose serious points if I don't see a play while I'm in New York."

He motioned toward an angry Avett, screaming on the sidewalk.

"A play's not exactly Avett's thing, as surprising as that sounds..."

"Very," I said.

"So… what do you think? Do you want to come?"

He didn't move closer, but he did look up. He looked up and met my eyes.

"Let's not consider it a date," he said. "It will be a onetime thing. We'll agree on that going in. Just dinner and a play. Nice to meet you."

"Because of our policies?" I said.

His smile returned, open and generous. "Yes," he said. "Because of them."

"What's that smell?" Bailey asks.

I'm pulled from my memory to find Bailey standing in the kitchen doorway. She looks irritated standing there in a chunky sweater—a messenger bag slung over her shoulder, her purple-streaked hair caught beneath its strap.

I smile at her, my phone cradled under my chin. I have been trying to reach Owen, unsuccessfully, the phone going to voice mail. Again. And again.

"Sorry, I didn't see you there," I say.

She doesn't respond, her mouth pinched. I put my phone away, ignoring her perma-scowl. She's a beauty, despite it. She's a beauty in a way that I've noticed strikes people when she walks into a room. She doesn't look much like Owen—her purple hair naturally a chestnut brown, her eyes dark and fierce. They're intense—those eyes. They pull you in. Owen says that they're just like her grandfather's (her mother's father), which is why they named her after him. A girl named Bailey. Just Bailey.

"Where's my dad?" she says. "He's supposed to drive me to play practice."

My body tenses as I feel Owen's note in my pocket, like a weight.

Protect her.

"I'm sure he's on his way," I say. "Let's eat some dinner."

"Is that what smells?" she says.

She wrinkles her nose, just in case it isn't clear that the smell to which she is referring isn't one she likes.

"It's the linguine that you had at Poggio," I say.

She gives me a blank look, as though Poggio isn't her favorite local restaurant, as though we weren't there for dinner just a few weeks before to celebrate her sixteenth birthday. Bailey ordered that night's special—a homemade multigrain linguini in a brown butter sauce. And Owen gave her a little taste of his glass of Malbec to go with it. I thought she loved the pasta. But maybe what she loved was drinking wine with her father.

I put a heaping portion on a plate and place it on the kitchen island.

"Try a little," I say. "You're going to like it."

Bailey stares at me, trying to decide if she is in the mood for a showdown—if she's in the mood for her father's disappointment, should I snitch to him about her fast, dinnerless exit. Deciding against it, she bites back her annoyance and hops onto her barstool.

"Fine," she says. "I'll have a little."

Bailey almost tries with me. That's the worst part. She isn't a bad kid or a menace. She's a good kid in a situation she hates. I just happen to be that situation.

There are the obvious reasons why a teenage girl would be averse to her father's new wife, especially Bailey, who had a good thing going when it was just the two of them together, best friends, Owen her biggest fan. Though, those reasons don't cover the totality of Bailey's dislike for me. It isn't just that I got her age wrong when we first met. It comes down to an afternoon shortly after I moved to Sausalito. I was supposed to pick her up at school, but I got stuck on a call with a client—and I arrived five minutes late. Not ten minutes. Five. 5:05 P.M. That was what the clock said when I pulled up to her friend's house. But it may as well have been an hour. Bailey is an exacting girl. Owen will tell you that this is a quality we have in common. Both his wife and his daughter can decipher everything about someone else in five minutes. That's all it takes. And in the five minutes Bailey was making her decision about me I was on a telephone call I shouldn't have taken.

Bailey twirls some pasta onto her fork, studying it. "This looks different than Poggio."

"Well, it's not. I convinced the sous chef to give me the recipe. He even sent me to the Ferry Building to pick up the garlic bread he serves with it."

"You drove into San Francisco to get a loaf of bread?" she says.

It's possible that I try too hard with her. There is that.

She leans in and puts the whole bite in her mouth. I bite my lip, anticipating her approval—a small yum escaping her lips, in spite of herself.

Which is when she gags on it. She actually gags, reaching for a glass of water.

"What did you put in that?" she says. "It tastes like… charcoal."

"But I tasted it," I say. "It's perfect."

I take another bite myself. She's not wrong. In my confusion over my twelve-year-old visitor and Owen's note, the butter sauce had transformed from its slightly malted, foamy richness into actually just being burnt. And bitter. Not unlike eating a campfire.

"I gotta go anyway," she says. "Especially if I want to get a ride from Suz."

Bailey stands up. And I picture Owen standing behind me, leaning down to whisper in my ear, *Wait it out.* That's what he says when Bailey is dismissive of me. Wait it out. Meaning—she'll come around one day. Also meaning—she's leaving for college in two and a half short years. But Owen doesn't understand that this doesn't comfort me. To me, this just means I'm running out of time to make her want to move toward me.

And I do want her to move toward me. I want us to have a relationship, and not just because of Owen. It's more than that—what draws me toward Bailey even as she pushes me away. Part of it is that I recognize in her that thing that happens when you lose your mother. My mother left by choice, Bailey's by tragedy, but it leaves a similar imprint on you either way. It leaves you in the same strange place, trying to figure out how to navigate the world without the most important person watching.

"I'll walk over to Suz's," she says. "She'll drive me."

Suz, her friend Suz, who is also in the play. Suz who lives on the docks too. Suz who is safe, isn't she?

Protect her.

"Let me take you," I say.

"*No.*" She pulls her purple hair behind her ears, checks her tone. "That's okay. Suz is going anyway…"

"If your father isn't back yet," I say, "I'll come and pick you up. One of us will be waiting for you out front."

She drills me with a look. "Why wouldn't he be back?" she says.

"He will. I'm sure he will. I just meant… if I come get you, then you can drive home."

Bailey just got her learner's permit. It'll be a year of her driving with an adult until she can drive alone. And Owen doesn't like her driving at night, even when she's with him, which I try to utilize as an opportunity.

"Sure," Bailey says. "Thanks."

She walks toward the door. She wants out of the conversation and into the Sausalito air. She would say anything to get there, but I take it as a date.

"So I'll see you in a few hours?"

"See ya," she says.

And I feel happy, for a just a second. Then the front door is slamming behind her. And I'm alone again with Owen's note, the inimitable silence of the kitchen, and enough burnt pasta to feed a family of ten.

Don't Ask a Question You Don't Want the Answer To

At 8 P.M., Owen still hasn't called.

I take a left into the parking lot at Bailey's school and pull into a spot by the front exit.

I turn down the radio and try him again. My heartbeat picks up when his phone goes straight to voice mail. It's been twelve hours since he left for work, two hours since the visit from the soccer star, eighteen messages to my husband that have gone unreturned.

"Hey," I say after the beep. "I don't know what's going on, but you need to call me as soon as you get this. Owen? I love you. But I'm going to kill you if I don't hear from you soon."

I end the call and look down at my phone, willing it to buzz immediately. Owen, calling back, with a good explanation. It's one of the reasons I love him. He always has a good explanation. He always brings calmness and reason to whatever is going on. I want to believe that will be true even now. Even if I can't see it.

I slide over so Bailey can jump into the driver's seat. And I close my eyes, running through different scenarios as to what could possibly be going on. Innocuous, reasonable scenarios. He is stuck in an epic work meeting. He lost his phone. He is surprising Bailey with a crazy present. He is surprising me with some sort of trip. He thinks this is funny. He isn't thinking, at all.

This is when I hear the name of Owen's tech firm—The Shop—coming from my car radio.

I turn the radio up, thinking I imagined it. Maybe I was the one who said it in my message to Owen. *Are you stuck at The Shop?* It's possible. But then I hear the rest of the report, coming from the NPR host's slick, grippy voice.

"Today's raid was the culmination of a fourteen-month investigation by the SEC and the FBI into the software start-up's business practices. We can confirm that The Shop's CEO, Avett Thompson, is in custody. Expected charges include embezzlement and fraud. Sources close to the investigation have told NPR that, quote, *there is evidence Thompson planned to flee the country and had set up a residence in Dubai.* Other indictments of senior staff are expected to be handed down shortly."

The Shop. She is talking about The Shop.

How is this possible? Owen is honored to work there. Owen has used that word. *Honored.* He told me that he took a salary cut to join them early on. Nearly everyone there had taken a salary cut, leaving bigger companies behind—Google, Facebook, Twitter— leaving big money behind, agreeing to stock options in lieu of traditional compensation.

Didn't Owen tell me they did this because they believed in the technology The Shop was developing? They aren't Enron. Theranos. They are a software company. They were building software tools set to privatize online life— helping people control what was made available about them, providing child-easy ways to erase an embarrassing image, make a website all but disappear. They wanted to be a part of revolutionizing online privacy. They wanted to make a positive difference.

How could there be fraud in that?

The host goes to commercial and I reach for my phone, flipping to Apple News.

But just as I'm pulling up CNN's business page, Bailey comes out of the school. She has a bag swung over her shoulder and a needy look on her face that I don't recognize, especially directed at me.

Instinctively, I turn the radio off, put my phone down.

Protect her.

Bailey gets in the car quickly. She drops into the driver's seat and buckles herself in. She doesn't say hello to me. She doesn't even turn her head to look in my direction.

"Are you okay?" I ask.

She shakes her head, her purple hair falling out from behind her ears. I expect her to make a snide remark—*Do I look okay?* But she stays quiet.

"Bailey?" I say.

"I don't know," she says. "I don't know what's going on…"

This is when I notice it. The bag she has with her isn't her messenger bag. It is a duffel bag. It's a large black duffel bag, which she cradles in her lap, gently, like it's a baby.

"What is that?" I say.

"Take a look," she says.

The way she says it makes me not want to look. But I don't have much of a choice. Bailey hurls the duffel bag onto my lap.

"Go on. Look, Hannah."

I pull back the zipper just a bit and money starts spilling out. Rolls and rolls of money, hundreds of hundred-dollar bills tied together with string. Heavy, limitless.

"Bailey," I whisper. "Where did you get this?"

"My father left it in my locker," she says.

I look at her in disbelief, my heart starting to race. "How do you know?" I say.

Bailey hands me a note, more like tosses it in my general direction. "Call it a good guess," she says.

I pick the note up off my lap. It's on a sheet from a yellow legal pad. It is Owen's second note that day, on that piece of yellow legal paper.

The other half of my note. *BAILEY* is written on the front of hers, underlined for her twice.

> *Bailey,*
>
> *I can't help this make sense. I'm so sorry. You know what matters about me.*
> *And you know what matters about yourself. Please hold on to it.*
> *Help Hannah. Do what she tells you.*
> *She loves you. We both do.*
> *You are my whole life,*
>
> *Dad*

My eyes focus on the note until the words start to blur. And I can picture what preceded the meeting between Owen and the twelve-year-old in shin guards. I can picture Owen running through the school halls, running by the lockers. He was there to deliver this bag to his daughter. While he still could.

My chest starts heating up, making it harder to breathe.

I consider myself to be pretty unflappable. You could say that how I grew up demanded it. So, there are only two other times in my life that I've felt this exact way: the day I realized my mother wasn't coming back and the day my grandfather died. But looking back and forth between Owen's note and the obscene amount of money he's left, I feel it happening again. How do I explain the feeling? Like my insides need to get out. One way or another. And I know if there is ever a moment I could vomit all over the place, it's now.

Which is what I do.

We pull up to our parking spot in front of the docks.

We've kept the car windows wide open for the duration of the ride and I'm still holding a tissue over my mouth.

"Do you feel like you're going to hurl again?" Bailey asks.

I shake my head, trying to convince myself as much as I'm trying to convince her. "I'm fine," I say.

"'Cause this could help…" Bailey says.

I look over to see her pull a joint out of her sweater pocket. She holds it out for me to take.

"Where did you get that?" I say.

"It's legal in California," she says.

Is that an answer? Is it even true for a sixteen-year-old?

Maybe she doesn't want to give me the answer, especially when I'm guessing she got the joint from Bobby. Bobby is more or less Bailey's boyfriend. He's a senior at her school and on the surface he's a good guy, if a bit nerdy: University of Chicago bound, head of student government. No purple streaks in his hair. But there is something about him Owen doesn't trust. And while I want to write off Owen's dislike to overprotection, it doesn't help that Bobby encourages Bailey's disdain toward me. Sometimes after spending time with him, she'll come home and lob an insult my way. While I've tried not to take it personally, Owen has been less successful. He had an argument with Bailey about Bobby just a few weeks ago, telling her he thought she was seeing too much of him. It was one of the only times I saw Bailey look at Owen with the dismissive glare she normally reserves for me.

"If you don't want it, don't take it," she says. "I was just trying to help."

"I'm good. But thanks."

She starts to put the joint back in her pocket and I flinch. I try to avoid making any big parenting moves with Bailey. It's one of the few things she seems to like about me.

I start to turn away, making a mental note to discuss this with Owen when he gets home—let him decide whether she keeps the joint or hands it over. But then it hits me. I have no idea when Owen will be home. I have no idea where he is now.

"You know what?" I say. "I'm going to take that."

She rolls her eyes but hands the joint over. I shove it into the glove compartment and reach down to pick up the duffel bag.

"I started counting it..." she says.

I look up at her.

"The money," she says. "Each roll has ten thousand dollars in it. And I got to sixty. When I stopped counting."

"Sixty?"

I start grabbing the loose rolls of money that have fallen on the seats, on the floor, and put them back inside the bag. Then I zip it closed, so she won't have to contemplate the enormous stash inside anymore. So neither of us will.

Six hundred thousand dollars. Six hundred thousand dollars and counting.

"Lynn Williams reposted all these *Daily Beast* tweets to her Insta Stories," she says. "All about The Shop and Avett Thompson. How he's like Madoff. That's what one of them said."

I go back through what I know—sharp, fast. Owen's note to me. The duffel bag for Bailey. The radio report suggesting embezzlement and massive fraud. Avett Thompson the mastermind of something I'm still trying to understand.

I feel like I'm in one of those twisted dreams that only happen when you go to sleep at the wrong time, the afternoon sun or midnight chill greeting you upon waking, disorienting you—and leaving you to turn to the person next to you, the person you trust most, looking for clarity. It was only a dream: There is no tiger under the bed. You weren't just chased through the streets of Paris. You didn't jump off the Willis Tower. Your husband didn't disappear, leaving you no explanation, leaving his daughter six hundred thousand dollars. And counting.

"We don't have that information yet," I say. "But even if it's true that The Shop is involved in something, or if Avett did something illegal, that doesn't mean that your father had anything to do with it."

"Then where is he? And where did he get this money!"

She is yelling at me because she wants to be yelling at him. It's a feeling I can relate to. *I'm just as angry as you are,* I want to say. And the person I want to say it to is Owen.

I look at her. Then I turn away, stare out the window, out at the docks, the bay, at all the night-lit houses in this strange little neighborhood. I can see directly into the Hahns' floating home. Mr. and Mrs. Hahn are sitting on the couch, side by side, eating their nightly bowls of ice cream, watching television.

"What do I do now, Hannah?" she says. My name hangs there like an accusation.

Bailey pushes her hair behind her ears, and I can see her lip start to quiver. It is so strange and unexpected—Bailey has never cried in front of me—that I almost reach out to hold her to me, like it's something we do.

Protect her.

I unbuckle my seat belt. Then I reach over and unbuckle hers. Simple movements.

"Let's go into the house and I'll make some phone calls," I say. "Someone's going to know where your father is. We'll start there. We'll start by finding him, so he can explain this all."

"Okay," she says.

She opens her car door and steps outside. But she turns back to look at me, her eyes blazing.

"But Bobby's coming over," she says. "I won't say anything about my father's special delivery, but I really want him here."

She isn't asking. What choice do I have anyway, even if she were? "Just stay downstairs, okay?"

She shrugs, which is as close to an agreement as we are going to reach on the matter. And before I can worry too much about it, I see a car pulling up, headlights blinking at us, bright and demanding.

My first thought is: *Owen. Please be Owen.* But my second thought feels more precise and I prepare myself. It's the police. It has to be the police. They're probably here to find Owen—to gather information about his involvement in his firm's criminal activities, to assess what I know about his employment at The Shop, and about his current whereabouts. As if I have any information to pass along to them.

But I'm wrong on that count too.

The lights go off and I see that it's a bright blue Mini Cooper and I know it's Jules. It's my oldest friend, Jules, hustling out of her Mini Cooper and racing toward me at top speed, her arms wide and outstretched. She is hugging us, hugging both Bailey and me, as hard as she can.

"Hello, my loves," she says.

Bailey hugs her back. Even Bailey loves Jules, despite the fact that I'm the one who brought her into Bailey's life. This is who Jules is to everyone who is lucky enough to know her. Comforting, steady.

It may be why of everything I'm guessing she'll say to me in that moment, the one thing I don't expect is what actually comes out of her mouth.

"It's all my fault," she says.

Think What You Want

"I still can't believe this is happening," Jules says.

We sit in the kitchen, at the small breakfast table in the sun nook, drinking coffee spiked with bourbon. Jules is on her second mug, her oversize sweatshirt concealing her small frame, her hair pulled back in two low pigtails. They make her look like she is trying to get away with something, sneaking some more bourbon into the mug. They make her look a little like her fourteen-year-old self, the girl I met our first day of high school.

My grandfather had just moved us from Tennessee to Peekskill, New York—a small town on the Hudson River. Jules's family had moved there from New York City. Her father was an investigative journalist for the *New York Times*—a Pulitzer Prize–winning journalist—not that Jules had any airs about her. We met while applying for after-school jobs at Lucky's, a local dog-walking service. We were both hired. And we took to walking our assigned dogs together every afternoon. We must have been a sight: two small girls, fifteen rowdy dogs surrounding us at any given time.

I was a freshman at the public high school. Jules was at a prestigious private school a few miles away. But those afternoons were just the two of us together. I'm still not sure how we would have gotten through high school without each other. We were so removed from each other's actual lives that we told each other everything. Jules once compared it to how you confide in a stranger you meet on a plane. From the beginning, this is what we've been to each other: safe, airborne. Complete with a thirty-thousand-foot perspective.

That hasn't changed, now that we're the grown-ups. Jules has followed in her father's footsteps and works for a newspaper. She's a photo editor at the *San Francisco Chronicle*, focusing primarily on sports. She eyes me, worried. But I'm eyeing Bailey in the living room, snuggled into Bobby on the couch, the two of them talking low. It seems harmless. And still, my thought is, *I have no idea what harmless looks like.* This is the first time Bobby has been over when Owen hasn't been home. This is the first time when it's been up to me alone.

I try to check on them while pretending not to check on them. But Bailey must feel my gaze. She looks up at me, less than pleased. Then she stands up and deliberately closes the glass living room door with a thud. I can still see her, so it's more of a ceremonial slamming. But it's a slamming all the same.

"We were sixteen once too, you know," Jules says.

"Not like that," I say.

"We only wish," she says. "Purple hair rocks."

She makes a move to pour some more whisky into my coffee cup, but I cover the mug with my hand.

"You sure? It'll help," she says.

I shake my head no. "I'm okay," I say.

"Well, it's helping me."

She pours herself some more and moves my hand out of the way, topping me off. I smile at her, even though I have barely taken a sip of what I already have. I'm too stressed, too physically off—too close to standing up and busting into the living room, pulling Bailey by the arm into the kitchen with me just to feel like I'm accomplishing something.

"Have you heard from the police yet?" Jules says.

"No, not yet," I say. "And why isn't someone from The Shop banging down the door? Telling me what to do when they show up?"

"Bigger fish to fry," she says. "Avett was their primary target and the police just took him into custody."

She circles the rim of her mug with her fingers. And I take her in—her long eyelashes and high cheekbones, the one wrinkle between her eyes in overdrive today. She is nervous, the way she gets, the way we both get, before we have to tell each other something that we know isn't going to be fun for the other person to hear—like the time she told me she saw my quasi-boyfriend Nash Richards at the Rye Grill, kissing another girl. It was less that she thought I'd be upset about Nash, who I wasn't particularly into, and more that the Rye Grill was Jules's and my favorite place to eat french fries and cheeseburgers. And when she threw her soda in Nash's face, the manager told her we were permanently banned.

"So are you going to tell me, or what?" I say.

She looks up. "Which part?" she says.

"How this is all your fault?"

She nods, readying herself, blowing out her cheeks. "When I got to the *Chronicle* this morning, I knew there was something going on. Max was giddy, which almost always means bad news. Murder, impeachment, Ponzi scheme."

"He's a peach, that Max," I say.

"Yeah, well…"

Max is one of the few investigative journalists still at the *Chronicle*—handsome, smarmy, brilliant. He is also crazy about Jules. And, despite her assurances to the contrary, I kind of suspect Jules feels the same way about him.

"He was looking particularly smug, hovering around my desk. So I knew that he knew something and wanted to gloat. He's old fraternity brothers with someone at the SEC who apparently had the scoop on what was going down with The Shop. With the raid this afternoon."

She looks at me, not wanting to continue.

"He told me that the FBI has been investigating the firm for over a year. Shortly after their stock went public, they got a tip that the market listing was fraudulently overstated in connection with the IPO."

"I don't know what that means," I say.

"It means The Shop thought the software would be ready earlier than it was. So they went to market too soon. And then they were stuck, pretending they had functional software when in reality they couldn't sell it yet. So to compensate, and keep the stock prices high, they began falsifying their financial statements."

"How did they do that?"

"So they have their other software, video, apps, their bread-and-butter business. But their privacy software, the game changer Avett was touting, wasn't functional yet, right? They couldn't start selling it. But it was far enough along that they could do demos for potential large buyers. Tech firms, law offices, that sort of thing. And then when those companies showed interest, they put it down as a future sale. Max says it's not dissimilar to what Enron did. They declared they were making all kinds of money on future sales, to keep the stock price rising."

I'm starting to understand where she's driving.

"And to buy themselves some more time to fix the problem?" I say.

"Exactly. Avett wagered that the contingent future sales would turn into actual sales as soon as the software was functional. They were using the faux-financials as a stopgap to keep the stock nice and healthy, until the software was fixed," she says. "Except they got caught before they got it there."

"And there's the fraud?" I say.

"And there's the fraud," she says. "Max says it's massive. Stockholders will lose half a billion dollars."

Half a *billion* dollars. I try to wrap my head around that. It's the least of it, but we are large shareholders. Owen wanted to put his faith in the place he worked, in the software he was working on. So when the company went public he held on to all of his stock options. He even purchased more stock. How much were we going to lose? Most of our savings? Why would he put us in the position to lose so much if he knew anything bad was going on? Why would Owen invest our savings, our future, in a faulty operation?

It gives me hope that he didn't.

"So if Owen invested in The Shop, that must mean that he didn't know, right?"

"Maybe..." she says.

"That doesn't sound like maybe."

"Well there's also the possibility he did what Avett did. That he bought the stock to help inflate the value with the idea that he'd sell before anyone found out."

"Does that sound like Owen to you?" I say.

"None of this sounds like Owen to me," she says.

Then she shrugs. And I hear the rest—what's rattling around in her mind, what's rattling around in mine: Owen is the chief coder. How could he not know that Avett was inflating the value of the software that he was working on, the software that wasn't yet working? If anyone would know, wouldn't it have to be him?

"Max did say that the FBI thinks most of the senior staff were either in on it, or complicit in looking the other way. Everyone thought they could fix the glitch before anyone caught on. Apparently, they were close. If not for this one tip to the SEC, they might have pulled it off."

"Who tipped them off?"

"No idea. But that's why the raid. They wanted to shut it all down before Avett disappeared. With the two hundred and sixty million dollars' worth of stock he's quietly been off-loading..." She pauses. "For months now."

"Holy crap," I say.

"Yep. Anyway, Max found out ahead of time. About the raid. So the FBI cut a deal with him. If he agreed not to break the story before they went in, they'd give him a two-hour lead on the raid. The *Chronicle* beat everyone. The *Times*. CNN. NBC. Fox. He was so proud of himself that he had to tell me. And I don't know... My first instinct was to call Owen. Well, my first instinct was to call you, but I couldn't reach you. So then I called Owen."

"To warn him?"

"Yes," she says. "To warn him."

"Why are you feeling badly about that? Because he ran?" I say.

It's the first time I have said it out loud. The obvious truth. And yet saying it out loud makes me feel better somehow. At least it's honest. Owen ran. He is running. He isn't, just simply, gone.

Jules nods and I swallow hard, fight back against the tears rising up.

"That's not on you," I say. "You could have lost your job warning him. You were trying to help. How on earth would I be mad at you for that? I'm just mad at Owen." I pause, considering that. "I'm not even exactly mad at Owen. I'm more numb. And just trying to figure out what he's possibly thinking. How he thinks this isn't bad for him, to take off like this."

"What have you come up with?" she asks.

"I don't know. Maybe he is trying to exonerate himself? But why not do that from here? Get a lawyer. Let the system clear you..." I say. "I just can't shake the feeling that I'm missing something, you know? I'm missing what kind of help he is looking for."

She squeezes my hand, tightly, gives me a smile. But she doesn't look at all like we are on the same page, which is when I realize she isn't telling me whatever it is that is beneath that look. She isn't saying the worst of it.

"I know that look," I say.

She shakes her head. "It's nothing," she says.

"Tell me, Jules."

"The thing is, and I can't believe it myself exactly, but he wasn't surprised," she says. "He wasn't surprised when I told him about the raid."

"I'm not following you."

"I learned this early on from my father. Sources can't hide it when they know something. They forget to ask the obvious questions they'd want to know, if they were as in the dark as you were. Like, the questions you just asked me about what exactly happened…"

I stare at her, waiting for the rest, as something starts shifting in my head. I look through the glass at Bailey. She is lying against Bobby's chest, her hand on his stomach, her eyes closed.

Protect her.

"The thing is, if Owen didn't know anything about the fraud, he would have wanted more information from me. He would have needed a lot more information about what was going on at The Shop. He'd have said something like, *Slow down, Jules. Who do they think is guilty? Does it look like Avett spearheaded the fraud alone or is the corruption more widespread? What does it look like happened, how much has been stolen?* But he didn't want to know more. Not about any of it."

"What did he want to know?" I say.

"How long he had to get out," she says.

Twenty-Four Hours Earlier

Owen and I sat on the dock, eating Thai food straight from the take-out containers. Drinking ice cold beer.

He was in a sweatshirt and jeans, bare feet. There was barely a sliver of moon, the Northern California night chilly and wet, but Owen wasn't cold at all. I, on the other hand, was wrapped in a blanket, two pairs of socks, puffy boots.

We were sharing a papaya salad and spicy lime curry. Owen was tearing up, the heat from the chilies going straight to his eyes.

I stifled a laugh. "If you can't hack it," I said, "we can order the curry mild next time."

"Oh, I can hack it," he said. "If you can hack it, I can hack it…"

He stuffed his mouth with another bite, his face turning red as he struggled to swallow. He reached for his beer and guzzled it down.

"See?" he said.

"I do," I said.

Then I leaned in to kiss him.

After I pulled back, he smiled at me, touched my cheek.

"What do you think? Can I get under that blanket with you?" he asked.

"Always."

I moved over, wrapping the blanket over his shoulders, feeling the heat of his body. His barefooted body, a good ten degrees warmer than mine.

"So tell me," he said. "What was your favorite thing today?"

This was something we sometimes did on days we got home late—on days we were too tired to get into the big stuff. We each picked one thing from the day to tell each other about. One good thing from our separate lives.

"I actually think I have a pretty cool idea for a little treat for Bailey," I said. "I'm going to re-create the brown butter pasta for dinner tomorrow night. You know, the one we had on her birthday at Poggio? Don't you think she'll love that?"

He wrapped his arm more tightly around my waist, kept his voice low. "Are you asking me if she'll love that? Or if that will make her love you?"

"Hey. Not nice."

"I'm trying to be nice," he said. "Bailey's lucky to have you. And she's going to come around to that. Pasta experiment or not."

"How do you know?"

He shrugged. "I know things."

I didn't say anything, not exactly believing him. I wanted him to do more to bridge the gap between Bailey and me, even if I didn't know what that could possibly be. If he wasn't going to do that, I at least wanted him to tell me I was doing everything I could.

As if hearing my thoughts, he pushed my hair off my face. He kissed the side of my neck.

"She really loved that pasta though," he said. "It's a sweet thing to do."

"That's all I'm saying!"

He smiled. "I should be able to duck out of work early tomorrow. If you're in the market for a sous chef?"

"I am," I said.

"Count me in then," he said. "I'm yours."

I put my head on his shoulder. "Thank you," I said. "Okay. Now you."

"Favorite part of my day?" he said.

"Yes," I said. "And don't cop out and say right now."

He laughed. "Shows how well you know me," he said. "I wasn't going to say right now."

"Really?"

"Really," he said.

"What were you going to say?"

"Sixty seconds ago," he said. "It was cold outside the blanket."

Follow the Money

Jules doesn't leave until after 2 A.M.

She offers to stay over, and maybe I should have let her because I barely get any sleep.

I lay awake most of the night on the living room couch, unable to face my bedroom without Owen. I wrap myself up in an old blanket and wait out the dark, playing it over and over in my head—the last thing Jules said before she left.

We stood at the front door and she leaned in to give me a hug. "One thing," she said. "Did you keep your own checking account?"

"Yes," I said.

"That's good," she said. "That's important."

She smiled approvingly, so I didn't add that I'd done so at Owen's insistence. Owen was the one who wanted to keep some of our money separate for a reason he never fully explained. I assumed it had something to do with Bailey. But maybe I was wrong about that. Maybe it had to do with leaving what was mine untouched.

"I ask because they're probably going to freeze all his assets," Jules said. "That's the first thing they'll do while they're trying to figure out where he went. What he knew. They always follow the money."

Follow the money.

I feel a little bit queasy, even now, as I think about the duffel bag shoved under the kitchen sink, a bag full of money that Owen probably knows they can't follow. I didn't tell Jules about the duffel because I know what it looks like to any reasonable person. I know what it should look like to me too. It looks like Owen is guilty. Jules had already decided as much, and a mysterious bag of money would only convince her further. Why wouldn't it? She loves Owen like a brother, but it isn't about love. It's about what points toward Owen's involvement in this mess: that he's running, that he acted suspiciously with Jules on the phone. Every single thing.

Except this. Except what I know.

Owen wouldn't run because he is guilty. He wouldn't leave to save himself. He wouldn't leave to avoid prison or to avoid looking me in the eye and admitting what he's done. He wouldn't leave Bailey. He would never leave Bailey unless he absolutely had to. How can I be so sure of this? How can I trust myself to be sure of anything when I'm obviously biased in what I'm willing to see?

Partially it's because I've spent my life *needing* to see. I've spent my life paying incredibly close attention. When my mother left for good, I didn't see it coming. I missed it. I missed the finality of that departure. I shouldn't have. There were so many hasty exits before that, so many nights she slipped out and left me with my grandfather without so much as a goodbye. There were so many times she didn't come back for days, or weeks, only offering up an occasional phone call, an occasional check-in.

When she finally left for good, she didn't say she wasn't coming back. She sat down on the edge of my bed and brushed my hair off my face and said she had to go to Europe—that my father needed her with him. But she said she'd see me soon. I assumed that meant she'd be back soon—she was always coming and going. But I missed it. The language of it. "Seeing me soon" meant she was never coming back, not in a substantial way. It meant I'd spend an afternoon or an evening with her twice a year (never overnight).

It meant she was lost to me.

That's the part that I missed: My mother didn't care enough not to be lost to me.

That's the part I've sworn to myself I would never miss again.

I don't know if Owen is guilty. And I'm furious he left me to deal with this alone. But I know he cares. I know he loves me. And, more than that, I know he loves Bailey.

He would only leave *for* her. It has to be that. He left the way he did to try and save her. From something or someone.

It all comes down to Bailey.

The rest is just a story.

The sunlight streams through the undraped living room windows, soft and yellow, against the harbor.

I stare outside. I don't turn on the television or flip open my laptop to check the newsfeed. I know the most important thing. Owen is still gone.

I head upstairs to shower and find Bailey's door uncharacteristically open, Bailey sitting up in her bed.

"Hey there," I say.

"Hi," she says.

She pulls her knees to her chest. She looks so scared. She looks like she is trying hard to hide it.

"Can I come in for a sec?" I say.

"Sure," she says. "I guess."

I walk over and sit down on the edge of her bed—as if that is something I know how to do, as if that is something I've done before.

"Did you sleep at all?" I say.

"Not much," she says.

The outline of her toes is visible through the sheets. She curls them tight together, like a fist. I start to reach for her foot, hold it, but then think better of it. I clasp my hands together and look around her room. Her bedside table is littered with theater books and plays. Her blue piggy bank rests on top of them—the piggy bank that Owen won for her at a school fair shortly after they moved to Sausalito. It's a female piggy bank, complete with bright red cheeks and a bow on top.

"I just keep going over it in my head," she says. "I mean... my father doesn't make things complicated. At least not with me. So explain what he wrote in his note to me."

"What do you mean?"

"*You know what matters about me...* what's that even mean?"

"I think he means that you know how much he loves you," I say. "And that he's a good man despite what people may be saying about him."

"No, that's not it," she says. "He meant something else. I know him. I know he meant something."

"Okay..." I take a deep breath. "Like what?"

But she is shaking her head. She is already onto something else.

"And what am I supposed to do with that money? All that money he left me?" she says. "That's the kind of money that someone leaves you when they're not coming back."

That stops me. Cold. "Your father's coming back," I say.

Her face fills with doubt. "How do you know?"

I try to think of a comforting answer. Luckily it also feels like the truth. "Because you're here."

"So why isn't he?" she says. "Why did he take off like he did?"

It feels like she isn't actually looking for an answer. She is looking to fight when I give her an answer that she doesn't want. It makes me furious with Owen for putting me in this position, regardless of the reason. I can tell myself that I'm sure of Owen's intentions—that, wherever he is, he's there because he is trying to protect Bailey. But I'm left sitting here, without him, anyway. Doesn't that make me as ridiculous as my mother is? Doesn't it make me the same as her? Both of us putting our faith in someone else above everything else—calling it love. What good is love, if this is where it leads you?

"Look," I say. "We can talk about this more later, but you should probably get ready for school."

"I should get ready for school?" she says. "Are you serious?"

She isn't wrong. It's a lousy thing to say. But how can I say what I want to say? That I've called her father dozens and dozens of times, that I don't know where he is. And I certainly have no idea when he's coming back to us.

Bailey gets out of bed and heads toward the bathroom and the terrible day ahead of her, ahead of both of us. I almost stop her and tell her to come back to the bed. But that seems more about what I need. Isn't what's best for her to get out of this house? Go to school? Forget about her father for five minutes?

Protect her.

"I'm going to drop you off," I say. "I don't want you walking to school alone this morning."

"Whatever," she says.

She's apparently too tired to argue. One break.

"I'm sure we're going to hear from your father soon," I say. "And things will start to make a lot more sense."

"Oh, you're sure of that?" she says. "Wow, that's a relief."

Her sarcasm can't mask it—how tired she is, how alone she feels. It makes me miss my grandfather, who would know exactly how to make Bailey feel better. He'd know how to give her the thing she needs, whatever that thing might be, to know she's loved in a moment like this. To know she can trust. The same way he did for me. How many months after my mother left did he find me upstairs in my room, trying to write a letter to her? Asking her how she could desert me?

I was crying and angry and scared. And I'll never forget what he did next. He was wearing his overalls and these thick work gloves—purple, and ridged. The gloves were a recent purchase. He got them made special in purple because that was my favorite color. He took the gloves off and he sat down on the floor next to me and helped me finish the letter, exactly as I wanted to write it. No judgment. He helped me spell out any words I was having trouble with. He waited while I figured out exactly how I wanted the letter to end. Then he read the entire letter out loud so I could hear it for myself, pausing when he got to the sentence in which I asked my mother how she could have left me behind. *Maybe that's not the only question we should be asking,* my grandfather said. *Maybe we should also think about whether we'd really want it to be different. We could think about whether she actually did us a favor in her own way...* I looked at him, starting to understand where he was gently leading me. *After all, what your mother did... it gave me you.*

The most generous thing to say. The most comforting and generous thing. What would he say to Bailey now? When am I going to figure out how to say it too?

"Look, I'm trying here, Bailey," I say. "I'm sorry. I know I keep saying the wrong things to you."

"Well," she says as she closes the bathroom door behind herself, "at least you know."

Help Is on the Way

When we decided I was moving to Sausalito, Owen and I talked about how to make the transition as easy as possible for Bailey. I felt strongly, probably more strongly than Owen even did, that we shouldn't move Bailey out of the only home she'd ever known—the home she'd been living in for as long as she could remember. I wanted her to have continuity. Her floating home—complete with its wooden beams and bay windows, its storybook views on Issaquah Dock—was her continuity. Her safe haven.

But I wonder if it didn't just make it more apparent: Someone moved into her most cherished space and there was nothing she could do about it.

Still, I did everything I could to not disturb the balance. Her balance. Even in the way that I moved into the house, I tried to keep the peace. I put my stamp on Owen's and my bedroom, but the only other room I redecorated wasn't a room at all. It was our porch, lovingly hugging the front of the house. Before I arrived, the porch was empty. But I lined it with potted plants, rustic tea tables. And I built a bench to put by the front door.

It is a great rocking bench—shingled in white oak, striped pillows for comfort.

Owen and I have made it our weekend ritual to sit on the bench together, drinking our morning coffee. It's our time to catch up on the week as the sun rises slowly over the San Francisco Bay, catching the bench in its warmth. Owen is more animated in those conversations than during the work week—a load lifted as the day stretches out before him, empty and relaxed.

That's partially why the bench makes me so happy, why I take comfort even passing by it. And why I nearly jump out of my skin when I walk outside to take out the trash and there is someone sitting on it.

"Garbage day?" he says.

I turn around to see a man I don't recognize leaning against the bench's arm, like he belongs there. He wears a backward baseball cap and a windbreaker, holds tight to a cup of coffee.

"Can I help you?" I say.

"I'm hoping so." He motions toward my wrists. "But you may want to put those down first."

I look down to see that I'm still holding the trash, the two weighty garbage bags in my hands. I drop the bags into the trash cans. Then I look back up and take him in. He is young—maybe in his early thirties. And he is good-looking in a way that's disarming, complete with a strong jaw, dark eyes. He is almost too good-looking. But the way he smiles gives him away. He knows it better than anyone.

"Hannah, I take it?" he says. "It's nice to meet you."

"Who the hell are you?" I say.

"I'm Grady," he says.

He bites the edge of the coffee cup, holding it between his lips as he points at me to give him a second. Then he reaches in his pocket and pulls out something that looks like a badge. He holds it out for me to take.

"Grady Bradford," he says. "You can call me Grady. Or Deputy Bradford if you prefer, though that seems awfully formal for our purposes."

"And what are those?"

"Friendly," he says. Then he smiles. "Friendly purposes."

I study the badge. It has a star with a circular ring wrapped around it. I want to run my finger around that circle, through the star, as if that will help me determine whether the badge is genuine.

"You're a police officer?"

"A U.S. marshal actually," he says.

"You don't look like a U.S. marshal," I say.

"And what does a U.S. marshal look like?" he says.

"Tommy Lee Jones in *The Fugitive*," I say.

He laughs. "It's true, I'm younger than some of my colleagues, but my grandfather was with the service, so I got an early start," he says. "I assure you it's been a legitimate one."

"What do you do for the Marshals' office?"

He takes his badge back and stands up, the bench rocking back and forth as it loses the weight of him.

"Well, primarily, I apprehend people who are defrauding the U.S. government," he says.

"You think my husband's done that?"

"I think The Shop has done that. But no, I'm not convinced your husband has. Though I'd need to speak to him before I could properly assess his involvement," he says. "Seems like he doesn't want to have that conversation though."

That sticks to me for some reason. It sticks to me as not the entire truth, at least not Grady's entire truth as to what he's doing on my dock.

"Can I see your badge again?" I say.

"512-555-5393," he says.

"Is that your badge number?"

"That's the phone number for my branch office," he says. "Give a call there, if you like. They'll confirm for you who I am. And that I just need a few minutes of your time."

"Do I have a choice?"

He gives me a smile. "You always have a choice," he says. "But I'd certainly appreciate if you talked to me."

It doesn't feel like I have a choice, at least not a good one. And I don't know if I like him, this Grady Bradford, with his practiced drawl. But how much would I like anyone who is about to ask me a bunch of questions about Owen?

"What do you say?" he says. "I was thinking we could take a walk."

"Why would I take a walk with you?"

"It's a nice day," he says. "And I got you this."

He reaches under my rocking bench and pulls out another cup of coffee, piping hot, fresh from Fred's. EXTRA SUGAR and SHOT OF CINNAMON are written on the side of the cup in large black letters. He hasn't just brought me a cup of coffee. He's brought me a cup of coffee just the way I take it.

I breathe the coffee in, take my first sip. It's the first bit of pleasure since this whole mess started.

"How do you know how I take my coffee?" I say.

"A waiter named Benj helped me out. He said you and Owen get coffees from him on the weekend. Yours with cinnamon, Owen's black."

"This is bribery."

"Only if it doesn't work," he says. "Otherwise it's a cup of coffee."

I look at him and take another sip.

"Sunny side of the street?" he says.

We leave the docks and walk toward the Path, heading toward downtown— Waldo Point Harbor peeking out at us in the distance.

"So I take it no word from Owen?" he says.

I think about our kiss goodbye by his car yesterday, slow and lingering. Owen wasn't anxious at all, a smile on his face.

"No. I haven't seen him since he left for work yesterday," I say.

"And he hasn't called?" he says.

I shake my head.

"Does he usually call from work?"

"Usually," I say.

"But not yesterday?"

"He may have tried me, I don't know. I went to the Ferry Building in San Francisco, and there are a bunch of dead zones between here and there, so…"

He nods, completely unsurprised, almost like he knows this already. Like he is playing way past it.

"What happened when you got back?" he says. "From the Ferry Building?"

I take a deep breath and think about it for a minute. I think about telling him the truth. But I don't know what he will make of the information about the twelve-year-old girl and the note she gave to me, about the note Owen left for Bailey at the school. About the duffel bag of money. Until I figure it out for myself, I'm not including someone I just met.

"I'm not sure what you mean," I say. "I made Bailey dinner, which she hated, and she went to play practice. I heard about The Shop on NPR while I was waiting for her in the school parking lot. We came home. Owen didn't. No one slept."

He tilts his head, takes me in, like he doesn't believe me, entirely. I don't judge him for that. He shouldn't. But he seems to be willing to let it go.

"So… no call this morning, correct?" he says. "No email either?"

"No," I say.

He pauses, as though something is just occurring to him.

"It's a crazy thing when someone disappears, isn't it? No explanation?" he says.

"Yes," I say.

"And yet... you don't seem all that mad."

I stop walking, irritated that he thinks he knows enough about me to make a judgment call on how I feel.

"I'm sorry, I didn't realize there was an appropriate way to respond when your husband's company is raided and he disappears," I say. "Am I doing anything else you deem inappropriate?"

He thinks about it. "Not really."

I look down at his ring finger. No ring there. "I take it you're not married?"

"No," he says. "Wait... do you mean ever or currently?"

"Is it a different answer?"

He smiles. "No."

"Well, if you were, you'd understand that I'm more worried about my husband than anything else."

"Do you suspect foul play?"

I think of the notes Owen has left, of the money. I think of the twelve-year-old's story of running into Owen in the school hallway, of Owen's conversation with Jules. Owen knew where he was going. He knew he needed to get away from here. He chose to go.

"I don't think he was taken against his will, if that's what you're asking."

"Not exactly."

"So what are you asking, Grady? Exactly?"

"Grady. I like that. I'm glad we're on a first-name basis."

"What's your question?"

"Here you are, left to pick up the pieces of his mess. Not to mention take care of *his* daughter," he says. "That would make me mad. And you don't seem to be that mad. Which makes me think there is something you know that you're not telling me..."

His voice tightens. And his eyes darken until he seems like what he is— an investigator—and I'm suddenly on the other side of whatever line he draws to separate himself from the people he suspects of wrongdoing.

"If Owen told you something about where he disappeared to, about *why* he left, I need to know," he says. "That's the only way for you to protect him."

"Is that your primary interest here? Protecting him?"

"It is. Actually."

That does feel true, which unnerves me. It unnerves me even more than his investigator mode.

"I should get home."

I start to move away from him, Grady Bradford keeping me a little off-balance standing so close.

"You need to get a lawyer," he says.

I turn back toward him. "What?"

"Thing is," he says, "you're going to get a lot of questions about Owen, certainly until he's around again to answer them for himself. Questions you're under no obligation to answer. It's easier to push them off if you tell them you have a lawyer."

"Or I can just tell them the truth. I have no idea where Owen is. And I have nothing to hide."

"It's not that simple. People are going to offer you information that makes it seem like they're on your side. And Owen's side. They aren't. They aren't on anyone's side but their own."

"People like you?" I say.

"Exactly," he says. "But I did make a phone call for you this morning to Thomas Shelton. He's an old buddy of mine who works on family law for the state of California. I just wanted to make sure you're protected in case someone comes out of the woodwork seeking temporary custody of Bailey during all of this. Thomas will pull some strings to make sure that temporary custody is granted to you."

I let out a deep breath, unable to hide my relief. It has occurred to me that, if this goes on for too much longer, losing custody of Bailey is a possibility. She has no other family to speak of—her grandparents deceased, no close relatives. But we aren't blood relatives. I haven't adopted her. Couldn't the state take her away at any time? At least until they determine where her one legal guardian is, and why he has left his kid behind?

"He has the authority to do that?" I say.

"He does. And he will."

"Why?"

He shrugs. "Because I asked him to," he says.

"Why would you do that for us?" I ask.

"So you'd trust me when I tell you the best thing you can do for Owen is lie low and get a lawyer," he says. "Do you know one?"

I think of the one lawyer I know in town. I think of how little I want to talk to him, especially now.

"Unfortunately," I say.

"Call him. Or her."

"Him," I say.

"Fine, call him. And lie low."

"Do you want to say it again?" I ask.

"Nah, I've said it enough."

Then something in his face changes, a smile breaking through. Investigator mode apparently behind us.

"Owen hasn't used a credit card, not a check, nothing for twenty-four hours. And he won't. He's too smart, so you can stop calling his phone because I'm sure he dumped it."

"So why did you keep asking if he called?"

"There are other phones he could have used," he says. "Burner phones. Phones that aren't readily traceable."

Burner phones, paper trails. Why is Grady trying to make Owen sound like a criminal mastermind?

I start to ask him, but he presses a button on his key chain, a car across the street shining its lights, coming to life.

"I won't keep you longer, you have enough to deal with," he says. "But when you do hear from Owen, tell him I can help him if he lets me."

Then he hands me a napkin from Fred's, his name written down, GRADY BRADFORD, with two phone numbers beneath it, his numbers I presume—one of them marked cell.

"I can help you too," he says.

I pocket the napkin as he crosses the street and gets into his car. I start to walk away, but as he turns on the engine, something occurs to me and I walk toward him.

"Wait. With which part?" I say.

He lowers his window. "With which part, what?"

"Can you help?"

"The easy part," he says. "Getting through this."

"What's the hard part?"

"Owen's not who you think he is," he says.

Then Grady Bradford is gone.

These Are Not Your Friends

I go back into the house just long enough to grab Owen's laptop.

I'm not going to sit there thinking about what Grady said, and all the things he seemed to leave out, which are bothering me more. How did he know so much about Owen? Maybe Avett wasn't the only one who they've been following closely for the last year and change. Maybe Grady's nice guy act—helping me with Bailey's custody, offering advice—was so I'd slip up and tell him something Owen wouldn't want him to know.

Did I slip up? I don't think so, even as I go back through our conversation. But I'm not going to risk doing it in the future, not with Grady, or with anyone

else. I'm going to figure out what's going on with Owen first.

I take a left off the docks and head toward my workshop.

I need to make a stop first though at Owen's friend's house. It's a stop that I'm not particularly eager to make, but if anyone will have insight into what Owen is thinking, into what I might be missing, it's Carl.

Carl Conrad: Owen's closest friend in Sausalito. And one of the only people on whom Owen and I disagree. Owen thinks I don't give him a fair shake, and maybe that's true. He's funny and smart and totally embraced me from the minute I arrived in Sausalito. But he also habitually cheats on his wife, Patricia, and I don't like knowing that. Owen doesn't like knowing that either, but he says he's able to separate it out in his mind because Carl has been such a good friend to him.

This is how Owen is. He values the first friend he made in Sausalito more than he judges him. I know that's how my husband works. But maybe he hasn't been judging Carl for other reasons. Maybe Owen doesn't judge him because Carl returns the favor, by not judging a secret Owen felt safe confiding in Carl.

Even if that theory is wrong, I still need to talk to him.

Because Carl's also the only lawyer I know in town.

I knock on the front door, but no one answers. Not Carl, not Patty.

It's odd because Carl works from home. He likes to be around for his kids—his two young kids—who usually nap at this time. Carl and Patty are sticklers for their children's schedule. Patty lectured me about it during our first night out together. Patty had just celebrated her twenty-eighth birthday, which made the lecture all the more enjoyable. If I was still able to have children—that was how she said it—I was going to have to be careful not to let them rule the roost. I'd have to show them who was in charge. That meant a schedule. That meant, in her case, a 12:30 P.M. nap every day.

It's 12:45. If Carl isn't home, why isn't Patty?

Except that through the living room blinds, I see that Carl is home. I see him standing there, hiding behind those blinds, waiting for me to go.

I knock on the door again, pressing hard on the doorbell. I'm going to ring the doorbell for the rest of the afternoon until he lets me in. Kids' naps be damned.

Carl swings the door open. He is holding a beer; his hair is neatly combed. Those are the first indicators that something strange is going on. His hair is usually uncombed, which he thinks makes him look sexy. And there is something in his eyes—a strange mix of agitation and fear and something else I can't name, probably because I'm so shocked that he hid from me.

"What the hell, Carl?" I say.

"Hannah, you need to go," Carl says.

He's angry. Why is he angry?

"I just need a minute," I say.

"Not now, I can't talk right now," he says.

He moves to close the door, but I hold it open. My force surprises both of us, the door escaping his grasp, opening wider.

Which is when I see Patty. She stands in the living room doorway, holding her daughter Sarah in her arms, the two of them dressed in matching paisley dresses—their dark hair pulled back into soft braids. The identical attire and haircut only further highlight what Patty wants people to see when they look at Sarah: an equally presentable but smaller version of herself.

Behind them—filling up the living room—a dozen parents and toddlers watch a clown make balloon animals. A HAPPY BIRTHDAY SARAH banner hangs above their heads.

It's their daughter's second birthday party. I had totally forgotten about it. Owen and I were supposed to be here celebrating. Now Carl isn't even opening the door.

Patty offers a confused wave. "Hey there…" she says.

I wave back. "Hi."

Carl turns back toward me, his voice controlled but firm. "We'll talk later," he says.

"I forgot, Carl. I'm sorry." I shake my head. "I didn't mean to show up during her party."

"Forget it. Just go."

"I will but… would you just please step outside and talk to me for a couple of minutes? I wouldn't ask but it's urgent. I think I need a lawyer. Something's happened at The Shop."

"Do you think I don't know that?" he says.

"So why won't you talk to me then?"

Before he can answer, Patty walks toward us and hands Sarah to Carl. Then she gives her husband a kiss on the cheek. A big show. For him. For me. For the party.

"Hi," she says, kissing me on the cheek too. "Glad you could make it."

I keep my voice down. "Patty, I'm sorry for walking in on the party, but something's happened to Owen."

"Carl," Patty says, "let's get everyone out back, okay? It's time for ice cream sundaes."

She looks to the group and flashes her smile at them.

"Everyone head out back with Carl. You too, Mr. Silly," she says to the clown. "It's ice cream time!"

Then—and only then—she turns back toward me. "Let's talk out front, yeah?" she says.

I start to tell her that Carl is really who I need to speak with, Carl who is walking away with Sarah on his hip, but Patty is pushing me onto the front porch. She closes the thick red door and I am on the wrong side of it again.

This is when, on the privacy of her porch, Patty turns back to me, eyes blazing. Smile gone.

"How dare you show up here," she says.

"I forgot about the party."

"Screw the party," she says. "Owen broke Carl's heart."

"Broke his heart... how?" I say.

"Gee, I don't know. Maybe it has something to do with him stealing all our fucking money?"

"What are you talking about?" I say.

"Owen didn't tell you that he convinced us to go in on The Shop's IPO? He sold Carl on the software's potential, sold him on the enormous returns. Failed to mention that the software was dysfunctional."

"Patty, look..."

"So all of our money is now tied up in The Shop's stock. Actually, I should say, what's left of our money is tied up in stock, which on my last check was down to thirteen cents."

"Our money was there too. If Owen had known, why would he do that?"

"Maybe he didn't think they'd get caught. Or maybe he's a freaking moron, I can't tell you that," she says. "But I can promise you that if you don't leave my house, right now, I'm calling the cops. I'm not kidding. You're not welcome here."

"I understand why you're upset with Owen. I do. But Carl may be able to help me find him and that is the fastest way to get this sorted out."

"Unless you're here to pay for our kids' college, we have nothing to say to you."

I'm not sure what to say to her, but I know I have to say something before she walks back inside. After seeing him in person, after seeing the look in his eyes, I can't shake the feeling that Carl may know something.

"Patty, can you take a breath please?" I say. "I'm in the dark here too. Just like you."

"Your husband aided in a half-a-billion-dollar fraud, so I'm not so sure I believe you," she says. "But if you're telling me the truth, you're the biggest fool in the world, not seeing who your husband really is."

It doesn't seem like the greatest time to tell her that, in terms of playing the fool, she isn't avoiding it either. Her husband has been sleeping with his coworker on and off since Patty was pregnant with the child that Mr. Silly is entertaining in the backyard. Maybe we are all fools, one way or another, when it comes to seeing the totality of the people who love us—the people we try to love.

"Do you really expect me to believe that you didn't know what was going on?" she says.

"Why would I be here looking for answers if I did?" I say.

She tilts her head, considers. Perhaps that penetrates, or perhaps she realizes she just doesn't care. But her face softens.

"Go home to Bailey," she says. "Just go. She's going to need you."

She starts to walk back inside. Then she turns back.

"Oh. And when you speak to Owen? Tell him to go fuck himself."

With that, she closes the door.

On the walk to my workshop, I move fast.

I keep my eyes down as I turn onto Litho Street and pass LeAnn Sullivan's house. I clock that she and her husband are sitting on their front porch, drinking their afternoon lemonade. But I pretend to be busy on my phone. I don't stop the way I normally would to say hello to them. To join them for a glass.

My workshop is in a small craftsman house next door to their home. It is 2,800 square feet with an enormous backyard—the kind of space I only dreamed of having when I was in New York, the kind of space I did dream about in New York every time I had to subway out to my friend's warehouse in the Bronx to work on pieces that wouldn't fit into my workshop on Greene Street.

I start to relax as soon as I walk through the front gate, closing it behind myself. But instead of heading inside, I circle around to the backyard and the small deck where I like to do my paperwork. I take a seat at the small table and open Owen's laptop. I push Grady Bradford out of my mind. I push out Patty's wrath. And I ignore that Carl wouldn't even look at me, let alone provide any insight. It centers me, in a way, knowing I have to figure it out myself. And I feel calmer being among my things, my work. Being in my favorite place in Sausalito. It makes it almost feel normal that I'm hacking into my husband's personal computer.

Owen's laptop powers up and I key in his first password. Nothing pops out at me as unusual. I click open his PHOTOS folder, which is essentially the Bailey bible. There are hundreds of photographs of her from elementary school and junior high, photographs from each and every birthday starting with her fifth birthday in Sausalito. I've seen these all many times. Owen loved narrating the parts of their life that I'd missed: Little Bailey playing in her first soccer game, which she was terrible in;

Little Bailey performing in her first school play in second grade (*Anything Goes*), which she was amazing in.

I don't find a lot of photographs of them from when Bailey was very little, back when they were still living in Seattle, at least not in the main folder.

So I click on a small subfolder labeled O.M.

This is the folder for Olivia Michaels. Owen's first wife. Bailey's mother.

Olivia Michaels née Olivia Nelson: high school biology teacher, synchronized swimmer, Owen's fellow Princeton alum. There are only a handful of photographs in this folder too—Owen said Olivia hated to be photographed. But the photographs he does have of her are beautiful, probably because she was beautiful. She was tall and lean with long red hair that ran halfway down her back and an intense dimple that made her look permanently sixteen.

We don't look exactly alike—she was prettier, for starters, more interesting-looking. But, if you swapped out some of the details, it would be fair to say there is a similarity between us. The height, the long hair (mine is blond to her red), maybe even something in her smile. The first time Owen showed me a photograph of her, I commented on the similarity. But Owen said he didn't see it. He didn't get defensive, he just said if I actually saw his first wife in person, I wouldn't think we had much in common.

I wondered if the photographs were also misleading in how little Olivia seemed to resemble Bailey—with the exception of my favorite photograph of Olivia. In that photograph, she is sitting on a pier in a pair of jeans, a white button-down shirt. She has her hand on her cheek and her head is thrown back as she laughs. The coloring is different, but there is something in that smile that may match her kid's—that I imagine matched Bailey in person. It pulls Olivia in as the missing piece, connecting Bailey to someone besides Owen.

I reach out and touch the screen. I want to ask her what I'm missing about her daughter, about our husband. She would most certainly know better than I do—I know that to be true—which feels like its own kind of injury.

I take a breath in, and click on the folder labeled THE SHOP. It includes fifty-five documents all devoted to code and HTML programs. If there is a code hidden within the actual codes, I certainly won't find it. I make a note to find someone who can.

Oddly, there is a document in THE SHOP titled MOST RECENT WILL. I don't like that it is in there, especially considering what is going on, but I relax when I open it. The will is dated shortly after our wedding. He has shown me this will before. And nothing has changed. Or almost nothing. I see a small note on the bottom of the last page of the will above Owen's signature. Was that there before and I didn't notice it? It names his conservator, someone I've never heard of. L. Paul. No address. No phone number.

L. Paul. Who is this person—and where have I seen his or her name before?

I'm making a note about L. Paul in my notebook when I hear a female voice behind me.

"Learn anything interesting?"

I turn to see an older woman standing at the edge of my backyard, a man standing next to her. She is put together in a navy pantsuit, her gray hair pulled back tight in a ponytail. The man is less put together, with heavy eyelids, a wrinkled Hawaiian shirt, and a thick beard that makes him look older than she is, even though I suspect he is closer to my age.

"What are you doing back here?" I say.

"We tried ringing the front bell," the man says. "Are you Hannah Hall?"

"I'd like a better answer as to why you're trespassing on my property before I tell you that," I say.

"I'm Special Agent Jeremy O'Mackey from the Federal Bureau of Investigation, and my colleague here is Special Agent Naomi Wu," he says.

"Call me Naomi. We were hoping we could talk with you?"

Instinctively, I close the computer. "It's actually not a great time," I say.

She gives me a sticky-sweet smile. "It'll just take a few minutes," she says. "Then we'll get out of your hair."

They are already walking up the stairs onto the deck, sitting down in the chairs on the other side of the small table.

Naomi pushes her badge across the table, Agent O'Mackey does the same.

"I hope we aren't interrupting anything important," Naomi says.

"I hope you didn't follow me here, that's what I hope," I say.

Naomi takes me in, looking more than a little surprised at my tone. I'm too irritated to care. I'm irritated and more than a little worried they'll demand to take Owen's computer before I figure out what it has to tell me.

There's also this. I'm thinking of Grady Bradford's warning: *Don't answer any questions you think you shouldn't answer.* I'm bracing myself to heed it.

Jeremy O'Mackey reaches forward, takes his badge back.

"I assume you're aware that we're in the process of investigating the technology firm where your husband works?" he says. "We were hoping you could shed some light on his current whereabouts?"

I put the computer in my lap, protecting it.

"I'd like to, but I have no idea where my husband is. I haven't seen him since yesterday."

"Isn't that odd?" Naomi says, as if this has just occurred to her. "To not have seen him?"

I meet her eyes. "Very, yes."

"Would you be surprised to learn that your husband hasn't used his cell phone or any of his credit cards since yesterday? No paper trail at all," she says.

I don't answer her.

"Do you know why that might be?" O'Mackey says.

I don't like the way they're looking at me, like they've already decided I am keeping something from them. It is another reminder I don't need that I only wish I were.

Naomi pulls a notepad from her pocket, flipping open a page.

"We understand you've been in business with Avett and Belle Thompson?" she says. "They have commissioned one hundred and fifty-five thousand dollars of work from you over the last five years?"

"I don't know off the top of my head if that's the correct amount. But, yes, they are clients."

"Have you spoken to Belle since Avett's arrest yesterday?" she says.

I consider the messages I left on her voice mail. Six of them. Messages that have gone unreturned. I shake my head no.

"She hasn't called you?" he says.

"No," I say.

She tilts her head, considers. "Are you sure about that?"

"Yes, I'm sure who I've spoken to and who I haven't spoken to."

Naomi leans forward, toward me, like she is my friend. "We just want to make sure you're telling us everything. As opposed to your friend Belle."

"What do you mean?"

"Let's just say it didn't help her proclamation of innocence that she made it after purchasing four flights to Sydney from different Northern California airports in an attempt to leave the country undetected. It doesn't scream *I know nothing*, does it?"

I'm careful not to react. How is this happening? How is Avett in jail and Belle trying to sneak off to her former home? And how is Owen nowhere to be found in the middle of it all? Owen who is smart, who often sees the whole picture. Do I really believe he missed so much of this picture?

"Did Belle discuss The Shop with you?" Naomi asks.

"She never said anything to me about Avett's work," I say. "Belle wasn't interested."

"That mirrors what she said to us."

"Where is Belle now?"

"At her St. Helena home with her passport in her lawyer's possession. She's maintaining her position that she's shocked to think her husband would be guilty of this wrongdoing," he says. He pauses. "But in our experience the wife usually knows."

"Not this wife," I say.

Naomi chimes in, almost as if I haven't answered them. "As long as you're sure," she says. "Someone has to think of Owen's daughter."

"I am."

"Good," she says. "Good."

It sounds like a threat. And I hear what she is pretending not to say. I hear her insinuation that they could take Bailey away. Didn't I have Grady's assurance that they wouldn't?

"We will need to talk to Bailey as well," O'Mackey says. "When she returns from school today."

"You will not be talking to her," I say. "She knows nothing about her father's whereabouts. She's to be left alone."

O'Mackey matches my tone. "I'm afraid that's not up to you," he says. "We can set up a time now or we can just show up at your house later this evening."

35

"We've retained legal counsel," I say. "If you want to talk to her, you will need to reach out to our lawyer first."

"And who is your lawyer?" Naomi says.

I say it before I let myself consider the implication of saying it. "Jake Anderson. He's based in New York."

"Fine. Have him reach out to us," she says.

I nod, trying to figure out how to defuse the situation, not wanting to undo whatever Grady promised that morning about Bailey staying put. That is the most important thing.

"Look, I know you're just doing your jobs," I say. "But I'm tired and as I already told the U.S. marshal this morning, I don't have many answers for you."

"Whoa... whoa. What?" O'Mackey says.

I look at him and the no-longer-smiling Naomi.

"The U.S. marshal who came by to see me this morning," I say. "We went through this already."

They look at each other. "What was his name?" O'Mackey asks.

"The U.S. marshal's name?"

"Yes," he says. "What was the U.S. marshal's name?"

Naomi looks at me with her mouth pinched, like the playing field has changed in a way she wasn't ready for. This is why I decide not to tell the truth.

"I don't remember," I say.

"You don't remember his name?"

I don't say anything else.

"You don't remember the name of the U.S. marshal who showed up at your doorstep this morning. That's what you are telling me?"

"I didn't get a whole lot of sleep last night, so things are a little foggy."

"Do you remember if this U.S. marshal showed you a badge?" O'Mackey says.

"He did."

"Do you know what a United States marshal badge looks like?" Naomi says.

"Am I supposed to?" I say. "I also don't know what an FBI badge looks like, now that you're mentioning things I don't know. I probably should confirm that you are who you say you are. Then we can continue this conversation."

"We're just a little confused because this case isn't in the jurisdiction of the U.S. Marshals' office," she says. "So we need to ascertain who exactly was speaking with you this morning. They shouldn't have been here without our approval. Did they threaten Owen in some way? Because you should know that if Owen's involvement is minimal, he may be able to help himself by testifying against Avett."

"That's true," O'Mackey says. "He isn't even a suspect yet."

"Yet?" I say.

"He didn't mean yet," Naomi says.

"I didn't mean yet," O'Mackey says. "I meant that there is no reason for you to be talking to a U.S. marshal."

"Funny thing is, Agent O'Mackey, he said the same thing about you guys."

"Did he?"

Naomi pulls herself together, smiles. "Let's just start over, okay?" she says. "We're all on the same team here. But, in the future, you might want your lawyer present before you talk to anyone who just shows up at your door."

I match her smile. "That's a great idea, Naomi. I'm going to start with that right now," I say.

Then I point toward the gate and wait for them to walk through it.

Don't Hold This Against Me

After I'm certain that the FBI agents are gone, I leave my workshop.

I walk back toward the docks, Owen's computer tightly clasped to my chest. I pass the elementary school just as the kids are getting out for the day.

I look up, feeling eyes on me. Several mothers (and fathers) are staring in my direction. Not exactly with anger—not like Carl and Patty—more like with concern, with pity. These people love Owen, after all. They've always loved him. They've embraced him. It's going to take more than seeing his firm's name in their newsfeed to make them doubt him. That's the thing about a small town, people protect their own. It takes a lot for them to turn on someone they love.

It also takes a lot to let anyone new in. Like me. They're still not sure about letting me in. And when I first moved to Sausalito, it was worse. Those curious eyes were scrutinizing me, but for a different reason. They were asking questions loudly enough that Bailey heard them, came home, and relayed them. They wanted to know who was this out-of-towner who Owen had decided to marry. They didn't understand how Sausalito's most eligible bachelor was off the market because of a woodturner, though they didn't call me that. They called me a carpenter—a carpenter who didn't wear makeup or trendy shoes. They said how strange for Owen to choose a woman like that—a fresh-faced woman, pushing forty, who probably wasn't going to give him more kids. A woman who apparently didn't stop playing with wood long enough to figure out how to have a family of her own.

They didn't seem to understand about me what Owen understood from the beginning. I had no problem being on my own. My grandfather had raised me to depend on myself. My problems came when I tried to fit myself into someone else's life, especially when that meant giving up a part of myself in the process. So I waited until I didn't have to—until it felt like someone fit effortlessly. Or maybe that's too easy. Maybe it's more accurate to say that what was required to be with Owen didn't feel like effort. It felt like details.

At the house, I lock the door behind me and take out my phone and look up a name in my contacts. JAKE. It's the last phone call I want to make at this moment, but I do it anyway. I call the other lawyer I know.

"This is Anderson…" he says when he picks up.

The sound of his voice takes me back to Greene Street, to onion soup and

Bloody Marys at The Mercer Kitchen on Sundays, to a different life. It takes me back because this is how my former fiancé has always answered the phone. Jake Bradley Anderson—University of Michigan JD/MBA, triathlete, excellent cook.

In the two years since we've last spoken, he hasn't made a change to his greeting, even though it comes off as smug. He likes that it comes off as smug. That is why he does it. He thinks it's a good thing—smugness, intimidation—considering what he does for a living. He is a litigator at a Wall Street law firm, on track to being one of their youngest senior partners. He isn't a criminal lawyer, but he is a great lawyer, as he would be the first to tell you. I'm just hoping that Jake's type of hubris will help me now.

"Hi there," I say.

He doesn't ask who it is. He knows who it is, even after all this time. He also knows something is really wrong for me to be calling him.

"Where are you?" he says. "Are you in New York?"

When I called Jake to tell him I was getting married, he said that one day I'd show up back home ready to be together again. He believed that. And apparently he thinks today is that day.

"Sausalito." I pause, dreading the words I don't want to say. "I could use your help, Jake. I think I need a lawyer…"

"So… you're getting divorced?"

It's all I can do not to hang up the phone. Jake can't help himself. Even though he was relieved when I called

off the wedding, even though he married someone else four months later (and shortly thereafter divorced her), he liked to play the victim in our relationship. Jake held on to the narrative that because of my history, I was too scared to truly let him in—that I thought he'd leave me like my parents did. He never understood that I wasn't scared of someone leaving me. I was scared that the wrong person would stay.

"Jake, my husband's the reason I'm calling you," I say. "He's in trouble."

"What did he do?" he says.

It's the best I can hope for from him so I proceed to tell him the whole story, starting with some background information about Owen's work, the investigation into The Shop and Owen's bizarre disappearance, walking him through the dual visits from Grady Bradford and the FBI, and how the FBI didn't know about Grady. I move him through how no one seems to know anything about where Owen is, or what he is planning next—least of all Bailey and me.

"And the daughter… she's with you?" he says.

"Bailey, yes. She's with me. Which is probably the last place she wants to be."

"So he left her too?"

I don't answer him.

"What's her full name?" he says.

I hear him typing on his computer, taking notes, making one of the charts that used to cover our living room floor. Owen, now, in its bull's-eye.

"First of all, don't be too worried that the FBI didn't know about the guy from the U.S. Marshals Service coming to talk to you. They could all be lying to you. And beyond that, there are often turf wars between different law enforcement agencies, especially when the scope of the investigation is still in question. Any word yet from anyone at the SEC?"

"No."

"There will be. You should refer all law enforcement to me, at least until we know what's going on. Don't say anything, just have them call me directly."

"I appreciate that. Thank you."

"Don't mention it," he says. "But I gotta ask... how wrapped up in this are you?"

"Well, he's my husband, so I would say intimately."

"They're going to show up with search warrants," he says. "I'm surprised they haven't already. So, if there is anything that implicates you, you need to get it out of your house."

"I can't be implicated," I say. "I have nothing to do with this."

I feel myself getting defensive. And I feel an uptick of anxiety, thinking of anyone showing up at my house with search warrants—thinking of the duffel bag they would find, still untouched, hidden beneath the kitchen sink.

"Jake, I'm just trying to figure out where Owen is. Why he thought the only way out was to get away from here."

"He probably doesn't want to go to jail, for starters."

"No, that's not it. He wouldn't run because of that."

"So what's your theory?"

"He's trying to protect his daughter," I say.

"From what?"

"I don't know. Maybe he thinks it's going to ruin her life if her father is falsely accused. Maybe he's off somewhere trying to prove he's innocent."

"Not likely. But... there is the possibility that something else is going on," he says.

"Like what?"

"Like worse things that he's guilty of," he says.

"Helpful, Jake," I say.

"Look, I'm not going to sugarcoat this. If Owen isn't running from The Shop, he is probably running from what The Shop might reveal about him. The question is what that might be..." He pauses. "I have a private investigator, a good one. I'll ask him to do some digging. But I'm going to need you to email me Owen's entire history. Anything you know. Where he went to school, where he grew up. And dates. Everything. Where and when his daughter was born."

I hear Jake start to bite on his pen. No one else in the world would decipher that is what he is doing, his secret habit. The one less-than-confident thing Jake does. But I can picture it as if I were sitting right there, staring at his mauled pen cap. It's a terrible thing to know everything about someone long after you want to.

"And do this for me. Keep your phone near you in case I need to get in touch. But don't answer for any numbers you don't recognize."

I think of Grady saying Owen threw his phone away—that he threw away the phone with the only number for him I'd recognize.

"What if it's Owen?"

"Owen's not calling right now," he says. "You know that."

"I don't know that."

"I think you do."

I don't say anything. Even though I suspect he's right, I'm not going to tell Jake he is. I'm not going to betray Owen in that way. Or Bailey.

"And you need to figure out why he ran, something more specific than he's trying to protect his kid..." he says. "And you better figure it out quickly. The FBI isn't going to ask nicely for long."

My head starts to spin, thinking about how unkindly the FBI has been asking already.

"Are you still there?" he says.

"I'm here."

"Just... try to stay calm. You know more than you think you do. You know how to get through this."

It's enough to make me cry, the way he says it—sweetly, assuredly—Jake's version of a deep kindness.

"But in the future," he says, "don't say someone is innocent, okay? Say he's not guilty, if you have to say something. But saying someone's innocent makes you sound like an idiot. Especially when most people are guilty as fuck."

And then there's that.

Six Weeks Ago

"We should take a vacation," Owen said. "We're overdue."

It was midnight. We were lying in bed, his hand cupping mine. He was resting it on his chest, on his heart.

"You should come with me to Austin," I said. "Or would that not count?"

"Austin?" he said.

"I have the woodturners symposium I told you about. We could turn it into a getaway. Spend a couple of days in Texas Hill Country..."

"It's in Austin? You didn't tell me it was in Austin..."

Then he nodded, like he was considering it, considering joining me—except I felt something shift in him. I felt something shut down in his body.

"What's wrong?" I said.

"Nothing," he said.

But he let go of my hand and started to play with his wedding band, turning it around and around his finger. I made him that wedding band. I made it to match mine, exactly: Two slim bands that, from a distance, looked like any other shiny, platinum ring. But I made ours out of brushed steel, a thick white oak. Rustic and elegant at once. I'd used my smallest lathe. Owen had sat on the floor beside me while I worked.

"Bailey also has that school trip to Sacramento coming up," he said. "We could hightail it to New Mexico, just the two of us, get lost in the white rock."

"I'd love that," I said. "I haven't been to New Mexico in a long time."

"Me neither. Not since back when I was in college. We drove up to Taos, spent a week on the mountain."

"You drove all the way from New Jersey?" I asked.

He kept twirling his ring, absentmindedly. "What?"

"You drove all the way from New Jersey to New Mexico? That must have taken you forever."

That stopped him, his fingers leaving his ring. "It wasn't during college."

"Owen! You just said you went to Taos during college."

"I don't know. It was a mountain somewhere. Maybe it was Vermont. All I remember was that the air was too thin."

I laughed. "What's going on with you?"

"Nothing. It just…"

I look at him, trying to follow what he isn't saying.

"It just brings back a weird part of my life."

"College?"

"College. After college." He shook his head. "Being stuck on a mountain I don't remember."

"Okay… so that's maybe the weirdest thing I think you've ever said to me."

"I know."

He sat up and turned on the light. "Shit," he said. "I really need that vacation."

"Let's take it," I said.

"Okay. Let's take it."

He lay down, again, put his hand on my stomach. And I could feel him relax again. I could feel him come back to me. So I didn't want to press him. I didn't want to press him right then on what he'd almost chosen to share.

"And we don't have to get into it now, but just for the record?" I said. "I spent most of college playing guitar in a Joni Mitchell cover band, attending poetry slams, and dating a philosophy grad student who was working on a manifesto about how television was the government's attempt to control a revolution."

"Not sure he was exactly wrong about that," he said.

"Maybe not, but the point is, there's not a whole lot you could tell me about who you used to be that would change anything, at least not between us."

"Well," he whispered. "Thank God for that."

Bailey's No Good Very Bad Day

When Bailey gets back from school, she looks miserable.

I'm sitting on the bench, drinking a glass of red wine, a blanket covering my legs. I try to go back over the day—a day that began and will end without Owen, as impossible as that feels. As angry and sad and stressed and alone as that makes me feel.

She weaves down the docks, keeping her head down, until she gets to the house. Then she stops in front of me, right in front of the bench, and stands there. Eyes blazing.

"I'm not going back there tomorrow," she says. "I'm not going back to school."

I take in her eyes, her fear. There we are—mirror images of each other—the last way I wanted us to get here.

"They pretend they're not talking about it," she says. "About my dad. About me. It's worse than if they just said it to my face. Like I can't hear them whisper about it all day anyway."

"What were they saying?"

"Which part do you want to hear?" she says. "How Brian Padura asked Bobby after chemistry if my father was a criminal? Or when Bobby punched him in the mouth for it?"

"Bobby did that?"

"Yep…"

I nod, a little impressed with Bobby.

"It gets worse from there," she says.

I move down the bench slightly, making room for her. She sits down, but on the edge, as if she may change her mind and get up at any moment.

"Why don't you skip tomorrow?"

She looks at me, surprised. "Really?" she says. "You're not even going to fight me on that?"

"Would it help?"

"No."

"As far as I'm concerned, you're off the hook for school tomorrow. If your day was anything like mine, you deserve to be."

She nods, starts biting on her nails. "Thank you," she says.

I want to reach out and take her hand away from her mouth, hold it. I want to tell her it is going to be okay, that it will all get easier—one way or another. But even if it would comfort her to hear it, it wouldn't comfort her to hear it from me.

"I have no energy to cook anything, so your only form of nutrition tonight is coming from two extra-cheese pizzas with mushrooms and onions that are on their way to us in thirty minutes or less."

She almost smiles, which cracks it open in me, the question I know I need to ask her, the question that I hope will help me figure out what has been looming so large in my mind since getting off the phone with Jake.

"Bailey," I say, "I keep thinking about what you asked me earlier, about what your father meant in his note to you. What he meant by *you know what matters…*"

She sighs, apparently too exhausted for the eye roll that would usually accompany it.

"I know, my father loves me. You made your point," she says.

"Maybe I was wrong about that," I say. "About him meaning that. Maybe he meant something else."

She looks at me, confused. "What are you talking about?"

"Maybe he wrote that because you know something," I say. "You know something about him that he wants you to remember."

"What could I possibly know?" she says.

"I'm not sure."

"Well, I'm glad we cleared that up," she says. Then she pauses. "Everyone at school seems to agree with you though."

"What do you mean?"

"They all think I know why my father is doing whatever he's doing," she says. "Like he told me over breakfast that he was planning to steal half a billion dollars and disappear."

"We don't know that your father had anything to do with that," I say.

"No, we just know he isn't here."

She's correct about that. Owen isn't here. For all we know, he could be anywhere. It brings me back to what Grady Bradford said offhandedly to me that morning—the information he inadvertently gave me when he was trying to convince me I should talk to him, that he was on our side. He offered his phone number. He offered the phone number to his branch office. It had an area code I didn't recognize. 512. I reach into my back pocket, and pull out the napkin from Fred's. Two numbers on it—both of which start with 512. No address.

I reach for my cell phone on the tea table and call the office number, my heart racing as it starts to ring, as the automatic operator answers, telling me I have reached the U.S Marshals' office.

The Western Texas branch of the U.S. Marshals' office. Located in Austin, Texas.

Grady Bradford works out of the Austin office. Why is a U.S. marshal from Texas the one who shows up at my door? Especially a marshal who, if I believe O'Mackey and Naomi, has no authorization over the investigation? And if he does have authorization, why? What has Owen done that Bradford would be somehow involved in this?

What does Texas have to do with any of this?

"Bailey," I say, "did you and your father ever spend any time in Austin?"

"Austin, as in Texas? No."

"Think about it for a second. Did you ever pass through Austin on the way to somewhere else? Maybe before you guys moved to Sausalito. When you were still living in Seattle..."

"So when I was like... four years old?"

"I realize it's a long shot."

She looks up, searching her brain for a day or a moment she's long forgotten that all of a sudden she is being told is a little too important to forget. She looks upset that she can't find it. And upsetting her is the last thing I want.

"Why are you asking me anyway?" she says.

"There was a U.S. marshal here earlier from Austin," I say. "I was just thinking that maybe he was here because of some tie your father has to the city."

"To Austin?"

"Yes," I say.

She pauses, considers, reaching for something.

"Maybe," she says. "A long time ago... It's possible I was there for a wedding. When I was really little. I mean, I'm pretty sure I was a flower girl because they made me pose for all these photos. And I think someone told me we were in Austin."

"How sure are you?"

"Not sure," she says. "As not sure as you can get."

"Well what do you remember about the wedding?" I ask, trying to narrow down the window.

"I don't know… all I remember is we were all there."

"So your mother too?" I say.

"I think so, yeah. But the part I remember best I don't think she was with us for. My dad and I left the church and went on a walk, and he brought me to the football stadium. There was a game going on. I'd never seen anything like it. This enormous stadium. All lit up. Everything was orange."

"Orange?" I say.

"Orange lights, orange uniforms. I loved orange, I was obsessed with Garfield, so you know… that's what I remember. My father pointing to the colors and saying, it's like Garfield."

"And you think you were at a church?"

"Yeah, a church. Either in Texas or nowhere near Texas," she says.

"But you never asked your father after that where the wedding was? You never asked him for any details?"

"No. Why would I?"

"Good point."

"Besides, it makes him upset if I bring up the past," she says.

That surprises me. "Why do you think?"

"'Cause of how little I remember about my mother."

I stay quiet. But Owen did mention something similar to me. He'd taken Bailey to a therapist when she was little, her mom seemingly blocked from her mind. The therapist told Owen this was common. It was a defense mechanism to ease the abandonment of losing a parent as young as Bailey was when she'd lost Olivia. But Owen thought it was bigger than that, and, for some reason, he seemed to blame himself for it.

Bailey closes her eyes, as if thinking of her mother is too much, as if thinking about her father is now too much too. She wipes at her eyes, but not before I see a tear escape. Not before she knows I see it. She's not even trying to hide how alone she feels. And I know something then, brushing up against Bailey in that kind of pain. I will do anything I can to make it go away. To help her. I'll do anything to make her feel okay again.

"Can we talk about something else?" she says. Then she puts her hand up. "You know what? I take that back. Can we talk about nothing? What I want is to talk about nothing at all."

"Bailey…" I say.

"No," she says. "Can you just leave me alone?"

Then she leans back, waiting for her pizza and for me to go away, in whichever order she can make those things happen.

What Don't You Want to Remember?

I go inside, honoring Bailey and her request to be left alone. I have no desire to push her. I have no desire to demand she come inside. She is confused and angry, wondering if her father is who she thinks he is—wondering if she can still trust in the person she has always known him to be. Stable, generous, hers. She is angry that she has to question that—angry at him, angry at herself. It is a feeling I can relate to.

Protect her.

But from what? From what Owen was involved in at The Shop? From what he let happen there? Or does Owen want Bailey protected from something else? Something I can't see yet? Something I don't want to see yet?

I pace back and forth in my bedroom. I don't want to antagonize Bailey, but I feel an urgent need to pull at any thread I can find. It's all I can think to do—to reconsider (to ask her to consider) our foggy, gentle memories of Owen. To juxtapose them against these last twenty-four hours. Where do they meet?

Suddenly, one way they meet comes firing back. Austin. Something else I know about Austin and Owen. Shortly before I moved to Sausalito, I was offered a job there. A movie star who lived there was redoing her house, a ranch house on Westlake Drive, hugging Lake Austin.

She wanted help getting rid of her ex-husband's aura. Her ex-husband had loved everything modern and hated anything rustic. Her interior designer had suggested my woodturning pieces. But she wanted to be involved, which meant I needed to go to Austin for two weeks and go through the process with her.

I asked Owen to come with me, and he shut the idea down. He was upset that I'd want to go anywhere that would delay my move to Sausalito—that would delay us beginning our lives together in the real way that we had been planning for.

I was anxious to get to California too—and less-than-anxious to work side by side with the increasingly demanding client. So I turned down the job. I clocked his strange behavior though. It was out of character for Owen to react that way—needy, controlling. When I raised it with him, he apologized for reacting badly. He said the move was just making him nervous. He was nervous about how Bailey would adjust to having me in her home. It always came down to Bailey for Owen. Any changes that upended her were going to upend him. I understood the anxiety. I let it go.

But I think about the other Austin red flag. When I asked him to come with me to Austin for my woodturners symposium, he went dark for a minute. He didn't balk at the suggestion, but he pivoted. He did pivot. So maybe it wasn't just about Bailey. Maybe it had something to do with Austin itself. Something he didn't want me to run into there. Something he had run from.

I reach for my phone and call Jake, a diehard football fan: college, the NFL, classic games on YouTube at eight in the morning.

"It's late where I am," he says, instead of hello.

"What can you tell me about the Austin football stadium?" I say.

"I can tell you it's not called that," he says.

"Do you know anything about their football team?"

"The Longhorns? What do you want to know?"

"Their colors?"

"Why?"

I wait.

He sighs. "Orange and white," he says.

"You positive?"

"Yes, burnt orange and white. Uniforms, mascot. Goalposts. The end zone. The entire stadium. It's midnight. It's after midnight. I'm sleeping. Why are you asking?"

I can't seem to tell him the truth, which sounds crazy. The U.S. marshal who showed up at our house is based out of there. Bailey remembers being there. Maybe. And Owen got weird about the idea of us going there, two different times. Two different times I can now recall.

I don't want to tell him that Austin is all I have.

I think of my grandfather. If he were alive, and sitting here with me, I could tell him. He wouldn't think I was crazy. He'd just sit there and help me go through it all until I figured out what I needed to do. That's why he was good at his job—at helping me understand what my job was. The first lesson he ever taught me was that it wasn't just about shaping a block of wood into what you wanted it to be. That it was also a peeling back, to seeing what was inside the wood, what the wood had been before. It was the first step to creating something beautiful. The first step to making something out of nothing.

If Owen were here, he would understand that too. I could tell him too. He would look at me and shrug. *What do you have to lose*? He would look at me, and see it—what I'd already decided.

Protect her.

"Jake? I'll call you back," I say.

"Tomorrow!" he says. "Call me back tomorrow."

I hang up, and I go back outside. I find Bailey where I left her, staring out at the bay, sipping on my glass of wine, like it belongs to her.

"What are you doing?" I say.

The glass is almost empty. It was full when I left it. Now it is almost empty. The wine covers her lips, the corners of her mouth stained red.

"Can you not?" she says. "I just had a little."

"I don't care about the wine."

"So then why are you looking at me like that?" she says.

"You should go and pack a bag," I say.

"Why?" she says.

"I was thinking about what you said, about the wedding. About Austin. And I think we should go," I say.

"To Austin?"

I nod.

She looks at me, confused. "That's crazy. How is going to Austin going to help anything?" she says.

I want to give her an honest answer. If I try to quote my grandfather and tell her this could be the peeling back, will she be able to hear that? I doubt it. And if I tell her what I've put together so far—a wobbly formulation at best—she will rebel and refuse to go.

So I tell her something that she can hear, something that is also the truth. Something that sounds like what her father would say.

"It's better than sitting here," I say.

"What about school?" she says. "I'm just going to miss school?"

"You said you weren't going tomorrow anyway," I say. "Didn't you just finish saying that?"

"Yeah," she says. "I guess."

I'm already heading into the house. I'm already on the way.

"So pack."

— Part 2 —

Each species of wood has its own distinctive patterns and colors, which are revealed when the bowl is turned.

—Philip Moulthrop

Keep Austin Weird

We get on a 6:55 A.M. flight out of San Jose.

It's been forty-six hours since Owen left for work, forty-six hours since I've heard a word from him.

I give Bailey the window seat and take the aisle, passengers knocking into me as they make their way to the one bathroom in the back of the plane.

Bailey leans against the window as far away from me as she can get, her arms folded tightly against her chest. She is wearing a Fleetwood Mac tank top, no sweatshirt, goose bumps running up her arms.

I don't know if she is cold or upset. Or both. We have never flown together before, so I didn't think to remind her to put a sweatshirt in her carry-on. Not like she would have heeded my advice anyway.

Still, suddenly, this feels like Owen's greatest crime. How did he not provide me with a point of reference before he disappeared? How did he not leave behind a set of rules on how to take care of her? The first rule: Tell her to pack a sweatshirt when she gets on a plane. Tell her to cover her arms.

Bailey keeps her eyes glued to the window, avoids eye contact. It's just as well that she has no desire to talk. I start taking notes in my notebook instead. I work on making a game plan. We land at twelve thirty local time, which means it will probably be close to two before we make it to downtown Austin and check into the hotel.

I wish I knew the city better, but I've been to Austin only once before, during my senior year of college. It was Jules's first professional assignment (she was paid to the tune of $85 and a hotel room) and she invited me to tag along. She was photographing the *Austin Chronicle*'s Annual Hot Sauce Festival for a Boston food blog. We spent most of our time in Austin at that festival, burning our mouths off on a hundred different kinds of spiced ribs and fried potatoes and smoked veggies and jalapeño sauces. Jules took six hundred photographs.

It wasn't until shortly before we were heading out of town that we wandered outside of the gardens in East Austin where the festival was being held. We found a hilltop that gave us the most incredible view of the downtown skyline. There were as many trees as skyscrapers, more clear sky than clouds. And the coziness of the lake somehow made Austin feel less like a city and more like a small town.

Jules and I decided then and there that we were going to move to Austin after graduation. It was far less expensive than New York, far easier than Los Angeles. We didn't really consider it when the time came, but in that moment, that's what it felt like, looking down over the city. It felt like looking at our future.

This certainly isn't the future I'd imagined.

I close my eyes, trying to not let it subsume me, the questions that keep rolling through my head on a terrible loop, the questions I need answers to: Where is Owen? Why did he need to run? And what did I miss about him that he was too afraid to tell me himself?

That's part of the reason I'm sitting on this plane. I have this fantasy that by leaving the house, it will trigger something in the universe that makes Owen come home home again and offer up the answers himself. Isn't that how it's supposed to work, the kettle boils once you stop watching? As soon as we land in Austin, there will be a message from Owen asking where we are, telling me that he is sitting in our empty kitchen waiting on us, as opposed to the other way around.

"What can I get you ladies?"

I look up to see the flight attendant standing by our aisle, her silver drink cart in front of her.

Bailey doesn't turn her head from the window, her purple ponytail the only thing facing out.

"Regular Coke," she says. "Lots of ice."

I shrug, a peace offering for Bailey's shortness. "Diet, please," I say.

The flight attendant just laughs, unoffended. "Sixteen?" she whispers.

I nod.

"I have a sixteen-year-old myself," she says. "Twins actually. Believe me, I get it."

This is when Bailey turns around.

"I'm not hers," she says.

It's true. It's also something Bailey may have said on another day, eager to correct the record. But just now it sounds different and it stings in a way I have trouble hiding on my face. It isn't just about how it makes me feel. It's also about the reckoning that's coming for her on the heels of her comment—the impossible realization that hating or disavowing me is a whole lot less fun when, at the moment, I'm the only person that she has.

Her face tightens as it hits her. I stay quiet, staring at the television screen on the seat in front of me, an episode of *Friends* playing silently, Rachel and Joey kissing in a hotel room.

I pretend not to notice Bailey's despair, but I don't put on my headphones either. It's the best I can come up with for giving her some breathing room while trying to let her know I'm there if she wants me.

Bailey rubs at the goose bumps on her arms, not saying anything, not for a while. Finally, she takes a sip of her soda. Then she makes a face.

"I think she switched our drinks," she says.

I turn and look at her. "What's that?"

She holds out her ice-filled cup, her soda brimming to the top. "This is diet," she says. "The flight attendant must have given me yours…"

I try not to look too surprised as she hands her drink over. And I don't argue. I hand Bailey my drink and wait for her to take a sip.

Bailey nods, like she is relieved to have her correct drink. Except we both know the flight attendant delivered us the correct drinks in the first place. And only now—only since Bailey's gesture, her attempt to relieve the tension—are the drinks mixed up.

If this is Bailey's way of reaching toward me, I'm going to meet her there.

I take a sip of the Coke. "Thank you," I say. "I thought mine tasted weird."

"No worries…" she says. Then she returns to looking out the window. "No big deal."

We get into an Uber at the airport and I scroll through the news reports on my phone.

Stories about The Shop plaster CNN's home page, the *New York Times*, the *Wall Street Journal*. Many of the recent headlines focus on a press conference held by the head of the SEC, offering up such clickbait as THE SHOP IS CLOSED FOR GOOD.

I click on the most recent article in the *New York Times*, which covers the SEC announcement that they're filing civil fraud charges against Avett Thompson. And which quotes a source in the FBI about how senior staff and top executives will *most certainly* be named as people of interest.

Owen isn't mentioned by name. At least not yet.

The Uber pulls onto Presidential Boulevard and heads toward the hotel, which is on Lady Bird Lake near the Congress Avenue Bridge. It's away from the hubbub of the busiest part of the city, across the bridge from the heart of downtown Austin.

I reach into my bag and pull out a printout of our hotel reservation, sweeping over the details. Jules's full name, Julia Alexandra Nichols, stares back at me. Jules suggested reserving the room on her credit card as a safety measure. I have her credit card and her ID in my wallet, further safety measures, in case anyone is tracking us.

Of course, there is a record of our flight to Austin. Jules put the flights on her credit card, but our real names are on the plane tickets. There's a clear way to track us here, if anyone is inclined to do so. But even if they track that we're in Austin, they don't need to know exactly where in Austin. I'm not helping the next Grady or Naomi to show up at my door, unannounced.

The driver—a young guy in a bandanna—looks at Bailey in the rearview mirror. He isn't much older than she is and he keeps trying to make eye contact with her. He keeps trying to get her attention.

"Is this your first time in Austin?" he asks her.

"Yep," she says.

"What do you think so far?" he says.

"Based on the fourteen minutes since we left the airport?" she says.

He laughs, as though she is joking with him, as though she is inviting him to keep talking.

"I grew up here," he says. "You can ask me anything about this city and I can tell you even more than you wanted to know."

"Good to know," she says.

I can see that Bailey is totally tuned out so I try to engage him in case any of it will turn out to be useful later.

"You grew up here?" I say.

"Born and raised. I lived here when this was a small town," he says. "It's still a small town in a lot of ways, but there are a helluva lot more people and a lot bigger buildings."

He pulls off the highway and I feel a clinching in my chest as downtown Austin comes into view. I know this was the plan, but looking out the window at this strange city, it all seems so much crazier.

He points out the window, motions toward a skyscraper.

"That's the Frost Bank Tower," he says. "Used to be the tallest building in Austin. Now I'm not even sure it cracks the top five. Have you heard of it?"

"Can't say I have," I say.

"Yeah, crazy story behind it," he says. "If you look at it from certain angles it looks like an owl. Exactly like an owl. Might be hard to see from here but it's wild if you can make it out..."

I open my window and take in the Frost Building—the tiers on top, like ears, the two windows that look like eyes. There is definitely an owl similarity.

"This is a UT town, but the architects all went to Rice University and the owl is Rice University's mascot. So that's like a f-you to our mascot and to the Longhorns in general," he says. "And I mean, some people say it's just a conspiracy theory, but look at it. The building looks like an owl! How can that be an accident?"

He turns onto South Congress Bridge and I can see our hotel in the distance.

"Are you guys here looking at UT?" he asks. He directs the question toward Bailey, again trying to meet her eyes in the rearview.

"Not exactly," she says.

"So... what are you doing here?"

She doesn't answer. She opens the window in an attempt to discourage further questions. I don't blame her for that. I don't blame her for not being particularly anxious to explain to a stranger why she is here—in a city she is trying to remember whether she's been to before, searching for information about her missing father.

"Just fans of Austin," I say.

"Right on," he says. "A little vacay. I can get behind that."

He pulls up to the hotel and Bailey is opening the door before the car even stops moving.

"Wait, wait! Let me give you my number. In case there is anything I can show you guys while you're in town."

"There isn't," Bailey says.

Then she shifts her bag higher on her shoulder. And starts walking toward the hotel's entrance.

I grab the suitcases from the trunk, hurry to keep up. I catch up to her by the revolving doors.

"That guy was so annoying," she says.

I start to say he was just trying to be friendly, but she isn't interested in friendly. And since I have to pick my battles, I decide this isn't going to be the one I choose.

We head into the hotel and I look around the lobby: high atrium, the bar, a Starbucks off to the side. Hundreds of rooms. Just the type of nondescript hotel I was hoping for, an easy place to get lost in. Except maybe I'm looking around a moment too long because a hotel employee catches my eyes.

She has a name tag on, AMY, her hair in a short bob.

We get in line at reception, but it's too late. She walks over, a smile plastered to her face.

"Hi there," she says. "I'm Amy, the hotel concierge. Welcome to Austin! Is there anything I can help you with while you're waiting to check in?"

"We're good. Unless you happen to have a map of the campus?" I say.

"Of UT-Austin?" she says. "Absolutely. I also could help set you up on a campus tour. And there is some outstanding coffee that you won't want to miss when you head to that part of town. Are you coffee drinkers?"

Bailey eyes me as though it's my fault Amy is hovering and jabbering on—and maybe she isn't wrong. I did ask for a map as opposed to just telling chatty Amy to move along. But I want a map. I want to hold something in my hands that makes it seem a little more like I know what I'm doing.

"Can I set up a shuttle service to take you there?"

We get to the front of the line, where a desk clerk named Steve is holding out two glasses of lemonade.

"Hiya, Amy."

"Steve! I was just about to set these two ladies up with some college maps and good flat whites."

"Excellent," Steve says. "I'll get you settled into your digs. What brings you to our little corner of the world? And how can I go about making it your favorite corner?"

That's it for Bailey. She gives up and starts to walk away—Steve the final nail in the aggressively friendly coffin. She heads toward the elevator bank, drilling me with a final look as she goes. A look of blame for these conversations she can't handle, for being far from home, for being in Austin at all. Any goodwill I managed to accrue on the plane is apparently gone.

"So, Ms. Nichols, you'll be staying on the eighth floor with a great view of the Lady Bird Lake," he says. "We have a pretty great spa in the hotel if you're looking to refresh from your flight before heading up to the room. Or I can set you up with a late lunch?"

I put up my hands in surrender.

"A room key, Steve," I say. "Just a room key. As quick as you can hand it over."

We drop our suitcases upstairs. We don't stop to eat anything.

At two thirty, we leave the hotel and head back toward the Congress Avenue Bridge. I decide we should walk. I figure a long walk may help jog a memory in Bailey, assuming there is a memory to jog. And this walk will lead us through the heart of downtown Austin and up toward the campus and the Darrell K Royal Stadium, the only football stadium in the city.

As soon as we make it over the bridge, the downtown splays out before us—vibrant and spinning, even in the early afternoon. It somehow feels more like it's nighttime: music playing, bars open, garden restaurants packed with people.

Bailey keeps her head down, eyes on her phone. How is she going to recognize anything if she isn't paying attention? But when we stop at a traffic light on Fifth Street, the DON'T WALK sign flashing before us, she does look up.

She looks up and I catch her do a double take.

"What?" I say.

"Nothing."

She shakes her head. But she keeps staring.

I follow her eyes to a sign for Antone's, written in blue script. HOME OF THE BLUES written below it. A couple cuddles by the front door, taking a selfie.

She points at the club. "I'm pretty sure that my father has a John Lee Hooker record from there," she says.

I know she's correct as soon as she says it. I can picture the album cover: *Antone's* logo on the front of it—the sleek lettering in script. And Hooker

singing into a microphone, hat and sunglasses on, guitar in hand. I remember a night last week—how could it possibly have been last week?—when Bailey was at play practice, and the two of us were in the house alone. Owen strummed on his guitar. I can't remember the words of the song now, but Owen's face while he sang—that I remember.

"He does," I say. "You're right."

"Not that it matters," she says.

"I don't think we know what matters yet," I say.

"Is that supposed to be uplifting or something?" she says.

Uplifting? Three days ago, we were all together in our kitchen, a million miles from this reality. Bailey was eating a bowl of cereal, talking to her father about the weekend. She wanted Owen to let her take a drive down to the Peninsula with Bobby, who wanted to go on a long bike ride around Monterey. *Maybe we can all go,* Owen said. Bailey rolled her eyes, but I could see that she was considering it, especially after Owen said that we could stop in Carmel on the way home. He wanted to stop and get clam chowder at a small restaurant she loved near the beach, a restaurant where he's been taking her since shortly after they moved to Sausalito.

That was three days ago. Now the two of us are in a new reality where Owen is missing, where we spend our time trying to figure out where he is. And why. A new reality where I'm constantly asking myself whether I'm wrong to hold on to the belief that the answers to those questions aren't going to upend my most central ideas of who Owen is.

I'm not aiming for uplifting. I'm just trying to say something neutral so she doesn't know how angry I am too.

When the light changes, I walk quickly across the street, turning onto Congress, picking up speed as I go.

"Try to keep up," I say.

"Where are we going?" Bailey says.

"Somewhere better than here," I say.

About an hour later, we round the capital and circle onto San Jacinto Boulevard. And the stadium comes into view. It is enormous, demanding—even from several blocks away.

As we walk toward it, we pass the Caven-Clark Sports Center. It seems to be the student rec center complete with a series of matching orange-laced buildings, Clark Field, and a large track. Students are playing tag football and doing sprints up the stairs and lounging on benches, making this part of campus feel at once completely separate and still a part of its city. Seamlessly integrated.

I look down at my campus map and start moving toward the closest stadium entrance.

But Bailey stops walking suddenly. "I don't want to do this," she says.

I meet her eyes.

"Even if I was at the stadium, then what? What's that going to tell us about anything?"

"Bailey..." I say.

"Seriously, what are we doing here?"

She won't respond well if I tell her that I stayed up last night reading about childhood memories—how we forget them. And how we get them back. They often come from returning to a place and then being allowed to experience it in the same way you experienced it the first time. That is what we are doing here. We are following her instinct. We are tapping into her memory that she's been here before. And my instinct, from the minute I realized where Grady Bradford came from, that we should.

"There are things your father hasn't told us beyond what's going on at The Shop," I say. "I'm trying to figure out what they are."

"That sounds pretty general," she says.

"It'll get less general the more you remember," I say.

"So... this is on me, then?"

"No, it's on me. If I was wrong to take you here, I'll be the first to say it."

She gets quiet.

"Look, will you just come inside? Can you do that?" I say. "We've come this far."

"Do I have a choice?" she says.

"Yes," I say. "Always. With me you always do."

I can see it flash across her face—her surprise that I mean it. And I do mean it. We are a hundred feet from the closest stadium entrance, GATE 2, but it is up to Bailey. If she wants to turn around, I won't stop her. Maybe this frees her to keep going, because that's what she does.

She walks up to the gate, which feels like a victory. A second victory: a stadium tour group seems to be congregating and we are able to latch on to them, walking past security without so much as a look from the distracted student manning the desk.

"Welcome to DKR," the tour guide says. "I'm Elliot, I'll be taking you around today. Follow me!"

He leads the group into the end zone and gives everyone a second to take in the stadium, which is epic. There is seating for more than a hundred thousand fans, TEXAS spelled out large on one end of the field, LONGHORNS on the other. It is so large—so imposing—that it feels like the kind of place you might remember, you might hold on to, especially at an early age.

Elliot starts walking the group through what happens on game night—how a cannon is fired after each touchdown, how Bevo, the mascot, is an actual steer bull and how there are a group of Texas cowboys who march him around the field, who tend to him.

As he finishes his spiel and starts to lead everyone up to the press box, I motion for Bailey to hang back, and we head to the bleachers.

I take a seat in the front row, Bailey following suit. I stare out at the field, watching her out of the corner of my eye as she settles in. And then she sits up taller.

"I can't be sure if it was here," she says. "I don't know. But I remember my father talking to me about how one day I'd love football the way he did. I remember him telling me not to be scared of the mascot."

That seems wrong—not the mascot part, which sounds exactly like Owen, but the loving football part. Owen doesn't care at all about football. At least since we've been together, I've barely seen him watch a whole game. No long afternoon football games taking over our weekends. No Monday night recapping. One of many refreshing changes from Jake.

"But I must be remembering wrong," she says. "My father doesn't love football, right? I mean… we never even watch games."

"That's what I was thinking. But he may have loved it then. When he thought he would make a fan out of you."

"When I was a toddler?"

I shrug. "Maybe he thought he could mold you into a Longhorn?"

Bailey turns back toward the field. Nothing left, apparently, to add to her memory. "I do think that's what it was. It wasn't about football, in general. He loved this team." She pauses. "Or whatever team it was, in their orange uniforms…"

"Just walk me through what you know, as if this were the place," I say. "Did you come after the wedding? Was it night?"

"No, it was during the afternoon. And I was in my dress. The flower girl dress. I know that. Maybe we had come from the wedding. The ceremony part."

She pauses.

"Unless I'm imagining all of this. Which feels equally possible."

I feel her getting frustrated. More than likely, Bailey remembered what she could back in Sausalito, and that's where we should've stayed. In our floating home, empty without Owen. The two of us existing in the terrible space he left there.

"I don't know what to say," she said. "Any stadium I might feel this way."

"But it does look familiar?"

"Yeah, it kinda does."

Then something occurs to me. It comes fast and I can see the rest, depending on what her answer is.

"So you walked here?"

She gives me a strange look. "Yes, with you."

"No, I mean, didn't you say you walked here from the wedding? That day with your father? Assuming it was here..."

She shakes her head, as if that was a crazy question, but then her eyes get wider. "Yeah, I think we did. If I was in the dress, we probably came right from the church."

I don't know if this conversation is creating the memory, or not, but she suddenly becomes more definitive.

"We definitely did," she says. "I mean we only came to the game for a little while, after the ceremony. We walked over. I'm pretty sure of it..."

"So it has to be near here."

"What does?" she says.

I look down at the map and see the options marked for us: a Catholic Church not too far from here; two Episcopal chapters, and a synagogue even closer than that. They are all within walking distance. They are all potentially the place Owen took Bailey before he took her here.

"You don't remember by chance what kind of ceremony it was? Like denominationally?"

"You're joking, right?"

I'm not. "Of course I am," I say.

Who Needs a Tour Guide?

I circle the churches on the map and we head out of the stadium through a different exit. We head down the steps and past a statue honoring the Longhorn Band, UT's Etter-Harbin Alumni Center just behind it.

"Wait," Bailey says. "Slow down a sec..."

I turn around. "What?"

She looks up at the building, at the sign in front: THE HOME OF THE TEXAS-EXES.

Then she turns back to the stadium. "This looks familiar," she says.

"Well, it looks a little like the other gate entrance—"

"No, it's like it all looks familiar," she says. "Like this part of the campus looks familiar. Like I was here more than once, or something. It *feels* familiar."

She starts looking around.

"Let me get my bearings," she says. "Let me figure out why this place looks familiar to me. Isn't that the point of all this? That something here is supposed to look familiar?"

"Okay," I say. "Take your time."

I try to encourage her, even though I don't want to stop here. I want to get to the churches before they close for the day. I want to find us someone to talk to.

I stay quiet and focus on my phone. I focus on figuring out the time line. If Bailey is onto something, if we aren't walking completely down the wrong path, it has to have been in 2008 that Bailey was here—while Bailey and Owen were still living in Seattle, while Olivia was still alive. The next year, Bailey and Owen moved to Sausalito. And any time before that, she would have been too young to remember much of this, if any of it.

So 2008 was the sweet spot. If Bailey is right about any of it, that's when she was here. I search for the football schedule. I search for the home game schedule, from twelve years ago.

But as I start to pull the past schedules up, my cell rings, BLOCKED coming up on the caller ID. I hold it in my hand, unsure what to do. It could be Owen. But I think of Jake telling me not to answer any unknown numbers, and it feels risky. Who else it may be, what other trouble that may cause.

Bailey motions to my phone. "Are you going to get that? Or just stare at it?"

"Haven't decided yet."

What if it's Owen though? What if? I click accept. But I don't say anything, waiting to hear what the caller has to say first.

"Hello? Hannah?"

The woman on the other end has a high-pitched voice, lispy, irritating. It's a voice that I recognize.

"Belle," I say.

"Oh what a mess this is," she says. "What an *outrage*. Are you okay? And how is Owen's daughter?"

It's Belle's attempt to be nice, but I note that she doesn't say Bailey. She says Owen's daughter because she can never remember Bailey's name. It's never been important to her to learn it.

"They didn't do this thing, you know..." she says.

They.

"Belle, I've been trying to reach you," I say.

"I know, I know, you must be beside yourself. I'm beside myself. I'm holed up in St. Helena like some kind of common criminal. Camera crews camped outside my door. I can't even leave the house! I had to have my assistant drop off roasted chicken and chocolate soufflés from Bouchon so I'd have *something* to eat," she says. "Where are you?"

I start to sidestep the question, but I don't need to. Belle isn't waiting for my answer. She just wants to keep talking.

"I mean this whole thing is just ridiculous," she says. "Avett is an entrepreneur, not a criminal. And Owen's a genius, though I don't need to tell you that. I mean, for crying out loud, why the hell would Avett need to do this thing anyway? Steal from his own company? This is, *what,* his eighth start-up? This late in his career he is going to start inflating values and lying and stealing? Or whatever the hell they say he is doing? Give me a break. We already have more money than we know what to do with."

She is fighting hard, arguing forcefully. But it doesn't change what she is leaving out, what she is refusing to acknowledge. Avett's previous success, the hubris that comes with it, could explain why he refused to fail now.

"Point is, it's a setup," she says.

"By who, Belle?"

"How the hell do I know? The government? A competitor? Maybe some hack who wants to get to the market first. That's Avett's theory. The point is that we are going to beat this. Avett has worked too hard for too long to be taken down by an accounting mishap."

And I hear it then, what people— Patty, Carl, Naomi—must hear when they're talking to me. I hear the crazy. She sounds crazy. Maybe that's what happens when the bottom falls out, you lose the ability to modulate—to make your words make sense to the rest of the world.

"So are you saying it was a setup or an accounting error?" I pause. "Or are you just saying it's everyone's fault except for Avett's?"

"Excuse me?" she says.

She's angry. I don't care. I don't have time for her, now that I know this conversation is going to a place where she wants something from me. I don't have anything left to give her.

I look at Bailey, who is watching me with questions in her eyes: Why am I sounding increasingly angry? What does this mean for her father?

"I need to go," I say.

"Just wait," she says. Which is when she starts to get to it. What she actually needs.

"Avett's lawyers are having trouble reaching Owen," she says. "And we just want to make sure, we just want to know... he isn't talking to law enforcement, is he? Because that wouldn't be smart, for any of us."

"If Avett didn't do anything wrong, what does it matter what Owen says?"

"Don't be naive. It doesn't work that way," she says.

I can almost see Belle sitting at her kitchen island, on the stool I made for her, shaking her head incredulously, the gold hoops she never takes off slapping at her high cheeks.

"How does it work?"

"Uh... entrapment, forced confessions. Is Owen that stupid?" She pauses. "Is he talking to the police?"

I want to say, *all I know is that he isn't talking to me*. I don't offer Belle that though. I don't offer her anything. We are in different positions, she and I. She isn't worried about Avett's safety. She isn't sincerely questioning whether the government's acting in bad faith or whether Avett's guilty. Belle knows that her husband is guilty. She is just trying to spin it, to do what she needs to do, to stop him from paying for it.

My concern, on the other hand, is how to stop Bailey from paying for it.

"Avett's lawyers need to debrief with Owen as soon as possible, so the story stays consistent," Belle says. "We could use your help on this. We all need to stick together."

I don't answer her.

"Hannah? Are you still there?"

"No," I say. "Not anymore."

Then I hang up. I hang up and go back to pulling up the old UT-Austin football schedule.

"Who was that?" Bailey says.

"Wrong number," I say.

"Is that what you call Belle these days?" she says.

I look up at her.

"Why even pretend?" she says.

She's furious and she's scared. And, apparently, I'm making that worse as opposed to better.

"I'm just trying to protect you from some of this, Bailey," I say.

"But you can't," she said. "That's the thing. No one can protect me from this. So how about you agree to be the person who tells me the truth?"

She looks older than she is suddenly. Her eyes are unwavering, her lips pursed. *Protect her.* The one thing Owen asked me to do. The one impossible thing.

I nod, holding her gaze. She wants me to tell her the truth, as if that is a simple thing to do. Maybe it is simpler than I'm making it.

"That was Belle. And she essentially confirmed for me that Avett is guilty, or that, at the very least, he has things to hide. And she seems surprised that Owen has gone off the grid as opposed to helping Avett hide those things. All of which makes me wonder what your father is hiding. And why." I pause. "So I'd like to find these churches and see if that offers any clue as to why he felt like he had no choice but to leave us. I'd

like to figure out if it's just about The Shop or if what I'm suspecting is true."

"Which is?"

"What he's running from goes back further than that," I say. "And it's about him. And you."

She doesn't say anything. She stands in front of me with her arms crossed over her chest. Then suddenly, she drops them. She drops them and moves in a little closer to me.

"So... when I asked you to tell me the truth, I meant, like, don't lie about who is on the phone."

"I went a step too far?"

"In a good way," she says.

It may be the nicest thing she has ever said to me.

"Well, I was trying to listen."

"Thank you for that," she says.

Then she takes the map from my hands and studies it herself.

"Let's go," she says.

Three Months Ago

It was 3 A.M., and Owen was sitting at the hotel bar, drinking a tall glass of bourbon, straight.

He felt my eyes on him and looked up.

"What are you doing down here?" he said.

I smiled at him. "I believe that's my question for you..." I said.

We were staying in San Francisco, in a boutique hotel across from the Ferry Building. There had been a terrible storm. It was the type of rainstorm that didn't happen in Sausalito too often and it had forced us to evacuate our home, our floating home, due to flooding risks. It forced us to take refuge on the other side of the Golden Gate Bridge—the hotel filled up with other floating home expats. Though apparently Owen wasn't finding much refuge at all.

He shrugged. "Thought I'd come downstairs to have a drink," he said. "Do some work…"

"On what?" I said.

I looked around. He didn't have his laptop with him. No papers lying around. There was nothing on the bar at all, except his bourbon. And one other thing.

"Wanna have a seat?" he said.

I sat down on the barstool next to him, wrapping my arms more tightly around myself. I was chilly in the middle-of-the-night coolness. My tank top and sweatpants weren't much of a match.

"You're freezing," he said.

"I'm okay."

He pulled off his hoodie, putting it over my head. "You will be," he said.

I looked at him. And waited. I waited for him to tell me what he was really doing down here, what was worrying him enough that he left our room. That he left me in the bed, his daughter on the pullout couch.

"Work is just a little stressful. That's all. But nothing's wrong. Nothing I can't handle."

He nodded, like he meant it. But he seemed stressed. He seemed more stressed than I'd seen him before. When we were packing our bags to come here, I found him in Bailey's room, packing up Bailey's childhood piggy bank, putting it in his duffel bag. He'd looked embarrassed when I saw him and explained that it was one of the first presents he'd gotten her. He didn't want to risk anything happening to it. That wasn't the weird part—Owen was packing up all sorts of sentimental things (Bailey's first hairbrush, family photo albums) and dropping them in his overnight bag. The weird part was that the other thing on the bar, besides his drink, was Bailey's piggy bank.

"So, if you've got it handled, why are you sitting here by yourself, in the middle of the night, staring at your daughter's piggy bank?"

"Thinking of breaking it open," he said. "In case we need the money."

"What's going on, Owen?" I said.

"Do you know what Bailey said to me tonight? When I told her we had to evacuate? She said she wanted to go with Bobby's family instead. That they're staying at the Ritz and she wanted to be with him. It turned into a whole, big thing."

"Where was I?"

"Locking down your workshop."

I shrugged, trying to be gentle. "She's growing up."

"I know, it's totally normal, I get it, but… the strangest thing happened when I told her no," he said. "I watched her stomp after me toward the car. And I just kept thinking, *she's going to leave me.* Maybe it's being a single parent all this time, just trying to keep the two of us above water, but I don't think I ever fully thought about the fact... or maybe I just didn't let myself."

"So that's why you are downstairs, looking at her piggy bank in the middle of the night?"

"Maybe. Or maybe it's just a strange bed," he said. "Can't sleep."

He picked up his bourbon, held it near his lips.

"When she was a little girl, when we first got to Sausalito, she was scared to walk down the docks. I think it was because the day after we moved in, Mrs. Hahn slipped and fell and Bailey saw her almost go down, almost land in the water."

"That's terrible!" I say.

"Yeah, well, for those first couple of months, she would make me hold her hand the whole way down the docks. From our front door, all the way to the parking lot. And she'd ask as we went, *Daddy, you're going to keep me safe, right? Daddy, you're not going to let me fall?* It took us like six and a half hours to get from the front door to the car."

I laughed.

"It drove me crazy. The hundredth time I had to do it, I actually think I went a little crazy." He paused. "And you know the only thing worse than that? The day she stopped."

I put my hand on his elbow, held him there. My heart exploding a little at his love for her.

"There is going to come a time when I won't be able to keep her safe anymore, not from anything," he said. "I won't even be able to tell her no anymore."

"Well, I can relate to that," I said. "I can't even tell her no now."

He looked over at me, bourbon still in hand, and laughed. He really laughed— my joke breaking his sadness, splintering it for him.

He put down his drink and turned toward me. "On a scale of one to ten, how weird is it that I'm sitting here?"

"Without the piggy bank?" I said. "It would be a two, maybe a three..."

"With the piggy bank? Am I breaking six?"

"Afraid so."

He put the piggy bank on an empty stool, and motioned for the bartender.

"Would you please make my wonderful wife here the drink of her choice?" he said. "And I'll take a cup of coffee."

Then he leaned in, put his forehead against mine.

"Sorry," he said.

"Don't be. It's hard, I get it, but it's not happening tomorrow, she's not leaving tomorrow," I said. "And she loves you so much. She's never going to leave you completely."

"I don't know about that."

"I do."

He kept his forehead there, touching mine. "I just hope Bailey doesn't wake up and find us gone," he said. "If you look outside, you can see the Ritz."

Little White Churches

Elenor H. McGovern peers at Bailey over her bifocals.

61

"So let me get this straight," she says. "You want to know what?"

We are sitting in Elenor's office at an Episcopal church. It's a large church, one of the oldest cathedrals in Austin, more than a hundred years old. And just over a half mile from the football stadium. But most important, it is the only church we've walked into—the final of the six contenders—that Bailey said felt familiar to her.

"We are just looking for a list of weddings that were held here during the 2008 football season," Bailey says.

Elenor, who is in her early seventies and pushing six feet tall, looks at us, overwhelmed.

"It's less complicated than it sounds," I say. "We actually just need a list of the weddings your pastor performed during the home games of the 2008 season. And we don't need the weddings that fell on the other days of those weekends. Just the weddings that happened to actually take place during the Longhorns' home games. That's all."

"Oh, during the home games from twelve years ago. Is that all?"

I ignore her tone and plow forward, hoping to turn her around. "I actually already did the legwork," I say.

I nudge the list across the table toward her. I've created a chart with the Longhorns' schedule from twelve years ago. I had Jules cross-check it at the *San Francisco Chronicle*, using their research tools, just to be sure that we didn't miss any of the games, just to make sure we checked all the boxes.

There are only eight dates in question. There are only eight dates when a small Bailey could have been walking into the stadium with Owen, could have found herself sitting here.

Elenor stares at the list. But she doesn't make a move to pick it up.

I look around the office, for clues about her—clues that may help me win her over. Christmas cards and bumper stickers cover her desk; photographs of Elenor's family are lined up on the fireplace mantel; a large bulletin board is brimming over with photographs and notes from parishioners. The office reveals forty years of building relationships right in this room, in this church. She knows everything about this place. We just need to know one small piece of it.

"I know it seems like a lot," I say. "But, if you take a look, you'll see we have downloaded the home game schedule from the 2008 season. And we are looking at fewer than ten weekends. We have them all for you, ready to go. Even if your pastor officiated two weddings a weekend, it'd be fewer than twenty couples."

"Look," Elenor says. "I'm sorry. I'm simply not authorized to give out that information."

"I understand that's the policy and why that's the policy," I say. "But you must agree these are exceptional circumstances."

"Of course. It's terrible to hear that your husband is missing. It seems you are dealing with a lot because of his absence. But that doesn't change our policy."

"Can't you make an exception to your policy?" Bailey says, her tone too harsh.

"We clearly aren't serial killers or anything. We could care less who these people are."

I put my hand on Bailey's leg, trying to calm her.

"We can sit here while we read the names," I say. "No printouts or addresses even have to leave this room."

Elenor looks back and forth between us, like she is torn between helping us and kicking us out. But it looks like she is leaning toward kicking us out. I can't let that happen, not when it's possible we are onto something. If we can figure out what wedding Owen and Bailey attended, we'll understand their tie to Austin. And maybe that tie will help explain what Grady was doing on my doorstep, what Owen is doing so far away from it.

"I really think Bailey may have been at this church," I say. "It would be very helpful to her, to both of us, to know for sure. And if you knew what we've been through this week, without her father... let's just say, it would be an act of kindness."

I see the sympathy percolate in Elenor's eyes and feel hopeful suddenly that my plea has put her on the side of helping.

"I'd like to help you. I would. But it's not something I can do, dear. If you want to leave your number, I can check with the pastor, but I just don't think that he's going to want to provide our parishioners' personal details."

"Jesus, lady, you're not going to give us a break here?" Bailey says.

It's, admittedly, not great language for her to use.

Elenor stands up, her head dangerously close to hitting the ceiling. "I'm going to need to excuse myself now, friends," she says. "We have a Bible study group this evening that I need to prepare for in the conference room. So if you wouldn't mind showing yourselves out."

"Look, Bailey didn't mean to be rude to you, but her father is missing and we're just trying to find out why. It's putting our family under a great deal of stress. Family is everything to us, as I'm sure you can understand."

I motion toward the photographs lining the mantel above the fireplace—the Christmas shots of her children and grandchildren, the candid shots of her husband, their dogs, a farm. Several photographs of Elenor and, perhaps, her favorite grandchild, sporting some crazy streaked hair of his own. His in a shade of green.

"I'm sure you'd be the first to go to great lengths for your family," I say. "I can see that about you. Please just think about it for a second. If I were sitting there and you were sitting here, I'm just asking you, what would you hope I'd do? Because, I'd try to do it."

She pauses and straightens her dress. Then, miraculously, Elenor sits back down, pushing her bifocals higher on her nose.

"Let me see what I can do," she says.

Bailey smiles in relief.

"The names can't leave this room."

"They won't leave your desk," I say. "We will figure out if there is someone who can help our family. That's all."

Elenor nods and pulls my list across the desk. Then she picks it up. She looks down at it, in her hands, as though she can't believe she is doing this. She sighs so we know she can't believe she's doing this.

She turns to her computer, starting to type.

"Thank you," Bailey says. "Thank you so much."

"Thank your stepmother," Elenor says.

Which is when an amazing thing happens. Bailey doesn't cringe when I'm referred to that way. She doesn't thank me. She doesn't even look at me. But she doesn't cringe, which feels a little like the same thing.

I don't have any time to savor it though because my phone starts to buzz. I look down to see a text from CARL.

I'm outside your house, can you let me in? I've been knocking...

I look to Bailey, touch her hand. "That's Carl," I say. "I'm going to see what he wants."

Bailey nods, barely acknowledging me, her eyes focused on Elenor. I head out into the hallway and text him that I'm calling him now.

"Hey," he says when he picks up. "Can I come in? I've got Sarah with me. We were on a walk."

I picture him standing outside our front door, Sarah in her BabyBjörn, wearing one of the enormous bows Patty loves to stick on top of her head, Carl using his walk with his daughter as

an excuse with Patty—an excuse to come and talk to me without Patty knowing.

"We aren't home, Carl," I say. "What's going on?"

"It's really not a phone type of conversation," he says. "I'd rather talk in person. I can come back later if that's better. I walk Sarah at five fifteen, get her some fresh air before dinner."

"I'd rather hear what you have to say now," I say.

He pauses, not sure what to do. I can see him considering whether to insist we do this in person later, when it will be easier for him to spin whatever he needs to spin. Because I have no doubt—I've had no doubt since I saw the look on his face yesterday—that there is something he knows, something he is afraid to say.

"Look, I just feel real bad about what happened when you came to the house yesterday," he says. "I was caught off guard and Patty was already so pissed. But I owe you an apology. It wasn't right, especially when..."

He pauses, like he is still trying to figure out whether to say it.

"Well, maybe I should back up, I mean... I don't know exactly what Owen told you, but he was really struggling at work. He was really struggling with Avett."

"He told you that?" I say.

"Yeah, he didn't go into a whole lot of detail, but he said he was under a lot of pressure to get the software working," he says. "He told me that much. He told me it wasn't going as smoothly as Avett had let on. But that his back was against the wall…"

That stops me. "What do you mean 'his back was against the wall'?"

"He said he couldn't just walk away. Go get another job. That he had to fix what was happening."

"Did he say why?" I say.

"That part he didn't get into. I swear to you. And I tried to push him on it. No job is worth that kind of stress…"

I look back into Elenor's office, Elenor still staring at her computer, Bailey pacing back and forth.

"Thanks for letting me know."

"Wait… there's something else."

I can hear him struggle. I can hear him struggle with how to even put the words together.

"There's something else I need to tell you."

"Just say it, Carl."

"We didn't invest in The Shop, Patty and me," he says.

I think back to what Patty said to me—how she called Owen a crook, how she accused him of stealing their money.

"I don't understand."

"I needed to use that money for something else, something I couldn't tell Patty about, something to do with Cara," he says.

Cara. The coworker Carl's been involved with on and off since before Sarah was born.

"What exactly?" I say.

"I'd rather not get into details, but I thought you should know that…" he says.

I can imagine a variety of scenarios that would cost him tens of thousands of dollars—the one percolating to the surface involves another baby, in another BabyBjörn, who also belongs to him. To both of them.

But I'm guessing and I don't have time to guess. I also don't particularly care. What I care about is that Owen didn't do what Patty accused him of doing. It almost feels like a kind of proof—a piece lining up to help me prove it to myself—Owen is still Owen.

"So, even with what's going on, you're letting your wife think that Owen took the money from you? That he convinced you to invest your savings in a fraudulent company?"

"I realize it's messed up," he says.

"You think?"

"Can I at least get some points for telling the truth?" he says. "This is the last conversation I want to be having."

I think of Patty, self-righteous Patty, telling her book club, her wine club, her tennis group—telling just about anyone in ladies central who will listen to her that Owen is a crook. Telling everyone the false information her husband has fed her.

"No, Carl, the last conversation you want to be having is the one you are about to have. With your wife. Because either you're going to tell her the truth or I'll do it for you."

This is when I hang up, my heart racing. I don't give myself time to process the implications of what he's told me because Bailey is motioning for me to come back in.

I pull myself together and walk back into Elenor's office. "Sorry about that," I say.

"That's quite all right," Elenor says. "I'm just pulling everything up…"

Bailey starts to move around the desk toward Elenor, but Elenor stops her with her hand.

"Let me just print the records out," she says. "And you can have a look. But I do need to get to that meeting, so you're going to have to move quickly for me."

"We will," I say.

But then Elenor stops typing. She looks at the screen confused. "This is the 2008 season you're asking about?" she says.

I nod. "Yes, first home game was the first weekend in September."

"I see that from the document," Elenor says. "What I'm asking is, are you sure of the year?"

"Pretty sure," I say. "Why?"

"2008?"

Bailey is trying not to look irritated. "2008, yes!"

"We were closed that fall for construction," she says. "It was a major renovation. There had been a fire. Doors shut on September first and we didn't open again for services, no ceremonies of any kind, until March. No weddings."

Elenor moves the screen so we can see the calendar for ourselves—all the empty squares. My heart drops.

"Maybe you have your year wrong?" Elenor says to Bailey. "Let me check 2009 for you."

I reach out my hand to stop her. There is no point in checking 2009. Owen and Bailey moved to Sausalito in 2009. I have the records of that, and in 2007, Bailey would have been too young to remember much of anything. She has no memories of Seattle during that time, let alone a sole weekend trip to Austin. If we are being honest with ourselves, even 2008 is a stretch. But if her mother was at the wedding—and Bailey thinks she may have been—then 2008 is the only time it could have been.

"Look, it had to be 2008," she says.

Bailey's voice starts to shake as she looks at the empty screen.

"I was here. And that's the only time it could have been. We've gone over this. It was that fall. It would have had to have been then if my mother was with us."

"Maybe it was 2007?" Elenor says.

"I would've been too young to remember any of it then."

"Then it wasn't here," Elenor says.

"But that doesn't make sense," Bailey says. "I mean, I recognize the apse. I remember it."

I move toward Bailey, but she moves away. She isn't interested in being appeased. She is interested in getting to the bottom of this.

"Elenor," I say. "Are there other churches in walking distance of campus that look like yours? Something we may have missed that may have reminded Bailey of your church?"

Elenor shakes her head. "No, not with a cathedral that is reminiscent of ours," she says.

"Maybe a church that has since closed down?"

"I don't think so. But why don't you leave your phone number? I can ask the pastor, some of our parishioners. And I will call if I remember anything. You have my word on that."

"What are you possibly going to remember?" Bailey says. "Why don't you just say you can't help us?"

"Bailey, stop…" I say.

"Stop? You're the one who said if I remember something we need to track it down, and now you're telling me to stop?" she says. "Whatever, I'm so freaking done with this."

She stands up quickly, storming out of Elenor's office.

Elenor and I watch her go silently. She gives me a kind look once Bailey has gone.

"It's fine," she says. "I know it's not me that she's angry with."

"Actually it may be," I say. "But it's misplaced. She needs to be mad at her father, and he's not here to hear it. So she's turning it on everyone else."

"Understood," Elenor says.

"Thank you for your time," I say. "If you do think of anything, even if it feels unimportant, please call."

I write down my cell number.

"Of course."

She nods, putting the number in her pocket as I start walking to the door.

"Who does this to his family?" she asks.

I turn around, and meet her eyes. "Sorry?" I say.

"Who does *this* to his family?" she says again.

The best father I've ever known, I want to say.

"Someone without a choice," I say. "That's who. That's who does this to his family."

"We always have a choice," Elenor says.

We always have a choice. That's what Grady said too. What does that even mean? That there is a right thing to do and there is a wrong thing to do. Simple. Judgmental. And if you are the person someone is asking that question about, you have chosen wrong—as if the world is divided between the people who have never made a big mistake. And the people who have.

I think of Carl on the phone, telling me that Owen was struggling. I think of how he must be struggling wherever he is now.

I feel my own anger rising.

"I'll keep that in mind," I say, my tone matching Bailey's.

And I head out the door to join her.

Not Everyone Is a Good Helper

When we get back to the hotel, we order grilled cheese and sweet potato fries from room service. I turn on the television. There's an old romantic comedy playing on basic cable—Tom Hanks and Meg Ryan finding their way to each other, against all odds—its familiarity a sedative. It lulls us. Bailey falls asleep on her bed.

I stay up, watching the rest of the movie, waiting for the moment I know is coming, Tom Hanks promising Meg Ryan that he has her, that he will love her. For as long as they both shall live.

Then the credits roll. And it's back to the dark hotel room in this strange city and it returns with a terrifying jolt: Owen is gone. Without explanation. Gone.

This is the terrible thing about a tragedy. It isn't with you every minute. You forget it, and then you remember it again. And you see it with a stark quality: This is what is required of you now, just to get along.

I'm too riled up to sleep, so I start going back through my notes from the day, trying to construct another way to utilize the wedding weekend to spark Bailey's memory. What were she and Owen doing in Austin besides going to the wedding? Was it possible they were here longer than that? Maybe Bailey isn't wrong. Maybe that's the reason the campus looked familiar to her. Did she spend more time there than that one weekend? And why?

I'm relieved when my phone rings, interrupting my thoughts. No good answers to my questions.

I pick up the phone, JAKE coming up on the caller ID.

"I've been trying to reach you for hours," he says.

"Sorry," I whisper. "It's been a long day."

"Where are you?"

"Austin."

"Texas?" he says.

I head into the hallway, gently closing the hotel room door, careful not to wake Bailey.

"There's a longer explanation, but essentially Bailey had memories of being in Austin when she was young. I don't know, maybe I pushed her to think she had memories of being here. But between that and Grady Bradford showing up at my door... I thought we should come."

"So... you're chasing leads?"

"Apparently not well," I say. "We'll be on a plane home tomorrow."

I hate hearing how those words sound. And the thought of going home to an Owen-less house is terrible. At least here I'm able to harbor the illusion that I can help bring Owen back to me, that Bailey and I, together, can do that.

"Well, look, I need to talk to you," Jake says. "And you're not going to like it."

"You're going to need to start by telling me something I will like, Jake," I say. "Or I'm hanging up on you."

"Your friend Grady Bradford is legitimate. Great reputation in the service. He's one of the go-to guys in the Texas bureau. The FBI often brings him on when a suspect goes missing. And if he wants to find Owen, I'm guessing he will."

"How is that good news?"

"I'm not sure anyone else can find him," Jake says.

"What do you mean?"

"Owen Michaels doesn't exist," he says.

I almost laugh. That's how ridiculous those words sound—ridiculous and, of course, wrong.

"I'm not saying you don't know what you're talking about, Jake, but I can assure you, he exists. His daughter is sleeping fifteen feet from me."

"Let me rephrase," he says, *"your* Owen Michaels doesn't exist. Besides a birth certificate and social security number that match, for both Owen and his daughter, the rest of the details are inconsistent."

"What are you talking about?"

"The investigator I was telling you about, and he knows what he is doing, says that no Owen Michaels exists that fits your husband's biography. There are several Owen Michaels who grew up in Newton, Massachusetts, and a few who attended Princeton University. But the only Owen Michaels on record who grew up in Owen's hometown and attended Princeton is seventy-eight years old and lives with his partner, Theo Silverstein, in Provincetown, out on Cape Cod."

I'm having troubling breathing. I sit down on the hallway carpet, my back against the wall. I can feel it. A knocking in my head, a knocking in my heart. *No Owen Michaels is your Owen Michaels.* The words moving through me, unable to find a home.

"Should I go on?" he says.

"No thank you."

"No Owen Michaels purchased or owned a home in Seattle, Washington, in 2006 or enrolled his daughter, Bailey, in preschool that year or had a registered income tax return anytime before 2009..."

That stops me. "That was the year he and Bailey moved to Sausalito."

"Exactly. That's where the record for your Owen Michaels starts. And from then on pretty much what you told me matches up. Their home, Bailey's schooling. Owen's work. And, of course, it was smart of him to purchase a floating home as opposed to a real house. Less of a paper trail. He doesn't even own the land. It's more like a rental. Harder to trace."

I put my hands over my eyes, trying to stop the spinning in my head, trying to get steadier.

"Before they arrived in Sausalito, I haven't found one piece of data that supports the story your husband has told you about his life. He went by another name or he went by his current name and just lied to you about every other thing. He lied about who he was."

I don't say anything at first. Then I manage to get out the question. "Why?" I say.

"Why would Owen change his name? The details of his life?" he asks.

I nod as though he can see me.

"I asked the investigator the same thing," Jake says. "He says there are usually two reasons why someone changes his identity, and you're not going to like either of them."

"No kidding?"

"The most common reason, believe it or not, is the person has a second family somewhere. Another wife. Another child. Or children. And he's trying to keep the two lives separate."

"It's not possible, Jake," I say.

"Tell that to a client we have now, this oil magnate billionaire who has a wife in North Dakota at his family's ranch and another in San Francisco in some mansion in Pacific Heights. Down the street from Danielle Steel. Twenty-nine years he has been with both women. Five children with one, five children with the other. And they have no idea. They think he travels a lot for work. They think he's a great husband. We only know about his dual families because we put a will together for him... that's going to be a fun estate reading."

"What's the other reason Owen might have done this?" I say.

"Assuming he doesn't have another wife hanging out somewhere?"

"Yes. Assuming that."

"The other reason someone creates a false identity, which is the working theory here, is that he's involved in some sort of criminal activity," he says. "And he ran to avoid trouble, to start a new life, to protect his family. But, almost across the board, the criminal gets in trouble again, which is his undoing."

"So that would mean that Owen was in trouble with the law before? That he's not only guilty of what's happening at The Shop, but he's guilty of something else too?"

"It would certainly explain why he ran," Jake said. "He knew when The Shop imploded, he'd be outed. He was more worried about his past catching up to him than anything else."

"But, by that logic, isn't it possible he isn't a criminal?" I say. "That he changed his name to escape someone? Someone who wanted to hurt him or maybe even hurt Bailey?"

Protect her.

"Sure, that's possible," he says. "But why wouldn't he tell you that to begin with?"

I don't have a good answer. But I need another alternative—something else to explain why Owen isn't coming up as Owen.

"I don't know. Maybe he's in witness protection," I say. "That would explain Grady Bradford."

"I thought of that. But do you remember my buddy Alex? He has a friend who is pretty high up in the U.S. Marshals' office, so he looked into it for me. And Owen ain't being protected."

"Would he tell you?"

"Yeah."

"What kind of protection program is that?"

"Not a great one. Anyway, he doesn't match the profile of someone in witness protection," he says. "Not his job, which is high-rent, not Sausalito. Protected witnesses sell tires somewhere in Idaho. And those are the lucky ones. It's not what you see in the movies. Most witnesses just get dropped off in the middle of nowhere with a little cash in their wallets and some new IDs and are told good luck."

"So then what?"

"For my money? It's option two. He's guilty of something and he's been running from it for a long time. And maybe he got caught up in The Shop because of that. Or maybe it's unrelated. Hard to know. But it would have caught up with him if he was arrested, so he ran to save himself. Or, maybe it's like you said, and he ran because he thought it was the best way to protect Bailey. To not get her caught up in whatever he's done."

It's the first thing that Jake says that penetrates. It's what I keep coming back to myself. If it were just Owen's mistakes that were going to catch up with him, he would've stayed with us. He would've faced the firing squad. But if any of this would take Bailey down with him, he would make another decision.

"Jake, even if you're right, even if I don't know the whole story about the man I married... I know he would only leave Bailey behind if he absolutely had to," I say. "Forgetting me for a second, if he were running, without any intention of coming back, he'd take her with him. She's everything to him. Owen doesn't have it in him to leave her. And just disappear."

"Two days ago, did you think he had it in him to make up his entire life history? Because he did do that."

I stare at the ugly hotel hallway carpet with its patterns of fuchsia roses, trying to find in them something like solace.

This feels impossible. Every bit of this feels impossible. How do you begin to grapple with the idea that your husband is running from the person he used to be, a person whose real name you don't even know? You want to argue that someone is getting the story wrong. Someone is getting your story wrong. In your story, the one you know by heart, none of this makes sense. Not where this story began, not where it's going. And certainly not where it's threatening to end.

"Jake, how do I go back inside and tell Bailey that nothing about her father is

what she thinks? I don't know how to tell her that."

He gets uncharacteristically quiet. "Maybe tell her something else," he says.

"Like what?"

"Like you have a plan to get her away from this," he says. "At least until it's all sorted out."

"But I don't."

"But you could. You absolutely could get her away from this. Come to New York. Stay with me. Both of you, at least until this is all sorted out. I have friends on the board at Dalton. Bailey can finish out the school year there."

I close my eyes. How am I here again? On the phone with Jake? How is Jake the one who is helping me? When we ended our relationship, Jake said I'd always felt absent to him. I didn't argue with him—I couldn't. Because I was a little absent. It had felt like something was missing with Jake. The very thing I'd thought I had with Owen. But if Jake is correct about Owen, then Owen and I didn't have what I thought we did. Maybe we didn't have anything close to it, at all.

"I appreciate the offer. And right now it doesn't sound so bad."

"But..." he says.

"From what you're telling me, we got here because Owen ran away," I say. "I can't run away too, not until I get to the bottom of this."

"Hannah, you really need to think of Bailey here."

I open the hotel room door and peek in. Bailey is sound asleep on her bed. She is curled up in the fetal position, her purple hair sticking out like a disco ball on the pillows. I close the door, step back into the hall.

"That's all I'm thinking of, Jake," I say.

"Not yet it's not," he says. "Or you wouldn't be trying to find the one person that in my opinion you should be keeping her away from."

"Jake, he's her father," I say.

"Maybe someone should remind him," he says.

I don't say anything. I look out over the glass walls and into the atrium below. Work colleagues (complete with their laminated conference name tags) are lounging in the hotel bar, couples are heading out of the restaurant hand in hand, two exhausted parents are carrying their sleeping children and enough LEGOLAND paraphernalia to open a store. From this far away, they all look happy. Though, of course, I don't really know. But, for just a moment, I wish I could be any of them as opposed to the person I am. Hiding in a hotel hallway, eight floors up. Trying to process that her marriage, her life, is a lie.

I feel anger surging inside of me. Ever since my mother left, I pride myself on the details, seeing the smallest things about a person. And if someone asked me three days ago, I would have said I know everything there is to know about Owen. Everything that matters anyway. But maybe I know nothing. Because here I am, struggling to figure out the most basic details of all.

"Sorry," Jake says. "That was a little harsh."

"*That* was a little harsh?"

"Look, I'm just saying that you've got a place here if you decide you want it," he says. "Both of you do. No strings. But if you decide not to take me up on that, at least make another plan. Before you go ripping that girl's life apart, convince her you know what you're doing."

"Who knows what they're doing in a situation like this, Jake?" I say. "Who finds themselves in a situation like this?"

"Apparently you do," he says.

"That's helpful."

"Come to New York," he says. "That's as helpful as I know how to be."

Eight Months Ago

"I didn't agree to this," Bailey said.

We were standing outside a flea market in Berkeley. And Owen and Bailey were in a rare standoff. He wanted to go in. The only place Bailey wanted to go was home.

"You did agree," Owen said. "When you agreed to come to San Francisco. So how about sucking it up?"

"I agreed to get dim sum," she said.

"And the dim sum was good, wasn't it?" he said. "I gave you my last pork bun. As a matter of fact, so did Hannah. That's two extra pork buns."

"What's your point?" she says.

"How about being a good sport and heading inside with us for thirty minutes or so?"

She turned on her heels and walked into the flea market, ahead of us—the requisite ten feet ahead of us, so no one would guess we were all together.

She was done negotiating with her father. And, apparently, she was done celebrating my birthday.

Owen gave me an apologetic shrug. "Welcome to forty," he said.

"Oh, I'm not forty," I said. "I'm twenty-one."

"Oh, that's right!" He smiled. "Great. Then I have nineteen more chances to get this right."

I took his hand, his fingers locking around mine. "Why don't we just go home?" I said. "Brunch was so nice. If she's ready to go home..."

"She's fine."

"Owen, I'm just saying, this isn't a big deal."

"No, it isn't a big deal," he said. "It isn't a big deal for her to suck it up and enjoy a lovely flea market. She'll be fine walking around for a half hour."

He leaned down to kiss me and we started to head inside. To find Bailey. We were just through the front gate when a large man on his way out stopped walking and called out after Owen.

"No way," he said.

He was wearing a baseball cap and a matching jersey, stretched out over his stomach. And he was carrying a lampshade—a yellow, velvet lampshade with the price tag still on it.

He reached out to hug Owen, the lampshade awkwardly knocking Owen on the back.

"I can't believe it's you," he said. "How long has it been?"

Owen pulled away from him, careful to disentangle himself in a way that kept the lampshade safe.

"Twenty years? Twenty-five?" he said. "How does the prom king miss all the reunions?"

"I hate to tell you, pal, but I think you have the wrong guy," Owen said. "I've never been king of anything, just ask my wife."

Owen gestured to me.

And the guy, this stranger, smiled in my direction. "It's good to meet you," he said. "I'm Waylon."

"Hannah," I said.

Then he turned back to Owen. "Wait. So you're telling me that you didn't go to Roosevelt? Class of 1994?"

"Nope, I went to Newton High in Massachusetts," Owen said. "You got the year right though."

"Man, you are a dead ringer for this guy I went to school with. I mean the hair is pretty different and he was more jacked than you. No offense. I was more jacked too, back then."

Owen shrugged. "We all were."

"A dead ringer though." He shook his head. "It's probably a good thing you're not him though. He was kind of a dick."

Owen laughed. "Take it easy," he said.

"You too," Waylon said.

Then he started to walk toward the parking lot. But then he turned back.

"Do you know anyone who went to Roosevelt High in Texas?" he said. "Like a cousin or something? You've got to at least be related."

Owen smiled, gently. "Sorry, buddy," he said. "Hate to disappoint you, but I'm not even close to the right guy."

Sorry, We're Open

Jake's words pound in my head. Owen Michaels doesn't exist. Owen isn't Owen. He's deceived me about the most central details of his life. He deceived his daughter about the most central details of hers. How is that possible? It feels entirely impossible, considering the man I thought I knew. I *do* know him. I still believe this, despite the evidence to the contrary. And this belief in him (in us) will either show me to be a steadfast partner or a complete fool. Hopefully those don't turn out to be the same thing.

After all, this is what I thought I knew. Twenty-eight months ago a man walked into my workshop in New York City wearing a sports jacket and Converse sneakers. On the way to the theater that night, he took me to dinner at a small tapas restaurant on Tenth Avenue, and he started to tell me the story of his life. It began in Newton, Massachusetts, and included four years at Newton High followed by four years at Princeton University, a move to Seattle, Washington, with his college sweetheart, and then a move to Sausalito, California, with his daughter. There were three jobs and two degrees and one wife before me, who he'd lost in a car accident. It was a car accident he could barely talk about more than a decade later, his face cloudy and dark. Then there was his daughter. The highlight of his story—the highlight of his life—his headstrong, inimitable daughter. He moved with her to a small town in Northern California because she'd pointed to it on a map. And said, *let's try there.* And that was something he could give her.

This is what his daughter thought she knew. She'd spent the majority of her life in Sausalito, California, in a floating home with a father who never missed a soccer game or a school play. There were Sunday night dinners at restaurants of her choosing, and a weekly trip to the movies. There were lots of jaunts to San Francisco museums, plenty of neighborhood potlucks, and the annual barbecue. She didn't remember their life before Sausalito, except in vague snapshots: a birthday party with a great magician; a trip to the circus where she cried at the clown; a wedding somewhere in Austin, Texas. Bailey filled in the blanks with what her father told her. Why wouldn't she? That's how you fill in the blanks—with stories and memories from the people who love you.

If they lie to you, like he did, who are you then? Who is he? The person you thought you knew, *your* favorite person, starts to disappear, a mirage, unless you convince yourself the parts that matter are still true. The love was true. His love is true. Because, if it isn't, the other option is that it was all a lie, and what are you supposed to do with that? What are you supposed to do with any of this? How do you put the pieces together so he doesn't disappear completely?

So his daughter doesn't feel like she is going to disappear completely too?

Bailey wakes up, shortly after midnight.

She rubs her eyes. Then she looks over to find me sitting in the crappy hotel desk chair, watching her.

"Did I fall asleep?" she says.

"You did."

"What time is it?" she says.

"Late. You should go back to bed."

She sits up. "It's kind of hard with you staring at me," she says.

"Bailey, did you ever visit your father's childhood home in Boston?" I say. "Did he ever take you to see his house?"

She looks at me confused. "Like where he grew up?"

I nod.

"No. He never took me to Boston. He barely went back there himself."

"And you never met your grandparents?" I say. "You never spent any time with them?"

"They died before I was born," she says. "You know that. What's going on?"

Who is going to fill in this blank for her? This kind of hole? I don't know where to start.

"Are you hungry?" I say. "You must be hungry. You barely touched your dinner. And I'm famished."

"Why? You ate both our dinners all on your own."

"Get dressed, okay?" I say. "Would you get dressed?"

She looks at the fluorescent hotel radio-clock. "It's midnight," she says.

I put a sweater on and toss her sweatshirt to her. She looks down at it, splayed across her legs, her Converse sneakers peeking out beneath the hood.

She pulls the sweatshirt over her head, pushing the hood all the way down until her purple hair is sticking out.

"Can I at least get a beer?" she says.

"Absolutely not."

"I have a fake ID that says otherwise," she says.

"Please get dressed," I say.

Magnolia Cafe is an Austin institution, famous for all-night eats, which might explain why it is still busy—music playing, every booth taken—at 12:45 AM.

We get two large coffees and an order of gingerbread pancakes. Bailey seems to love the sweet, spice-filled pancakes dripping in butter and coconut sugar. Bananas on the side. And watching her take them down, if nothing else, makes me feel like I'm doing something good for her.

We sit by the door, a neon red SORRY WE'RE OPEN sign flashing above our heads. I blink against it and try to find the words to tell her what Jake told me.

"It seems that your father hasn't always gone by the name Owen Michaels," I say.

She looks up at me. "What are you talking about?" she says.

I speak softly but unapologetically, filling her in. I let her know that her father's name isn't the only thing he's changed. The details of his life—the story of his life—are something he has apparently altered as well. He didn't grow up in Massachusetts, he isn't a graduate of Princeton University, and he didn't move to Seattle at twenty-two. At least he hasn't done those things in a way that we can prove.

"Who told you that?"

"A friend back in New York. He works with an investigator who focuses on this kind of thing. The investigator believes that your father changed his identity shortly before you moved to Sausalito. He's sure of it."

She looks down at her plate, confused, like she's heard the words wrong—all of it feeling impossible to compute.

"Why would he do that?" she says, not meeting my eyes.

"My guess is he was trying to keep you safe from something, Bailey."

"Like what? Like something he did? 'Cause my father would be the first to say that if you're running from something, it's usually yourself."

"We don't know that for sure."

"Right. All we know for sure is that he lied to me," she says.

And I see it start to rise up in her. Her anger, her justifiable anger at being excluded from the most basic details of her life. Even if he was doing it for her own good. Even if he was doing it because he didn't have a choice. One way or another, she is going to have to decide whether that's forgivable. We both are.

"He also lied to me," I say.

She looks up.

"I'm just saying, he lied to me too."

She tilts her head, like she is trying to figure out whether she believes that, whether she can take that at face value. Why would she? Why would she

believe anyone at this point? But it feels critical to try and assure her anyway—assure her that she can trust me—that I didn't deceive her too. It feels like everything hinges on her believing that.

She looks at me with such vulnerability, it's hard for me to speak. It's hard for me to even hold her gaze without breaking down.

Which is when I understand, in a flash, what I've been doing wrong with her—what I've been doing wrong in how I've been trying to connect with her. I thought if I were nice enough, sweet enough, she'd understand she could count on me. But that's not how you learn you can count on someone. You learn it in the moments when everyone's too tired to be sweet, too tired to *try* hard. You learn it by what they do for you then.

And what I'm going to do for her now is what my grandfather did for me. I'll do whatever it takes for her to feel that she is safe.

"So... it wasn't just him, right?" she says. "If he did this, I'm not who he said I am either then, right? My name and everything... at some point he changed it."

"Yes," I say. "If Jake's correct, then, yes, you used to go by something else as well."

"And all the details are different too, right?" She pauses. "Like... my birthday?"

That stops me. The heartbreak in her voice when she asks that question.

"Like my birthday's not really my birthday?" she says.

"No, probably not."

She looks down. She looks away from me. "That seems like something a person should know about themselves," she says.

I fight back tears, gripping the table, the small table in this happy Austin restaurant—paintings on the wall, bright colors, all of it completely antithetical to how I feel. I will myself to stop, blinking the tears back. A sixteen-year-old girl, who apparently has no one but me, needs me not to cry. She needs me to be there for her. So I pull myself together, giving her the space to fall apart. Letting her be the one to do that.

She folds her hands on the table, tears filling her eyes. And I feel nearly leveled by it, watching her in that kind of pain.

"Bailey, I know this feels impossible," I say. "But you are you. Whatever details are around that, whatever your father didn't tell you, that doesn't change who you are. Not at your core."

"But how can I have no memory of being called something else? Of where I lived? I should remember, shouldn't I?"

"You just said it yourself, you were a kid. You were just coming into consciousness when you became Bailey Michaels. None of this is a reflection on you at all."

"Just on him?" she says.

I think again about the guy at the Berkeley Flea Market, the guy who called Owen a prom king. Owen's calm reaction to him. He was completely unfazed. Could he have faked that so well? And what did it say about him if he did?

"You don't remember anyone ever calling your father anything else, do you? Before Sausalito?"

"Like a nickname?" she says.

"No, more like... by another name completely?"

"I don't think so. I don't know..." She pushes her coffee across the table. "I can't believe this is happening."

"I know."

She starts twirling her hair in her hands, the purple getting mixed up with her dark nail polish, her eyes blinking wildly as she tries to think.

"I have no idea what anyone called him," she says. "I never paid attention, why would I?"

She sits back, done guessing about her father, done guessing about her past, and completely exhausted from feeling like she has to. Who can blame her? Who wants to be sitting in a strange Austin restaurant trying to figure out who the most important person in your world was pretending to be? And how you missed it. Who he actually was.

"You know what? Let's just go," I say. "It's late. Let's go back to the hotel and try to get some sleep."

I start to stand up, but Bailey stops me. "Wait..." she says.

I sit back down.

"Bobby said something to me a couple months ago," she says. "He was applying to college and wanted to ask my father for an alumni recommendation for Princeton. But when he looked him up in the list of alums, he said he couldn't find an Owen Michaels anywhere. Not as a graduate in the engineering school, not as a student in the regular college either. I said obviously he looked it up in the wrong place, and then he got into University of Chicago and just dropped it. I never even remembered to ask Dad, but I just assumed it was Bobby not knowing how to work the alumni database or whatever." She pauses. "Maybe I should have asked him."

"Bailey, why would you? Why would you assume he was lying to you?"

"Do you think he was ever going to tell me?" she says. "Did he plan to take me for a walk one day and let me in on who I really am? Honestly, was he going to tell me that basically everything I knew about my life was a lie?"

I look at her in the dim light. I think of my conversation with Owen, the conversation about taking a vacation to New Mexico. Was he actually thinking of letting me into some of this then? If I'd pushed a little harder, would he have?

"I don't know," I say.

I expect her to say how unfair that is. I expect her to get upset again. But she stays calm.

"What's he so scared of?" she says.

It stops me. Because that's it. That feels like the crux of all of this. Owen is running from something that he is terrified of. He has spent his life running from it. And, more important, he has spent his entire life trying to keep Bailey from it.

"I think when we figure that out, we'll know where he is now," I say.

"Oh, well, easy enough," she says.

Then she laughs. But the laughter turns, fast, tears filling her eyes. But just as I think she is going to say that she wants to get out of here—that she wants to go back to the hotel, to go back to Sausalito—she seems to find her center. She seems to find something like resolve.

"So what do we do now?" she says.

We. What do we do now. We are in this together, it seems, which warms my heart, even if it's taken us to this all-night diner in South Austin, far from our home. Even if it's taken us into territory we never wanted to be in. That I would give anything so that Bailey didn't have to be in. We are here together and we both want to keep going. We both want to find Owen, whatever he has been hiding— wherever he is now.

"Now," I say. "We fix this."

Two Can Play at That Game

I wait until the morning to call him. I wait until I feel calm and I'm sure I can do what I need to do.

I gather up all of my notes and throw on a sundress. I close the door to the hotel room quietly, careful not to wake Bailey. Then I head downstairs, through the bustling lobby, and go outside, where I can walk along the street, where I can control better what he hears in the background.

It is still quiet out—the lake placid and peaceful—even with the morning rush, commuters on their way over the Congress Street Bridge, heading into their offices, their children's schools, on their way to start their blessedly normal days.

I reach into my pocket and pull out the napkin from Fred's, Grady's cell phone number underlined twice.

I turn on my cell phone, pressing *67 first before I tap in the number, hoping this will help block my call a little bit longer—if he is so inclined to unblock it, if he's so inclined to try and figure out where I am.

"This is Grady," he says when he picks up.

I brace myself to lie. This is, after all, what there is left to do. "It's Hannah," I say. "I heard from Owen."

This instead of hello.

"When?" Grady says.

"Late last night, around two A.M. He said he couldn't talk in case someone was listening to the call. Tracking him. He called from a pay phone or something. It came up as a blocked number and he was talking fast. He wanted to know if I was okay, if Bailey was okay, and he was adamant that he didn't have any part in what is going on at The Shop. He said he'd had a feeling Avett was up to something, but he didn't know the depth of it."

I can hear Grady on the other end of the phone, rustling around. Maybe he is looking for a notepad, something on which to write down the clues he seems to think I'm going to give him.

"Tell me what he said exactly..." he says.

"He said it wasn't safe for him to stay on the phone, but that I should call you," I say. "That you'd tell me the truth."

The rustling stops. "The truth? About what?"

"I don't know, Grady. Owen made it sound like you'd know how to answer that."

Grady pauses. "It's early in California," he says. "What are you doing up so early?"

"Would you be able to go back to sleep if your husband called you at two A.M. and told you he was in trouble?"

"I'm a pretty good sleeper, so..." he says.

"I need to know what's going on, Grady. What's really going on here," I say. "Why does a U.S. marshal based in Austin, Texas, come all the way to San Francisco seeking out someone who isn't a suspect?"

"And I need to know why you're lying to me about Owen calling you when he obviously did not."

"Why are there no records of Owen Michaels before he got to Sausalito?" I say.

"Who told you that?" he said.

"A friend."

"A friend? You're getting some faulty information from your friend," he says.

"I don't think so," I say.

"Okay, well, did you remind your friend that one of the primary functions of The Shop's new software is to alter your online history? That it helps you erase a trail you don't want to leave, correct? No online trail as to who you are. That includes online databases to universities, housing records—"

"I know how the software works."

"So why hasn't it occurred to you that if anyone expunged Owen's record, it might have been the one man who has the capability to do so?"

Owen. He is saying Owen made the trail to his past run cold. "Why would he do that?" I say.

"Maybe he was testing out his software," he says. "I don't know. I'm just saying you're making up quite an elaborate story when there are a variety of explanations as to what your friend did or didn't find out about Owen's past."

He is trying to throw me off-balance. I won't let him. I won't let him try to control this narrative for his own agenda, which is feeling increasingly suspicious.

"What did he do, Grady? Before all of this? Before The Shop? Why did he change his identity? Why did he change his name?"

"I don't know what you're talking about."

"I think you do," I say. "I think that explains why you came all the way to San Francisco for an investigation you have no jurisdiction over."

He laughs. "My jurisdiction puts me firmly in charge of this investigation," he says. "I think you should probably worry a little less about that and more about some other things."

"Like what?"

"Like the fact your pal Special Agent Naomi Wu at the FBI is threatening to name Owen as an official person of interest."

I pause. I haven't said her name. He knew her name. He seems to know everything.

"We don't have a whole lot of time before her team shows up at your house with search warrants. I'm fighting hard to hold her off for the moment, but I can't guarantee you it will keep going this way."

I think of Bailey having to come home to see her room turned apart—her world turned apart.

"Why, Grady?"

"Excuse me?"

"Why are you fighting so hard to stop that from happening?"

"That's my job," he says.

He says it assuredly, but I'm not convinced. Because something has clicked in for me. Grady doesn't want any of this for Owen any more than I do. Grady wants to help keep Owen away from that fate. Why is that? If Grady were just investigating Owen, if he were just trying to bring him in, if he was just trying to end this, he wouldn't care as much as he does. But something else is going on here—something far more nefarious than Owen being implicated in simple fraud. And suddenly I feel terrified that *that* something is worse than anything I have imagined yet.

Protect her.

"Owen left us a bag of money," I say.

"What are you talking about?" he says.

"Really, he left it for Bailey. It's a lot of money, and if someone shows up with one of those search warrants you're threatening me with, I don't want them discovering it. I don't want it used against me or as an excuse to take Bailey from me."

"That's not how this works."

"I'm still new to how this works, so in the meantime, I'm telling you about the money," I say. "It's under my kitchen sink. I don't want anything to do with it."

He is quiet. "Well, I appreciate that, it's better that I take it than that they find it," he says. "I can have someone in our San Francisco office come out and get it."

I look out past Lady Bird Lake, at Austin's downtown, its gentle buildings, the trees letting through the morning light. Grady is probably in one of those buildings already, starting his day. Grady is closer than I suddenly want him to be.

"Now's not a good time."

"Why not?"

Everything in my body tells me to tell him the truth. We are in Austin. But I'm still not sure whether he is a friend or a foe. Or both. Maybe everyone is a little bit of both, Owen included.

"I need to get some work done before Bailey gets up," I say. "And I've been thinking… maybe I should take Bailey somewhere else until this all calms down."

"Like where?"

I think of Jake's offer. I think of New York.

"I'm not sure," I say. "But we don't have to be in Sausalito, do we? I mean,

we don't have to stay there for any legal reason, correct?"

"Not officially, but it won't look good," he says. Then Grady pauses. He pauses as if hearing something.

"Wait. Why did you just say 'there'?"

"What?"

"You said, *we don't have to stay there.* Talking about your house, talking about Sausalito. If you were home, you would have said 'here.' We don't have to stay here."

I don't say anything.

"Hannah, I'm sending one of my colleagues over to check on you," he says.

"I'll put on some coffee," I say.

"This isn't a joke," he says.

"I don't think it is."

"So then where are you?" Grady says.

If Grady wants to trace my phone call, I know he can do it. For all I know he is already trying to do it. I look out at Grady's hometown, wondering what it's been for my husband.

"Where are you worried I'll be, Grady?" I say.

Then, before he can answer, I hang up the phone.

One Year Ago

"You think you can just pop in here whenever you want?" I said.

I was joking. But I was surprised that Owen snuck up on me, showing up at my workshop unannounced, in the middle of the workday. He didn't usually do that. He spent his days at the offices in Palo Alto, sometimes heading to downtown San Francisco for a meeting. He was rarely home on a weekday, except when Bailey needed him for something.

"If I popped in whenever I wanted, I'd be here constantly," he said. "What are we making?"

He rubbed his hands together, happy to be in the studio with me. He loved my work, loved being a part of it. And every time I saw how genuinely he felt that way, it was another small reminder how lucky I was to love him.

"What are you doing home so early?" I asked. "Is everything okay?"

"That depends," he said.

He lifted my face shield to give me a kiss hello. I was in my work clothes— which consisted of a high-necked jacket and that face shield—a combination that made me look like I belonged in the future and the past at the same time.

"Is my chair finished?"

I kissed him back, draping my arms around his shoulders.

"Not quite yet," I said. "And it's not your chair."

It was a Windsor chair I was making for a client in Santa Barbara, for her interior design office, but as soon as Owen had seen it in progress—the dark, chiseled elm; a heightened hoop back— he decided we couldn't let it go. He decided it was meant for him.

"We'll see about that," he said.

This was when his phone buzzed. Owen looked down at the caller ID, his face darkening. He clicked decline.

"Who was that?" I said.

"Avett," he said. "I'll call him later."

He clearly didn't want to talk about it, but I couldn't leave it there—not when I felt the heat coming off him. Not when he was getting this worked up just from a call he didn't take. "What's going on with him?

"He's being a little irrational. That's all."

"About what?"

"The IPO," he said. "It's not a big deal."

But it was flashing in his eyes—a mix of anger and irritation. Two things he rarely displayed. Two things he had displayed more recently. And, of course, he was standing in my workshop as opposed to in his own office.

I tried to choose my words carefully, wanting to help, but not wanting to undermine him. I didn't have to work in an office, didn't have to deal with the politics of having a boss I had to answer to—someone, like Avett Thompson, with whom I might not agree. And yet, I wanted to figure out how to say it—that I saw Owen's stress level rising. That it was just a job. That, as far as I was concerned, he could always find another.

Before I said anything, the phone buzzed again. AVETT showing up on the caller ID. Owen looked down at his phone. He looked down at it, like he was going to pick it up, his fingers hovering there. But he hit decline again, pocketing his phone instead.

He shook his head. "It doesn't matter how many times I say the same thing. Avett doesn't want to hear it," he said. "What we need to make this all work."

"My grandfather used to say that most people don't want to hear the thing that will make it work better," I said. "They want to hear what will make it easier."

"And what did he say to do about that?"

"Find other people. You know, for starters."

He tilted his head, took me in. "How do you always know what to say to me?" he said.

"Well, it's really my grandfather saying it, but sure..." I said.

He reached for my hand, a smile spreading across his face. Like nothing happened, or at least like it wasn't as important as he'd thought it was.

"Enough about this," he said. "Let's go see my chair."

He started pulling me to the door, toward the backyard and the deck where the chair was drying—sanded, newly polished.

"You know you can't have that chair," I said. "Someone commissioned it. She is paying us a lot of money for it."

"Good luck to her," he said. "Possession is nine-tenths of the law."

I smiled. "What do you know about the law?"

"Enough to know if I'm sitting in that chair," he said, "no one else is going to take it."

Delete All History

At 10 A.M., the hotel café is already busy, the lights dimmed.

I sit at the bar, drinking an orange juice while most of the people around me are starting in on morning cocktails—mimosas and Bloody Marys, champagne, White Russians.

I stare at the row of televisions, all tuned to different news shows. They come at me in closed captions, most of them reporting on The Shop. PBS shows footage of Avett Thompson being handcuffed and escorted away. MSNBC has a preview of Belle's *Today* show interview, Belle calling Avett's arrest a travesty of justice. CNN's chyron keeps warning that more indictments are coming, on repeat. It's almost like a promise, mirroring Grady's promise, that Owen will be in even more trouble soon. That whatever he is running from is about to catch him.

This is what gnaws at me, over and over, when I think of my husband—that something is coming for him, for all of us, that he couldn't stop. That he has left me to try and stop it for him.

I take out my notepad and go back over what Grady said during our phone call—trying to recall every detail, trying to hone in on what may be important to glean from it. I keep coming back to how he said that Owen might have erased his own online history. And, as wrong as that feels, I try to move myself there, to that assumption, to see what it shows me.

Which is when I land on it. That there are certain things we can't erase, certain things that we reveal to the people closest to us despite what we may or may not know we are telling them.

There are things, that without meaning to, Owen has told only me.

So I make another list. A list of everything I know about Owen's past. Not the false facts—Newton, Princeton, Seattle. The other facts—the nonfacts: things I learned accidentally during our time together, things that in retrospect seem like strange encounters. Like the guy from Roosevelt High School. I look Roosevelt up, and find eighty-six of them spread across the United States. None of them are anywhere near Massachusetts. But eight of them—in places like San Antonio and Dallas—are spread out across Texas.

I put a pin in that and keep thinking, landing on the night with Owen at the hotel, the piggy bank on the bar. Which is when I realize something about that piggy bank—something I've been struggling to remember. Am I remembering it correctly now, or am I conjuring up the memory out of something like desperation? I shoot Jules a text to check it out for me and keep thinking.

I keep working my way through things only I know: the anecdotes and stories that Owen has told me late at night. Just the two of us. The way you only do with the person you've chosen, the witness to your life.

Those stories, the stories he shared when he didn't even realize he was sharing, can't all be false too. I refuse to believe it. I will refuse to believe it until I'm proven wrong.

I start rolling through them, Owen's greatest hits: the time he took a boat trip down the Eastern Seaboard with his father, barely sixteen years old, the only time he ever spent several days alone with his father. The time during his senior year of high school that he let his girlfriend's dog out to play and the dog ran away, Owen getting fired from his first job for spending that afternoon searching for the dog instead of returning to work. The time he snuck into the midnight screening of *Star Wars* with his pals, his parents awake at 2:45 A.M. when he finally walked in.

And a story he told me about college, about why he started to love engineering and technology so much. Owen's freshman year of college, barely nineteen years old, he took a mathematics course with a professor he adored, someone he credited with his current career. Even though the professor told Owen he was the worst student he'd ever had. Had he told me what the professor's name was? Tobias something. Was it Newton? Or was it Professor Newhouse? And didn't he have a nickname he went by?

I race upstairs and back into the hotel room to wake Bailey—the one person who maybe has heard the story about this professor more times than I have.

I pull the comforter off and sit down on the edge of her bed.

"I'm sleeping," she says.

"Not anymore," I say.

She reluctantly props herself up against the headboard. "What is it?"

"Do you remember the name of your father's professor? The one he loved so much, who taught him freshman year?"

"I have no idea what you're talking about," she says.

I fight my impatience, thinking of all the times Bailey has rolled her eyes at this story—at how Owen has used it as a teaching opportunity. He's used it to convince Bailey to stick with something that matters to her, to commit to her plan. He's used it when he was trying to convince her of the opposite.

"You know this story, Bailey. The professor taught that impossible course in gauge theory and global analysis. Your father loves talking about him. The professor who told him that he was the worst student he'd ever had. And how that actually made Owen want to do better. How it focused him?"

Bailey starts nodding, a slow recognition. "You mean the guy who put my father's midterm on the bulletin board, right...?" she says. "So he wouldn't forget all the ways he could improve."

"Exactly, yes!"

"Sometimes your passion takes work and you shouldn't give up on it just because it isn't easy..." She takes on Owen's voice, imitating him. "Sometimes, kid, you need to work harder to get to a better place."

"That's it. Yes. That's him. I think his first name was Tobias but I need to know his full name. Please tell me you remember it."

"Why?" she says.

"Just, can you remember it, Bailey?"

"He called him by his last name sometimes. A nickname for his last name. But it started with a *J*... didn't it?"

"Maybe. I don't know."

"No, I don't think that was it... It was Cook... He called him Cook. So maybe it was Cooker?" she says. "Or was it Cookman?"

I smile, almost laughing out loud. She's right. I know it as soon as I hear it. It's good to know I wasn't even close.

"What's so funny?" she says. "You're freaking me out."

"Nothing, that's great. That's what I needed to know," I say. "Go back to sleep."

"I don't want to," she says. "Tell me what you figured out."

I open my phone and I plug his name into the search engine. How many professors with the name Tobias Cookman could there be who teach college-level mathematics? And more specifically gauge theory and global analysis?

One that I find, one who is teaching theoretical mathematics. One who has dozens of accolades and awards for his teaching. One who, from the set of photographs that pop up, looks just as surly as Owen has described him. Wrinkled brow, a deep frown. And, for some reason, in many of the photographs he is also perpetually clad in red cowboy boots.

Professor Tobias "Cook" Cookman.

He has never worked at Princeton University.

But for the last twenty-nine years, he has been on the faculty at the University of Texas at Austin.

It's Science, Isn't It?

We take a cab this time.

Bailey stares down at her hands, not blinking, looking more than a little stunned. I'm spinning too, working to hold my center. It's one thing when a private investigator intuits that your husband's name is different, that the details of his life are different. But if this pans out—if Owen took this class with this Professor Cookman—it's our first piece of proof, real proof, that Owen lied about the story of his life. It's the first proof that my instinct was right, that his story, Owen's real story, somehow may begin and end in Austin. It feels like a victory that we are moving closer to the truth. But when the truth is taking you somewhere you don't want to go, you also aren't sure. You aren't sure you want that win.

The cab pulls up to the College of Natural Sciences—a collection of buildings that's bigger and more expansive than my entire liberal arts college, campus and dorms included.

I turn and look at Bailey. She is taking in the buildings—the relaxed green running through and around them.

Even considering the circumstances, it's hard not to be impressed, especially when we get out of the car and start walking through the green and over the small bridge that leads to the Department of Mathematics.

The building that is home to UT's mathematics, physics, and astronomy departments. The ego wall proudly showcases that this building graduates hundreds of the most impressive science and math students in America each year. And it's also home to Nobel Prize winners, Wolf Prize winners, Abel Prize winners, Turing Award winners, and Fields Medal winners.

Including our Fields Medal winner, Professor Cookman.

As we take the escalator up to his office, we see a large poster of Professor Cookman's face. Same frown, same wrinkled brow.

The poster reads: TEXAS SCIENTISTS CHANGE THE WORLD. And it lists some of Professor Cookman's research, some of his awards. Fields Medal winner. Finalist for the Wolf.

We arrive in front of his office and Bailey cues up her phone to a photograph of Owen, the oldest photograph either of us has with us in Texas—in the hope that Professor Cookman is someone who is willing to look at it.

The photograph is from a decade ago. Owen is hugging Bailey after her first school play. Bailey is still in costume and Owen has his arms wrapped proudly around her shoulders. Bailey's face is mostly obscured by the mess of flowers he gave her—gerbera daisies and carnations and lilies, a bouquet larger than her whole body. Bailey is peeking out from behind the flowers, a big smile on her face. Owen is looking at the camera. Happy. Laughing.

It's almost too much to look at the photograph, especially when I zoom in on Owen. His eyes bright and lively.

Almost like he's here. Almost like he could be here.

I try to give Bailey a supportive smile as we walk inside and find a graduate student sitting behind a desk in the outer office. She wears black wire-rim glasses and is focused on grading a thick stack of student papers.

She doesn't look up, doesn't put her red pen down. But she clears her throat.

"Can I help you?" she says, like it's the last thing she wants to do.

"We are hoping to speak with Professor Cookman," I say.

"That much is obvious," she says. "Why?"

"My father's an old student of his," Bailey says.

"He's teaching," she says. "Besides, you need an appointment."

"Of course, but what Bailey here is trying to explain to you is that she too is interested in becoming a student. At UT. Like her father. And Nielon Simonson, over in admissions, suggested that she sit in on Professor Cookman's class today."

She looks up. "Who in admissions?" she asks.

"Nielon?" I say, trying hard to sell the name I just made up. "He said if Cook can't convince Bailey to come here, no one can. He thought she should sit in on his class today."

She raises her eyebrows. My use of his nickname Cook stops her, makes her believe me.

"Well, class is half over, but if you want to sit in on the rest of it, I guess I can take you down there..."

"That would be great," Bailey says. "Thanks."

She rolls her eyes, uninterested. "So let's do this," she says.

We follow her out of the office and walk down several staircases until we arrive at a large lecture hall.

"When you walk in, you'll be at the front of the class," she says. "Don't stop. Don't look at Professor Cookman. Head up the stairs and go directly to the back of the lecture hall. Got it?"

I nod. "Sure."

"If you disrupt his class in any way, he'll ask you to leave," she says. "Believe me."

She opens the door and I start to thank her, but she puts her finger to her mouth, shushing me.

"What did I just say?"

Then she is gone, shutting the door behind her, leaving us inside.

We stare at the closed door. Then we do what she said. I keep my eyes straight ahead as we walk up the staircase, heading to the back of the lecture hall, passing the eighty-something students who fill the seats.

I motion to a spot against the back wall and we head there, trying to make ourselves invisible. Only then do we turn and face the room.

Professor Cookman stands at the front, behind a small podium. In person, he looks to be about sixty and no taller than five foot five, even in those red cowboy boots, which seem to add an extra few inches.

Everyone's eyes are on him. Everyone is focused. No one is whispering to his or her neighbor. No one is checking email. No one is sending texts.

As Professor Cookman turns to write something on the large blackboard, Bailey leans toward me.

"Nielon Simonson?" she whispers. "Did you make that up?"

"Are we standing here or not?" I say.

"We are."

"So what does it matter?"

I think we are being quiet, but we are loud enough that someone in the back row turns and looks at us.

What is worse, Professor Cookman stops writing on the blackboard and turns too. He glares at us, the whole class following suit.

I feel myself flush and look down. He doesn't say anything, but he doesn't turn away from us either. Not for a good minute. A minute that feels like it's lasting far longer than that.

Thankfully, eventually, he turns back to the blackboard and continues his lecture.

We observe the rest of class silently and it's easy to see why everyone is so focused on Professor Cookman. Despite his stature, he's an impressive man. He runs the class like a show, captivating his students. And maybe, also, scaring them. He only calls on students who aren't raising their hands. When they know the answer, Cookman looks away, no acknowledgment. When a student doesn't know the answer, he keeps his eyes on the offender. He stares until it is uncomfortable, a little like he looked at us. Only then does he call on someone else.

After he writes a final equation on the board, he announces that the class is over and he dismisses everybody for the day. The class streams out and we head down the stairs to where he stands by his desk, packing his messenger bag.

It seems like he doesn't see us, continuing to pack up his papers. But then he starts speaking.

"Do you make it a habit to interrupt lectures?" he says. "Or should I count myself as special?"

"Professor Cookman," I say. "I'm sorry about that. We didn't mean for you to hear us."

"Do you think that makes it better or worse?" he says. "Who are you exactly? And why are you in my classroom?"

"I'm Hannah Hall. And this is Bailey Michaels," I say.

He looks back and forth between us, searching for more. "Okay."

"We're looking for some information about a former student of yours," I say. "We're hoping you might be able to help us."

"And why would I do that?" he says. "Especially for young women who disrupt my class?"

"You might be the only one who can," I say.

He holds my eyes, as if taking me in for the first time. I motion to Bailey, who hands Professor Cookman her phone, the screen opened to the photograph of her with her father.

He reaches in his shirt pocket and pulls out a pair of glasses, turns his gaze to the phone.

"The man standing next to you in the photograph?" he says. "Is he the former student?"

She nods but stays quiet.

He tilts his head, takes in the photo, like he is truly trying to remember. I try to help jog his memory.

"If we have his correct graduation year, he took your class twenty-six years ago," I say. "We were hoping you might know his name?"

"You know he took my class twenty-six years ago?" he says. "And you don't know his name?"

"We know the name he goes by now, but we don't know his real name," I say. "It's a long story."

"I've got time for the short version," he says.

"He's my father," Bailey says.

They're the first words out of Bailey's mouth and they stop him. He looks up, meets Bailey's eyes.

"How did you tie him back to me?" he says.

I look to Bailey to see if she wants to answer, but she is quiet again. And she looks tired. Too tired for sixteen. She looks up at me and motions. She motions for me to jump in.

"It turns out that my husband made up a lot of details... about his life," I say. "Except he did tell us a story about you, about the influence you had on him. He remembers you fondly."

He looks back down at the photograph, and I think I see a flicker in his eyes when he stares down at Owen. When I look at Bailey, I know she thinks that she's noticed the same thing. But, of course, this is what we want to see.

"He goes by Owen Michaels now," I say. "But he used to go by a different name, when he was your student."

"And why did he change his name?" he says.

"That's what we're trying figure out," I say.

"Well, I've taught many students over the years and I can't say I know him," he says.

"If it helps, we're fairly certain it was your second year of teaching."

"Maybe memory works differently for you, but in my experience, it gets harder the further away you get."

"In my recent experience, it's all pretty much the same," I say.

He smiles, taking me in. And maybe he sees it, what we are going through, because his tone softens.

"Sorry, I can't be of more help..." he says. "Maybe try the registrar's office. They could possibly steer you in the right direction."

"And what are we going to ask them?" Bailey says.

She's trying to stay controlled. But I see it. I see her anger brewing.

"Excuse me?" he says.

"I'm just saying, what are we going to ask them? If they have a student on file who now goes by Owen Michaels but used to go by something else?" she says. "This person who has apparently evaporated into thin air?"

"Yes, well, you're not wrong. They probably wouldn't be able to help with that..." he says. "This really isn't my forte though."

He hands Bailey her cell phone.

"I wish you both luck," he says.

Then he puts his bag over his shoulder and starts walking toward the exit.

Bailey stares down at her phone, back in her hands. She looks scared—scared and desperate—Professor Cookman moving away from her, Owen moving nowhere closer. We thought we were getting closer. We found Owen's professor. We got here. But now Owen just feels farther away. Which may explain why I call out to Professor Cookman, why I refuse to just let him leave.

"My husband was the worst student you ever had," I say.

Professor Cookman stops walking. He stops walking and turns around, facing us again.

"What did you just say?" he says.

"He loves to tell this story about how he struggled in your class and, after killing himself studying for the midterm, you told him that you were going to keep his exam in a frame in your office as a lesson to future students. Not as a how-to on applying yourself, but more like, at least I'm not as bad as that guy is."

He stays quiet. I keep talking, filling the silence.

"Maybe that is something you do with a student every year, especially since you had him so early on, and really by then who could have been a worst anything? But it worked with him. He believed you. And instead of it frustrating him, it made him want to work harder. To prove himself to you."

He still doesn't say anything.

Bailey reaches for my arm, like that is something she does, trying to pull me back, to let him go.

"He doesn't know," she says. "We should go."

She is eerily calm, which is somehow worse than when I thought she was going to lose it.

But Professor Cookman isn't moving, even though he is off the hook.

"I did frame it," he says.

"What?" Bailey says.

"His exam. I did frame it."

He starts walking toward us.

"It was my second year teaching and I wasn't much older than the kids were. I was trying to prove my authority. My wife eventually made me take the exam down and throw it out. She said it was too mean for a crappy midterm to be any student's legacy. I didn't see it that way, at first. She is smarter than I am. I kept that thing framed for a long time. It scared the crap out of my other students, which was really the point."

"No one wanted to be that bad?" I say.

"Even when I told them how good he became afterward," he says.

He reaches his hand out for Bailey's phone, Bailey handing it over, both of us watching as he tries to put something together.

"What did he do?" he says. "Your father?"

He directs his question to Bailey. I think she is going to offer an abbreviated version of what is happening at The Shop and with Avett Thompson—and say that we don't know the rest of the story yet. We don't know how he fits into the fraud there, or why it led to him leaving us here alone, trying to put the pieces together. These impossible pieces. But, instead, she shakes her head and tells him the worst part of what Owen has done.

"He lied to me," she says.

He nods, like that is enough for him. Professor Cookman. First name Tobias. Nickname Cook. Award-winning mathematician. Our new friend.

"Come with me," he says.

Some Students Are Better Than Others

Professor Cookman takes us back to his office, where he puts on a pot of coffee, and Cheryl, the graduate student manning his desk, is much more attentive than earlier. She powers on several computers on Cook's workstation as a second graduate student, Scott, starts going through Cook's filing cabinet—both of them moving as quickly as they can.

While Cheryl downloads a copy of Owen's photograph onto the professor's laptop, Scott pulls out an enormous file, slamming the cabinet closed, and then walks back over to the desk.

"The exams you have in here only go back to 2001. These are from 2001–2002."

"Then why are you handing them to me?" he says. "What am I supposed to do with these?"

Scott looks dumbstruck as Cheryl puts the laptop on Professor Cookman's desk.

"Go and check the filing cabinets in the archives," he says. "Then call the registrar and get me the class list from 1995. Also get 1994 and 1996, just to be thorough."

Scott and Cheryl head out of the office, tasked, and Cook turns to his laptop, Owen's photograph covering the screen.

"So what kind of trouble is your father in?" he says. "If I may ask."

"He works at The Shop," Bailey says.

"The Shop?" he says. "Avett Thompson's operation?"

"Exactly," I say. "He did most of the coding."

He looks confused. "Coding? That's surprising. If your father is the same person that I taught, he was more interested in mathematical theory. He wanted to work for the university. He wanted to work in academia. Coding's not a natural extension of that, really."

That may be why he decided to do it, I almost say. It was a way to hide in a field adjacent to the field he was interested in, but far enough away that no one would look for him there.

"Is he officially a suspect?" Cook asks.

"No," I say. "Not officially."

He motions toward Bailey. "I imagine you're just interested in finding your father. Either way."

She nods. And Cook turns his attention to me.

"And how does the name change fit in, exactly?"

"That's what we're trying to figure out," I say. "He may have been in trouble before The Shop. We don't know. We're only just learning about all the inconsistencies between what he's told us and..."

"What's true?"

"Yes," I say.

Then I turn and look at Bailey, to see how she's processing that. She looks back at me, as if to say, *It's okay.* Not that she is okay with what's going on, exactly—but maybe that it's okay, all the same, that I'm trying to get to the bottom of things.

Professor Cookman stares at the computer screen, not saying anything at first. "You don't remember all of them, but I do remember him," he says. "Though I remember him having longer hair. And being much heavier. He looks quite different."

"But not entirely?" I say.

"No," he says. "Not entirely."

I take that in—trying to imagine Owen walking through the world, looking the way Professor Cookman is describing. I try to imagine Owen walking through the world as someone else. I look over at Bailey and I can see it on her face. I can see it in her frown. How she's doing the same thing.

Professor Cookman closes the laptop and leans across the desk, toward us.

"Look, I'm not going to pretend to imagine what this all feels like, but I will say, for whatever it's worth, in my years of teaching, I've discovered one thing above all else that makes me calm in moments like this. It's an Einstein theory originally, which is why it sounds better in German."

"You may have to go with English," Bailey says.

"Einstein said, *So far as the theories of mathematics are about reality, they are not certain; so far as they are certain, they are not about reality.*"

Bailey tilts her head. "Still waiting on the English there, Professor," she says.

"It basically means, we don't know shit about anything," he says.

Bailey laughs—softly but genuinely—and it's the first time she's laughed in days, the first time she's laughed since this all started.

I'm so grateful that I almost leap over the table to hug Professor Cookman.

Before I do, Scott and Cheryl walk back into the office.

"Here's the roster from the spring semester, 1995. In 1994, you were teaching two different senior seminars. And in '96 you taught graduate students exclusively. Spring '95 was when you taught underclassmen. So that's the class the student would have been in."

Cheryl hands over the roster triumphantly.

"There were seventy-three people in the class," she says. "Eighty-three the first day, but then ten dropped out. That is pretty common in terms of normal attrition. I'm assuming you don't need the names of the ten who dropped?"

"No," he says.

"That's what I figured, so I went ahead and crossed those out for you," she says, like she just discovered something smaller than the atom. And, in my book, she has.

As Professor Cookman studies the list, Cheryl turns to us. "There's not an Owen on the list. Or even a Michaels on the list."

"That's not a surprise," he says.

Cook keeps his eyes on the list, but he shakes his head.

"I'm sorry I don't remember his name," he says. "You think I would know, having had his work framed above my head for all that time."

"It was a long time ago," I say.

"Still. It'd be far more helpful if I could recall that much, but these names aren't adding up to anything for me."

Professor Cookman hands the list over and I take it from him, gratefully and quickly, before he changes his mind.

"Seventy-three names are a whole lot more manageable than a billion. This is a whole lot more manageable than having nowhere to start."

"Assuming he's on there," Professor Cookman says.

"Yes, assuming that."

I look down at the printout, seventy-three names staring back at me—fifty of them men. Bailey peers over my shoulder to look too. We need to find a way to go through them as quickly as possible. But I am more hopeful than I have been that we have somewhere to start from. That we have a list of names to cull from, Owen somewhere among them. I feel certain of this.

"You don't know how much we appreciate this," I say. "Thank you."

"My pleasure," he says. "I hope it helps."

We stand up to go, Cookman standing up as well. He is not particularly eager to get on with his day. Now that he is invested, he wants to find out more. He seems to want to know who Owen used to be, how that led him to where he is now—wherever that is.

We start walking toward the office door when Cookman stops us.

"I do want to say… I'm not sure what is going on with him now, but I can tell you that back then, he was a nice kid. And smart. It all starts to blend, but those early years I remember some of them. Maybe because we try harder in the beginning. But I do remember. I remember he was a really good kid."

I turn back toward him, grateful to hear something about Owen, something that feels like the Owen I know.

He smiles, offers a shrug. "It wasn't all his fault. The crappy midterm. He was just too focused on one of the women in the class. He wasn't the only one. In a class of mostly men, she stood out."

This is when my heart stops. Bailey turns back in Cookman's direction too. I can almost feel her, forgetting to breathe.

One of the few things Owen has told us about Olivia, repeatedly, one of the few things Bailey had to hold on to about her mother is that her father had fallen in love with her in college. He said they had been seniors—that she had lived in the apartment next door. Had that been a lie too? The smallest detail changed to avoid any trace of the actual past?

"Was she like… his girlfriend?" Bailey says.

"Can't speak to that. I only even remember her, at all, because he made the case that she was why his work was suffering. That he was in love. He made the case in a long letter and I told him I was going to put it up, right next to his terrible exam, unless his work improved."

"That's humiliating," Bailey says.

"Apparently it was also effective," he says.

I look down at the list, scanning the names of the women. Thirteen in total. I search the list for an Olivia, but don't see one. Though of course, it may not be an Olivia I need to find.

"I know this is asking a lot, but you don't remember her name, do you? The name of the woman?" I say.

"I remember she was a better student than your husband," he said.

"Wasn't everyone?" I say.

Professor Cookman nods. "Yes. There's that too," he says.

Fourteen Months Ago

"So how does it feel? Being a married woman?" Owen asks.

"How does it feel being a married man?" I say.

We were sitting at Frances, an intimate restaurant in the Castro, at the farm table where our small wedding dinner had taken place. The day had started with the two of us getting married at city hall. I wore a short white dress, Owen put on a tie and new Converse sneakers. And it was ending with the two of us, time rolling toward midnight—as we finished the champagne, shoes off, now that our handful of guests had left.

Jules had been there, and a few friends of Owen's—Carl, Patty. And Bailey. Of course, Bailey. In a rare display of generosity toward me, she arrived at city hall on time and stayed at the restaurant until after we cut the cake. She even gave me a smile before leaving to spend the night at her friend Rory's. I hoped that meant she was at least a little happy about the day. I knew it probably meant she was a little happy that Owen let her have champagne.

Either way, I was taking the win.

"It feels pretty great being a married man," Owen said. "Though I have no idea how we're getting home tonight."

I laughed. "It's not a bad problem."

"No," he said. "Not as far as problems go."

He reached for the champagne bottle, filled his glass, and refilled mine. Then he moved his chair away, sat down on the back of mine. I leaned back against him, breathing in.

"We've come a long way from our second date when you wouldn't even let me drive you to dinner," he said.

"I don't know about that," I said. "I was pretty crazy about you, even then."

"You had a funny way of showing it. I wasn't even sure I was going to get to see you again after that night."

"Well, you did ask an awful lot of questions."

"I had a lot to learn about you."

"All in one night?"

He shrugged. "I felt like I needed to learn about the could-have-been boys..." he said. "Thought it was my best shot at not becoming one."

I reached back and touched his cheek—first with the outside of my palm, then with the inside.

"You became the opposite," I said.

"I think that might just be the single best thing anyone has ever said to me," he said.

"It's true," I said.

And it was true. Owen was the opposite. He had felt like the opposite from day one, from that first meeting in my workshop, but it was more than just a feeling now. He had proven himself to be the opposite. It wasn't just that it was easy to be with him (though it was) or that I felt deepened by him in a way I never had in a relationship before. It wasn't even that we understood each other in that elusive way that you either had with someone or you could never quite find—that pervasive shorthand in which a look could tell us what the other person needed: *Time to leave the party; Time to reach for me; Time to give me room to breathe.*

It was a little bit of all of that and something far bigger than all of that. How do you explain it when you find in someone what you've been waiting for your whole life? Do you call it fate? It feels lazy to call it fate. It's more like finding your way home—where home is a place you secretly hoped for, a place you imagined, but where you'd never before been.

Home. When you weren't sure you'd ever get to have one.

That's what he was to me. That's who he was.

Owen pulled my palm to his lips, held me there. "So... are you going to answer my question about how it feels?" he said. "To be a married woman?"

I shrugged. "Not sure yet," I said. "Too soon to tell."

He laughed. "Okay, well, that's all right," he said.

I took a sip of my champagne. I took a sip, and laughed too. I couldn't help it. I was happy. I was just... happy.

"Turns out you have a little while to decide," he said.

"Like the rest of our lives?" I said.

"I hope longer than that," he said.

If You Marry the Prom King...

Seventy-three names, fifty of them men.

One of them is potentially Owen.

We walk quickly across campus toward the main research library, which Cheryl tells us is most likely to house the school yearbooks. If we can get our hands on the yearbooks from the years Owen was at UT, that could be the key to getting through this list as quickly as possible. The yearbooks will offer not just student names, but they'll offer photographs too. They'll potentially have a photograph of a young Owen, if he did anything at school besides fail math.

We head inside the Perry-Castañeda Library, which is enormous—six stories of books and maps and cards and computer labs—and head to the research librarian's desk. She informs us that we will need to put a request in at the archives to get the hard copies of the school yearbooks from that far back, but we can access the archive on a library computer.

We go to the second-floor computer lab, which is mostly empty, and sit at two computers in the corner. I pull up Owen's freshman and sophomore yearbooks on one computer. And Bailey pulls up his junior and senior years. And, side by side, we begin looking up students from Cookman's class one at a time, hitting the roster alphabetically. Our first candidate: John Abbot from Baltimore, Maryland. I find him in one grainy photograph with the ski club. He doesn't look much like Owen in the photograph—thick glasses, full beard— but it is hard to rule him out completely just based on that one photograph. We find too many potential hits when we google just his name, but when I cross-reference with skiing, I find that John Abbot (Baltimore native, UT-Austin grad) now lives in Aspen with his partner and their two kids.

We are able to rule out the next few male students on the list much more easily: one is five feet tall and has curly red hair; another is six foot four and a professional ballet dancer who resides in Paris; one is living in Honolulu, Hawaii, and running for state senate.

We are on the *E*s when my phone rings. HOME comes up on the caller ID. For a second, I imagine that it's Owen. Owen is back at the house, and calling to tell us that he has worked everything out, and we need to come home immediately. So he can explain the parts that don't make sense. Where he has been, who he was before I knew him. Why he has left these things out.

But it isn't Owen on the phone. It's Jules.

Jules is responding to the text I'd sent her at the hotel bar, asking her to head to the house, asking her to find the piggy bank.

"I'm in Bailey's room," she says when I pick up.

"Was anyone outside?" I say.

"I don't think so. I didn't see anyone strange in the parking lot, and there wasn't anyone on the docks."

"Would you close the blinds while you're there?"

"Already done," she said.

I look over at Bailey, hoping she's too busy with the yearbooks to pay close attention. But I clock her eyeing me, waiting to see what this phone call is about. Maybe hoping, against hope, this is going to be the call that gets her back to her father.

"And you were right," Jules says. "It does say Lady Paul on the side."

She doesn't say what it is, of course. She doesn't say it's a piggy bank that she is at our house to retrieve—Bailey's piggy bank—though it would sound pretty innocuous if she did say that out loud.

I hadn't imagined it. The small note on the bottom of the last page of Owen's will, listing the conservator, L. Paul. It was also the name on the side of the blue piggy bank in Bailey's room— LADY PAUL, written in black, beneath the bow. The same blue piggy bank Owen had taken when we evacuated, the one I found him with at the hotel bar in the middle of the night. I chocked it up to his being sentimental. But I was wrong. He had taken the piggy bank because it was something he needed to keep safe.

"But there is a bit of an issue," Jules says. "I can't open it."

"What do you mean you can't open it?" I say. "Just smash it with a hammer."

"No, you don't understand, there's a safe inside the piggy bank," she says. "And the thing's made of steel. I'm going to have to find someone who can crack a safe. Any ideas?"

"Not off the top of my head," I say.

"K, I'll deal with it," Jules says, "but have you checked your newsfeed? They indicted Jordan Maverick."

Jordan is the COO of The Shop, Avett's number two and Owen's counterpart on the business side of the firm. He was newly divorced and had been spending a little bit of time at our place. I invited Jules over for dinner, hoping they'd hit it off. They didn't. She thought he was boring. I thought there were worse things to be—or maybe I just didn't see him that way.

"For the record," she says. "No more setups."

"Understood," I say.

At a different moment this would have been all the encouragement I needed to ask her about her colleague Max, to make a joke about whether he was the other reason she wasn't interested in setups. But, in this moment, all it does is remind me that Max has an inside source. One that can potentially help us in regard to Owen.

"Has Max heard anything beyond Jordan?" I ask. "Has he heard anything about Owen?"

Bailey tilts her head, toward me.

"Not specifically," she says. "But his source over at the FBI did say the software just became functional."

"What does that mean?" I ask.

Except I can guess what that means. It means Owen probably thought he was out of the woods. He probably thought any contingency plan he needed to create could be put on the backburner again. It means that when Jules called Owen and said they were coming in, he couldn't believe it. He couldn't believe that this close to being safe, he was about to be caught.

"Max is texting me," Jules says. "I'll call you after I find a safecracker, okay?"

"I bet those are some words you thought you'd never say."

She laughs. "No kidding."

I say goodbye and turn to Bailey. "That was Jules," I say. "I'm having her look into something at the house."

She nods. She doesn't ask if I have anything to report on her father. She knows I'd tell her if I did.

"Any progress?" I say.

"I'm on *H*," she says. "No hits yet."

"*H* is progress."

"Yeah. Unless he's not on the list."

My phone rings again. I think it's going to be Jules calling back, but the number is one I don't recognize—one with a 512 area code. Texas.

"Who's that?" she says.

I shake my head that I don't know. Then I accept the call. The woman on the other end of the line is already talking to me. She is midway through a sentence that, apparently, she thought I was there to hear.

"Scrimmages," she says. "We should have accounted for them too. The scrimmages."

"Who's this?"

"It's Elenor McGovern," she says. "From the Episcopal church. And I think I may have found an answer for you about the wedding your stepdaughter attended. Sophie, one of our longtime parishioners, has a son who plays football for UT-Austin. She never misses a game. She was in here earlier, helping with the new member breakfast, and it occurred to me she might be the person to ask if I'd missed something. And she said that during the summer, the Longhorns have a series of intrasquad scrimmages."

My breath catches in my throat. "And they're held in the stadium?" I say. "Just like the regular season games?"

"Just like the regular season games. Usually with a fairly packed crowd. People go as if it's an actual game," she says. "I'm not much of a football fan so that didn't occur to me, at first."

"It occurred to you to ask her, that's pretty great," I say.

"Well, maybe. And this part certainly is. I did a cross-check for you on the dates of the scrimmages during the time we were open. We had one wedding that lines up with the final scrimmage of the 2008 season. One wedding that your stepdaughter might have been at. Do you have a pen? You should write this down."

Elenor is proud of herself, and she should be. She may have found a link to Owen—to what Owen had been doing in Austin that weekend, so long after graduation. And to why Bailey was with him.

"I'm writing it down," I say.

"It was the Reyes and Smith wedding," she says. "I have all the information on the wedding here. The ceremony took place at noon. And the reception was held off-site. It doesn't specify where."

"Elenor, this is amazing. I don't even know how to thank you for this."

"You're so welcome," she says.

I reach across Bailey to pick up the printout of Cookman's class. There it is. No Reyes. But one Smith.

Katherine. Katherine Smith. I point to her name and Bailey starts typing quickly, searching for the yearbook index. KATHERINE SMITH coming up. SMITH, KATHERINE. Ten page numbers by her name.

Maybe they were friends—or she had been Owen's girlfriend, the one that Professor Cookman remembered. And Owen had been in town for Katherine's wedding. He had brought his family back to help his old friend celebrate.

Maybe if I could find her, she could shed light on who Owen used to be.

"Was her first name Katherine, Elenor?"

"No, not Katherine. Let me see. Bride's first name is Andrea," Elenor says. "And... yes, there we are. Andrea Reyes and Charlie Smith."

I feel deflated that it wasn't Katherine herself, but maybe she is related to Charlie somehow. This could certainly still be the connection. But before I can repeat that to Bailey, she turns to a page featuring the debate society and President Katherine "Kate" Smith.

And the photograph comes up.

It's a group photograph of the entire debate team. They are sitting on barstools in a small, old-school bar, more like a cocktail lounge than a traditional pub: wooden rafters, a long brick wall, bourbon bottles lined up like presents. Lanterns line the bar top, backlighting those bottles, backlighting the dark wine bottles above them.

The caption under the photograph reads: DEBATE TEAM PRESIDENT KATHERINE SMITH CELEBRATES WINNING THE STATE CHAMPIONSHIP AT HER FAMILY'S BAR, THE NEVER DRY, WITH TEAMMATES FROM (L) TO (R)...

"No way!" Bailey says. "That could be the bar. Where the wedding was."

"What are you talking about?"

"I didn't say anything, but last night when we were at Magnolia Cafe, and you were asking me all those questions, I remembered being at a bar for the wedding," she says. "Or, more like, some sort of small restaurant. But then I figured it was late and I was just grasping for something... anything... so

I let it go. I didn't even mention it. But this place in the photo, this Never Dry bar, looks like the bar."

I cover the phone's mouthpiece, and look down at Bailey, who is pointing with fever, almost in disbelief. She points to a record player in the corner, a weird kind of proof.

"I'm not kidding," she says. "That's the bar. I recognize it."

"There are a million bars that look like that."

"I know. But there are two things I remember about Austin," she said. "And that bar is one of them."

Which is when Bailey makes the photograph bigger. The debate team faces growing less blurry, Katherine's face becoming delineated. Easy to see.

We both go silent. The bar doesn't matter anymore. Owen doesn't even matter, exactly.

All that matters is the face.

It isn't a photograph matching the woman I know as Bailey's mother—that, more important, Bailey knows to be her mother. Olivia. Olivia of the red hair and girlish freckles. Olivia who looks a little like me.

But the woman staring back at us—this woman Katherine "Kate" Smith—looks like Bailey. Exactly like Bailey. She has the same dark hair. She has the same full cheeks. And, most notably, she has the same fierce eyes—judgmental more than sweet.

This woman staring back at us—she could be Bailey.

Bailey shuts off the screen suddenly, as if it is too much to look at. The photograph, Kate's face matching her own. She looks over at me, wondering what I am going to do next.

"Do you know her?" she says.

"No," I say. "Do you?"

"No, I don't know," she says. "No!"

"Hello?" Elenor says. "Are you still there?"

I keep my hand over the speaker, but Bailey can hear her through the phone. She can hear her loud-pitched questions. It's making her even more tense than she is. Her shoulders are seizing. Her hands are reaching for her hair, pulling it tight behind her ears.

I'm not proud of this. But I hang up on Elenor.

Then I turn back to Bailey.

"We need to go there right now," Bailey says. "I need to go to this bar... to this Never Dry..."

She is already standing up. She is already grabbing her things.

"Bailey," I say. "I know you're upset, I know you are. I'm upset too."

We aren't saying it yet, not out loud, who we think Katherine Smith may be—who Bailey fears and hopes she is.

"Let's just talk this through for a second," I say. "I think our best chance to get to the bottom of all this is to keep going through the class roster. We are at most forty-six men away from getting an answer to who your father used to be."

"Maybe we are. Maybe we're not."

"Bailey..." I say.

She shakes her head. She doesn't sit back down.

"Let me say this another way," she says. "I'm going to the bar right now.

You can come with me or you can let me go alone."

She stands there and waits. She doesn't storm out. She waits to see what I will do. As if there is a choice.

"I go with you, of course," I say.

Then I stand up. And we walk together toward the door.

The Never Dry

In the cab ride on the way to The Never Dry, Bailey keeps pulling on her bottom lip—almost like a nervous habit she suddenly developed, her eyes darting from side to side, frantic and terrified.

I hear the questions she's not asking me out loud and I don't want to push her. I also can't just sit there and watch her suffer, so I search obsessively on my phone for Katherine "Kate" Smith, for Charlie Smith—for anything I can possibly tell her, any new information I can offer up, in an attempt to soothe her.

But I find way too much. Smith is too common of a last name, even with my subsearches (UT-Austin, Austin native, debate champion). There are hundreds of hits, and images—none for the Katherine who greeted us at the library.

Which is when I have an idea. I plug Andrea Reyes into my search, along with Charlie Smith, and I finally hit on something that may help us.

A Facebook profile for the correct Charlie Smith pops up. He is a 2002 graduate from the University of Texas at Austin with a B.A. in art history, followed by two semesters at the Graduate School of Architecture, and an internship at a landscape architecture firm in downtown Austin.

No work history after that.

No status updates or photographs since 2009.

But it says that his wife is Andrea Reyes.

"There it is," Bailey says.

She points out the window to a blue door, vines around it. You could almost miss it—THE NEVER DRY written on a small gold plaque. It sits there quietly, kitty-corner to West Sixth Street, a coffee shop on one side, an alley on the other.

We hop out of the taxi and, as I turn to pay the driver, I see that our hotel is visible across Lady Bird Lake. I feel a strange pull, wanting to call this off, head back there.

Then Bailey goes to open the blue door.

And as she does, something happens that has never happened before. Call it maternal instinct. I grab her arm before I know I am grabbing it.

"What the hell?" she says.

"You wait here."

"What?" she says. "No way."

I start thinking quickly, the truth not feeling possible to say. *What if we walk inside there and see her? This Katherine Smith. What if your father took you away from her? What if she tries to take you from me?* And yet, there it is, feeling possible enough that it is the first thing that occurs to me.

"I don't want you in there," I say. "They'll be more likely to answer my questions if you're not in there too."

"That's not good enough, Hannah," she says.

"Well, how's this?" I say. "We don't know whose bar this is. We don't know who these people are or whether they are dangerous. All we know is that it's looking more and more like your father may have taken you from here and, knowing him, if he did that there was something he was trying to protect you from. There may have been *someone* he was trying to protect you from. You cannot go inside there until I find that out."

She is quiet. She stares at me unhappily, but she stays quiet.

I motion toward the coffee shop next door. It looks quiet, almost empty, after the afternoon rush.

"Just go sit inside and get yourself a piece of pie, okay?"

"I literally couldn't want a piece of pie less," she says.

"Then get a cup of coffee and keep working on Professor Cookman's roster. See if you can pull anyone else up on a search. We still have a long way to go."

"I don't like this plan," she says.

I pull the roster out of my messenger bag. I hold it out for her. "I'll come and get you when it's all clear in there."

"Clear of what? Why don't you just say it?" she asks. "Why don't you say who you think is inside?"

"Probably for the same reason you're not ready to say it, Bailey."

This gets through to her. She nods her agreement.

Then she takes the roster out of my hand and turns toward the coffee shop. "Don't take too long, okay?" she says.

Then she opens the door to the coffee shop, a whoosh of purple as she heads inside.

I breathe a sigh of relief. And I open the blue door to The Never Dry. There is a winding staircase, which I take upstairs to a candlelit hallway and a second blue door, which is also unlocked.

I open that door and enter a small cocktail lounge. An empty cocktail lounge. There are maple rafters and a dark mahogany bar, velvety love seats surrounding small bar tables. It doesn't feel like a college town bar. The hidden doorway, the intimate room. It feels more like a speakeasy—guarded, sexy, private.

No one is standing behind the bar. The only indication that anyone is even there is the lit tea candles on the cocktail tables, Billie Holiday playing on an old record player.

I walk up to the bar, taking in the shelves behind it. They're filled with dark liquors, boozy bitters—and there is one shelf devoted to framed photographs in thick, silver frames, a few framed newspaper clippings. Kate Smith appears in several, often with the same lanky, dark-haired guy. Not Owen. Someone besides Owen. There are several photographs of the dark-haired guy alone as well. I lean over the bar to try and make out what one of the newspaper clippings says. It includes a photograph of Kate dressed in a gown, the lanky guy dressed in a tuxedo. An older couple bookends him. I start to read through the names beneath the photograph. Meredith Smith, Kate Smith. Charlie Smith...

Then I hear footsteps. "Hey, there."

I turn around to see Charlie Smith. The lanky guy from the photographs. He's wearing a crisp button-down shirt and holding a case of champagne. He looks older than in the fancy framed photographs. Less lanky. His dark hair is now graying, his skin weathered, but it's definitely him. Whoever he is to Bailey. Whoever Bailey is to Kate.

"We're not open just yet," he says. "We don't usually start serving until closer to six..."

I point back from the direction I came. "I'm sorry about that, the door was unlocked," I say. "I didn't mean to just let myself in."

"Not a problem, you can have a seat at the bar and take a look at the cocktail menu," he says. "I just have a couple more things to take care of."

"Sounds great," I say.

He puts the champagne on the bar and offers a kind smile. I force a smile back. It isn't easy being around this stranger who has the same coloring as Bailey—and his smile, when he points it at me, is hers too, complete with her same uptick, the same dimple shining through.

I hop up onto a stool as he moves behind the bar and starts unpacking the champagne.

"Can I ask you a quick question? I'm new to Austin and I think I got a bit turned around. I'm looking for the campus. Can I walk from here?"

"Sure, if you have forty-five minutes or so. Probably easier to just hop in an Uber if you're in any kind of rush," he says. "Where are you headed to exactly?"

I think of his bio, of what I just pulled up about him. "The School of Architecture," I say.

"Really?" he says.

I'm not a good actress, so trying to look casual while telling this lie is a stretch. It pays off though. He's interested suddenly, just like I hoped he would be. Charlie Smith: late thirties, almost architect, married to Andrea Reyes. Married to Andrea at a wedding Bailey and Owen attended.

"I took some classes at the School of Architecture, once upon a time," he says.

"Small world," I say. I look around to stop my heart from racing, to center myself. "Did you design this place? It's gorgeous."

"Can't really take that much credit. I did a bit of a redesign when I took it over. But the bones are the same."

He finishes putting the champagne away and leans across the bar.

"Are you an architect?" he asks.

"Landscape architect. And I'm in the running for a teaching position," I say. "Just a temp position while one of the professors is on maternity leave. But they want me to come have dinner with some of the faculty, so I'm hopeful."

"How about a little liquid courage?" he says. "What would you like to drink?"

"Dealer's choice," I say.

"That's dangerous," he says. "Especially when I've got a little time."

Charlie turns and studies his choices, reaches for a bottle of small batch bourbon. I watch as he preps a martini glass with ice, bitters, sugar. Then he slowly pours the rich bourbon. Finishing it with a slice of orange peel.

He slides the drink toward me. "The house specialty," he says. "A bourbon old-fashioned."

"That looks too pretty to drink," I say.

"My grandfather used to make the bitters himself. Now I do it, most of the time. I'm falling down on the job a bit, but it makes all the difference."

I take a sip of my drink, which is smooth and icy and strong. It runs straight to my head.

"So, this is your family's bar?"

"Yeah, my grandfather was the original proprietor," he says. "He wanted a place to play cards with his buddies."

He motions to the one velvet booth in the corner, a RESERVED sign on it. There are several black-and-white photographs above it—including a great one of a group of guys, sitting in that booth.

"He spent fifty years behind the bar before I took it over from him."

"Wow," I say. "That's incredible. What about your father?"

"What about him?" he says.

And I clock it—how uncomfortable he looks at the mention of his father.

"I was just wondering why you guys skipped a generation..." I say. "He wasn't interested?"

His face relaxes, my question apparently innocuous enough for him.

"No, not really his thing. This place was my mother's father's, and she was definitely not interested..." He shrugs. "And I wanted the gig. My wife, or ex-wife now, had just found out she was pregnant with our twins, so my days as a student needed to be over."

I force a laugh, trying not to react to the fact that he has kids. Plural. I try to figure out how to press on that, to wrap this conversation around to his wife, to the wedding. To where I need it to go. To Kate.

"Maybe that's why you look familiar," I say. "This is going to sound crazy, but I think we met a long time ago."

He tilts his head, smiles. "Did we?"

"No, I mean... I think I was here, at the bar, back when I was in college."

"So... it's The Never Dry that looks familiar?"

"I guess that's more accurate, yeah." I say. "I was in town with a girlfriend for the hot sauce competition. She was photographing it for a local paper..."

I figure as much truth as I can muster is a good thing.

"And I'm pretty sure we came in here that weekend. This place doesn't look like a lot of other bars around Austin."

"It's certainly possible... the festival isn't held too far from here." He turns and pulls a bottle of Shonky Sauce Co. Purple Hot Sauce off his shelf. "This was one of 2019's winners. I use it to make a pretty feisty Bloody Mary..."

"That sounds like a commitment," I say.

"It's not for the faint of heart, that's for sure," he says.

He laughs and I brace myself for what I'm about to do.

"If I'm remembering this place correctly, the bartender working here that night was a total sweetheart. She gave us all sorts of tips for places to eat. I remember her. Long dark hair. She looked a lot like you, actually."

"That's some memory you have," he says.

"I might be getting a little help."

I point toward the shelf of silver-framed photographs. I point toward one in which Kate is staring back at me.

"Maybe it was her," I say.

He follows my eyes toward the photograph of Kate and shakes his head. "No, not possible," he says.

He starts wiping down the bar, completely tightening up. And this is when I should drop it—this is when I would drop it—if I didn't need his help to get to it, who Kate Smith is.

"Weird. I could have sworn it was her. Are you guys related?" I say.

He looks up at me, the look in his eye changing from avoidance to irritation. "You ask a lot of questions," he says.

"I know. Sorry. You don't have to answer that," I say. "It's a bad habit."

"Asking too many questions?"

"Thinking that people want to answer."

His face softens. "No, it's fine," he says. "She's my sister. And it's just a little sensitive 'cause she's not with us anymore..."

His sister. He said she was his sister. And he said she isn't with them anymore. This breaks something in me. If this is Bailey's mother, she is lost to her. Bailey has lived her life thinking her mother is lost to her, but this will be in an entirely new way. She will be lost to her as soon as she found her. Which is why the next thing I say is the truth.

"I'm sorry to hear that," I say. "I'm really sorry."

"Yeah..." he says. "Me too."

I don't want to push him further on Kate, not now. I can check death certificates when I leave here. I can check with someone else to learn more.

I start to get up, but Charlie scans the shelf until he finds a specific photograph. It's a photograph of Charlie with a dark-haired woman and two little boys, both of the boys dressed in Texas Rangers jerseys.

"Maybe it was my wife, Andrea," he says. "That you met, I mean. She worked here for years. When I was in school, she put in more shifts than I did."

He hands me the picture frame. I look closely at the photograph, at this nice family staring back at me, at his now ex-wife, shining a lovely smile at the camera.

"It probably was her," I say. "It's weird, isn't it? I don't know where I put the room key for my hotel, but her face, I think I remember."

I hold on to the photograph.

"Your boys are adorable."

"Thank you. They're great kids. But I need some new photographs in here. They were five in this photo," he says. "And now they're eleven, which, as they would be quick to tell you, is essentially voting age."

Eleven. That stops me. Eleven would line up, almost precisely, with when he and Andrea got married. Andrea getting pregnant shortly before or shortly after the wedding.

"They play me a bit now though, since the divorce. Think I'll cave to all their demands just so I get to be the cool dad..." He laughs. "They win more often than they should."

"Probably okay," I say.

"Yeah." He shrugs. "You got kids?"

"Not yet," I say. "Still looking for the guy."

This is truer than I want it to be. And Charlie smiles at me, perhaps wondering if I mean it as an invitation. I know this is the moment, the moment to ask the question I need an answer to most.

I stall as I think of how to get there.

"I should probably get going, but maybe I'll head back if I get done early enough."

"Definitely," he says. "Come back, we'll celebrate."

"Or commiserate."

He smiles. "Or that."

I stand up, as if I'm about to leave, my heart threatening to beat out of my chest.

"You know... this is a bizarre question. Is it okay if I ask you? Before I head out? I figure you know a lot of locals."

"Far too many," he says. "What do you need to know?"

"I'm trying to find this guy. My girlfriend and I met him when we were here that time... a lifetime ago. He lived in Austin, probably still does. And my friend had this huge crush on him."

He looks at me, intrigued. "Okay…"

"Anyway, she's going through a crappy divorce and he's stuck in her head. That sounds ridiculous, but since I'm back in town, I thought I'd try to find him. It would be a nice thing to be able to do for her. They had a connection. A million years ago, but connections are hard to find so…"

"Do you have a name?" he says. "Not that I'm great with names."

"How about faces?" I say.

"I'm pretty good with faces," he says.

I reach into my pocket and pull out my phone, click through to the photograph of Owen. It's the photograph that we showed Professor Cookman—the one on Bailey's phone, the one I asked her to text me. Bailey's face covered with flowers, Owen smiling, happy.

Charlie looks down at the photograph.

And it happens so quickly. He throws my phone down, cracking it against the countertop. He is over the bar and in my face. He isn't touching me, but he is so close that he could.

"Do you think this is funny?" he says. "Who are you?"

I shake my head, frightened.

"Who sent you?" he says.

"No one."

I back up against the wall, and he moves closer to me—his face in my face, his shoulder almost touching my shoulder.

"This is my family you're messing with," he says. "Who sent you here?"

"Get away from her!"

I look in the doorway to see Bailey standing there. She is holding the class roster in one of her hands, a cup of coffee in the other.

She looks scared. But more than that, she looks angry, like she is going to hurl a barstool at him, if she needs to.

Charlie looks like he has seen a ghost.

"Holy shit," he says.

He moves away from me slowly. I take in a deep breath and then another, my heartbeat slowing down.

We are in a weird standstill. Bailey and Charlie stare at each other as I pull myself off the wall. There are no more than two feet between any of us, but no one is moving. Not toward each other or away. Charlie, all of a sudden, in tears.

"Kristin?" he says.

At the sound of him calling her by a name, even a name I don't recognize, I stop breathing.

"I'm not Kristin," she says.

Bailey shakes her head, her voice catching.

I reach down and pick my cell phone up from the floor, the screen cracked. But it's working. It's still working. I could dial 911. I could get help. I inch backward, toward Bailey.

Protect her.

Charlie puts his hands up in surrender as I reach Bailey, the blue door right behind us. The stairs and the outside world just beyond that.

"Look, I'm sorry about that. I can explain. If you just sit down," he says. "Take a minute. Can you both do that?

Have a seat. I'd like to talk, if you'll let me."

He motions toward a table where we can all sit. And he steps away from us, as if giving us a choice. And I can see he means it—in his eyes. He looks more sorrowful than mad.

But his skin is still bright red, and I don't trust the anger I saw, the fear. Wherever it came from, I can't have Bailey around it, not until I know what his stake in this is. What I suspect his stake in Bailey is.

So I turn to Bailey. I turn to Bailey and grab her shirt at the small of her back, roughly, pulling her toward the door.

"Go!" I say. "Now!"

And, as though it is something we know how to do, we run down the stairs, together, then outside into Austin's streets and away from Charlie Smith.

Careful What You Wish For

We move quickly down Congress Avenue.

I'm trying to get back to our hotel room on the other side of the bridge. I need to get us somewhere private where we can collect our things and I can figure out the fastest way out of Austin.

"What happened in there?" Bailey says. "Was he going to hurt you?"

"I don't know," I say. "I don't think so."

I put my hand on the small of her back, steering her in and out of the after-work crowd—couples, groups of college kids, a dogwalker handling a dozen dogs. I move sideways, hoping to make it harder for Charlie to follow us—in case he is trying to follow us—this man who was so angry at seeing a photograph of Owen that he exploded.

"Faster, Bailey."

"I'm going as fast as I can," she says. "What do you want me to do? It's a clusterfuck."

She isn't wrong. Instead of the crowds letting up as we get closer to the bridge, there are more people, all clamoring to get onto the bridge's narrow walkway.

I turn back to make sure Charlie isn't following us. Which is when I see him— several blocks behind. Charlie. He is moving at a fast clip but he hasn't spotted us yet. He looks to the left and to the right.

The Congress Avenue Bridge is straight ahead. I grab onto Bailey's elbow and we head onto the bridge's walkway. But the foot traffic is moving slowly, if at all, the entire walkway jammed up with people. It's good in the sense that it is easier to blend in, but everyone seems to have stopped moving.

Mostly everyone on the bridge is at a standstill, many of them looking down at the lake below.

"Did these people forget how to move?" Bailey says.

A guy in a Hawaiian shirt, carrying a large camera—a tourist, if I were guessing—turns back and smiles at us. Apparently, he thinks Bailey's question is directed at him.

"We're waiting on the bats," he says.

"The bats?" Bailey says.

"Yeah. The bats. They feed every night right around now."

This is when we hear, "HERE THEY COME!"

And—in a bright flood—hundreds and hundreds of bats start to fly up from beneath the bridge out into the sky. The crowd cheers as the bats move in an almost ribbonlike formation—an enormous, orchestrated beautiful swarm of them.

If Charlie is still behind us, I can't see him. He is gone. Or we are gone, two revelers observing the bats take flight on a pretty Austin night.

I look up at the sky, flooded with the bats, moving as if in a dance together. Everyone applauds as they disappear into the night.

The guy in the Hawaiian shirt angles his camera to the sky, shooting pictures as they depart.

I slide past him and motion for Bailey to keep up. "We have to move," I say. "Before we get stuck here."

Bailey picks up the pace. And we make it over the bridge, both of us breaking into a jog. We don't stop until we turn down our hotel's long driveway. We don't stop until we are in front of the hotel, the doormen holding the door open.

"Just wait," Bailey says. "We need to stop for a second."

She puts her hands on her knees, catching her breath. I want to argue. We are so close to being on the safe side of the hotel's doors, so close to the privacy of our small room.

"What if I told you I remembered him?" she says.

I look over at the doormen, who are chatting with each other. I try to meet their eyes, get them to focus, as if they will keep us safe.

"What if I said I know him, Charlie Smith?"

"Do you?"

"I remember being called by that name," she says. "Kristin. Hearing him say it, all of a sudden I remembered. How do you forget something like that? How is that even possible?"

"We forget all sorts of things that no one helps us remember," I say.

Bailey gets quiet. Silent, actually. Then she says it, the words both of us have avoided saying out loud.

"You think that woman Kate is my mother, don't you?"

She pauses on the word *mother,* like it has fire in it.

"I do. I could be wrong, but I do."

"Why would my father lie about who my mother is?"

She meets my eyes. I don't try to answer her. I have no good answer for her.

"I'm just not sure who I should be trusting here," she says.

"Me," I say. "Just me."

She bites her lip, like she believes me, or at least like she is starting to believe me—which is more than I could hope for in this moment. Because you can't

108

tell people to trust you. You have to show them that they can. And I haven't had enough time.

The doormen are looking at us. I'm not sure they are listening, but they are looking. And I feel it. I feel how much I need to get Bailey out of here. Out of Austin. Immediately.

"Come with me," I say.

She doesn't fight me. We walk past the doormen and into the hotel lobby, head to the elevator bank.

But, as we step inside, a man gets on too—a young guy who I think is looking at Bailey strangely. He wears a gray sweater vest, piercings covering his ears. I know it is paranoid to think he is following us. I know it. If he is looking at Bailey, it is probably only because she is beautiful.

I'm not taking that chance though, so I move us off the elevator, and toward the back staircase, heart pounding.

I open the door, point toward the staircase. "This way," I say.

"Where are we going?" she says. "We're eight floors up."

"Just be glad it's not twenty."

Eighteen Months Ago

"Is there anything else I should know?" I asked. "Before this plane takes off?"

"Are we talking metaphorically or actually? Like the actual mechanics of the plane? Because I did do a brief stint at Boeing when I first got to Seattle."

We were on the flight from New York to San Francisco, a one-way ticket for me. The Shop had sprung for first class for both of us because Owen had been in New York for business in preparation for The Shop's IPO. Owen had stayed on for the initial reason he'd been planning to be in New York that week—to help move me out of it.

We had spent the last few days packing up my apartment, packing up my studio. And, when we landed, I'd move into his home. His and Bailey's. It would become my home too. And, soon, I would be his wife.

"I'm asking you what you left out. About you."

"While you can still get off the plane? We haven't started taxiing yet. There's probably still time..."

He squeezed my hand, trying to make light of it. But I was still jumpy. I was suddenly too jumpy.

"What do you want to know?" he said.

"Tell me about Olivia," I said.

"I've told you a lot about Olivia," he said.

"Not really. I feel like I know only the basics. College sweetheart, teacher. Georgia born and bred."

I didn't add the rest... that he lost her in a car accident. That he hadn't been involved, seriously, with anyone since.

"Now that I'm going to be in Bailey's life, in a serious way, I want to know more about her mother."

He tilted his head, like he was considering where to start.

"When Bailey was a baby? We all took a trip to Los Angeles. It was the weekend that a tiger escaped from the

Los Angeles Zoo. A young tiger, who had been at the zoo for only a year or so. He didn't just escape his cage, but the entire premises. And he ended up in a family's backyard in Los Feliz. When he got there, he didn't hurt anyone. He curled up under a tree and took a nap. Olivia was consumed with this story, which is probably how she found out the other part."

I smiled. "What's that?"

"The family whose backyard the tiger had curled up in had gone to the zoo only a few weeks before and one of their two young boys had been obsessed with the tiger. The boy had cried when he had to leave the tiger, not understanding why he couldn't take the tiger home with him. How do you explain that the tiger ended up at this boy's home? A coincidence? That was what the zoologists decided. The family lived pretty close to the zoo. But Olivia thought it served as proof. That sometimes you find your way to the place that wants you most."

"I love that story."

"You would have loved her," he said. Then he smiled, looked out the airplane window. "There was no way... not to love her."

I squeezed his shoulder. "Thank you."

He turned back toward me. "Do you feel better?"

"Not really," I said.

He laughed. "What else do you want to know?"

I tried to think of what I was asking for—it wasn't about Olivia. It wasn't even about Bailey. Not exactly, at least.

"I think... I think I need you to say it out loud," I said.

"Say what?"

"That we're doing the right thing."

That was the closest I could get to it—the closest way to express what I was actually worried about. I wasn't used to being a part of a family, not since I lost my grandfather. And that didn't exactly feel like a family. That felt like a twosome, plowing our way through the world, just me and him. His funeral was the last time I even saw my mother. Her calls on my birthday (or somewhere around my birthday) were our only form of communication at this point.

This was going to be something different. It would be the first time I was a part of an actual family. I felt completely unsure of how to do it properly, how to count on Owen, how to show Bailey she could count on me.

"We're doing the right thing," Owen said. "We're doing the only thing. I swear to you, on everything that matters to me, that's how I feel."

I nodded, calmed. Because I believed him. And because I wasn't really nervous, at least not about him. I knew how much I wanted him—how much I wanted to be with him. Even if I didn't know everything about him yet, I knew that he was good. I was nervous about everything else.

He leaned in and put his lips against my forehead. "I'm not going to be that asshole who says you kinda have to trust someone at some point."

"You're going to be the asshole who says it without saying it?"

The airplane started backing up, jolting us, before it turned, slowly heading toward the runway.

"Apparently," he said.

"I know I can trust you," I said. "I do. I trust you more than anyone."

He locked his fingers through mine.

"Metaphorically or actually?" he said.

I looked down at our fingers, locked together like that, just in time for takeoff. I stared down at them, finding comfort there.

"Here's hoping they're the same thing," I said.

The Good Lawyer

When we get back to the hotel room, I lock the dead bolt behind us.

I start looking around the room, our belongings strewn on the floor, our suitcases open.

"Start packing your stuff," I say. "Just throw it all in the suitcase, we're out of here in the next five minutes."

"Where are we going?"

"To rent a car and start driving home."

"Why are we driving?" she says.

I don't want to say the rest of it. That I don't even want to go to the airport. That I'm afraid they'll be looking for us there. Whoever they are. That I don't know what her father did, but I know who he is. And anyone who reacts to him the way that Charlie reacted to him is someone we can't trust. He's someone we need to get away from.

"And why are we leaving now? We're getting closer…" She pauses. "I don't want to leave until we figure this out."

"We will, I promise you, but not here," I say. "Not where you could be in danger."

She starts to argue, but I put up my hand. I rarely tell her what to do, so I know it may go south starting now. But still. She has to listen. Because we have to leave. We should be leaving already.

"Bailey," I say. "There's no choice. We're in over our heads."

Bailey looks at me surprised. Maybe she is surprised that I tell her the truth, that I don't sugarcoat it. Maybe she just wants to be done trying to convince me that I'm wrong to head back home. I can't read her expression. But she nods and stops arguing, so I decide to take the win.

"Okay," she says. "I'll pack."

"Thank you," I say.

"Yep…" she says.

She starts picking up her clothes and I walk into the bathroom, closing the door behind myself. I look into the mirror at my tired face. My eyes are bloodshot and dark, my skin pallid.

I splash water on my face and make myself take a few deep breaths in, trying to slow down my heartbeat—trying to slow down the crazy thoughts that are plowing through my mind, one of them finding its way to the surface anyway. What have I gotten us into here?

What do I know? What do I need to know?

I reach into my pocket, palm my phone. I cut my finger on the shattered screen, the small glass shards imbedding in my skin. I pull up Jake's contact and send a text.

> Pls get back to me on this ASAP. Katherine "Kate" Smith. That's her maiden name. Brother Charlie Smith. Austin, Texas. Cross-reference for birth of daughter, matching Bailey's age. Name "Kristin". Austin, Texas. Also check for marriage certificate and death certificate. Won't be reachable on my phone.

I put the phone under my foot and get ready to smash it. Even though it is the only way Owen can find us. It's also the way anyone else can. And if my suspicions are right, I don't want that. I want to get out of Austin without that happening. I want to get away from Charlie Smith and whoever may be with him.

But there is something gnawing at me, something I want to remember before I disconnect us from the world.

What is bothering me? What do I feel like I should be finding? Not Kate Smith, not Charlie Smith. Something else.

I pick up the phone and do another search for Katherine Smith, thousands of links popping up on Google for such a common name. Some that seem like they could be leading to the right Katherine but don't: an art history professor who graduated from University of Texas at Austin; a chef born and bred on Lake Austin; an actress, who looks quite a bit like the Kate I saw in the photos at the bar. I click on the link to the actress and pull up a photograph of her in a gown.

And it comes to me in a flash: what I am trying to remember, what struck me at The Never Dry.

There was that newspaper clipping I noticed when I first arrived at the bar.

The clip included a photograph of Kate dressed in a gown. Kate in a gown, Charlie dressed in a tuxedo, the older couple bookending them. Meredith Smith. Nicholas Bell. The headline read: NICHOLAS BELL RECEIVES THE TEXAS STAR AWARD. His name was also beneath the clipping.

Nicholas Bell. Husband of Meredith Smith. She was in other photographs, but he wasn't. Why was he in so few photographs except for that clipping? Why did his name sound familiar?

I plug in his name and then I know.

This is how the story started.

A young, handsome El Paso, Texas, Presidential Scholar was one of the first kids from his high school to attend college, let alone the University of Texas at Austin. Let alone law school.

He came from modest means, but money wasn't his motivation for becoming a lawyer. Even after a childhood where he didn't often know where his next meal was coming from, he turned down all sorts of job offers from firms in New York and San Francisco to become a public defender for the city of Austin. He was twenty-six years old. He was young, idealistic, and newly married to his high school sweetheart, a social worker, who had aspirations for beautiful babies, but none (at the time) for fancy houses.

His name was Nicholas but he quickly earned the nickname The Good Lawyer, handling the cases no one wanted, helping out defendants who wouldn't have gotten a fair shake with someone who cared less.

It is unclear how Nicholas went from there to becoming the bad lawyer.

It is unclear how he became the most trusted adviser to one of the largest crime syndicates in North America.

The organization was based out of New York and South Florida, where their top leaders lived in places like Fisher Island and oceanfront South Beach. They played golf and wore Brioni suits and told their neighbors they worked in securities. This was how the new regime operated. Quietly. Efficiently. Brutally. Their lieutenants preserved their stronghold in several core businesses—extortion, loan-sharking, narcotics—while also moving into more sophisticated revenue streams, like international online gaming and brokerage fraud on Wall Street.

Most notably, though, they bulked up their OxyContin business long before their competitors saw the opening there. And while these competitors were still primarily shilling the traditional illegals (heroin, cocaine), this organization became the largest trafficker of oxycodone in North America.

This is how Nicholas wound up in their orbit. One of the organization's young associates found himself in trouble in Austin while distributing OxyContin at UT-Austin. Nicholas managed to keep him out of prison.

Nicholas then spent the better part of the next three decades fighting on behalf of this organization—his work

leading to acquittals or mistrials on eighteen counts of murder, twenty-eight indictments for drug trafficking, sixty-one counts of extortion and fraud.

He proved himself invaluable and got wealthy in the process. But as the DEA and the FBI kept losing case after case against him, he became a target too. He remained unafraid they'd find anything that added up to his being anything more than a devoted attorney.

Until something went wrong. His grown daughter was walking down the street on her way home from her job, her beloved job. She was a clerk for the Texas Supreme Court—a year and change out of law school, a new mother. She was walking home, after a long week, when a car struck her.

It would have looked like any other accident, any other hit-and-run, except that she was hit on a small street near her Austin house and it was a clear day and it was a Friday afternoon. And Friday afternoons were when Nicholas spent time at his daughter's home, watching his granddaughter. Just the two of them. It was his favorite time of the week—picking his granddaughter up from music class and taking her to the park with the good swings, the park that was a block away from where his daughter was killed. So he'd be the one to find her. So he'd be the one to see it.

His clients said they had nothing to do with the accident, even though he had just lost a major case for them. And it seemed like the truth. They had a code. They didn't go after people's families. But someone had done it. As vengeance. As a warning shot. There was speculation that it had been members of a different organization who were aiming to secure his services for themselves.

None of these details mattered to his daughter's husband, though, who could only blame his father-in-law. The fact that it occurred on a Friday afternoon convinced him that his father-in-law's employers were involved, one way or another. And, regardless, he blamed his father-in-law for his deep entanglement with the kind of people that made it a question in the first place—that could bring this kind of tragedy to a family.

Not that The Good Lawyer had wanted his daughter to be hurt. He'd always been a great father and was devastated by her death, but his son-in-law was too angry to care. And his son-in-law knew things. He knew things The Good Lawyer had trusted him not to share with anyone else.

Which was why the son-in-law was able to turn state's evidence against his father-in-law and become the lead witness in a case that put his father-in-law in jail while casting a blow to the organization itself—eighteen members of the organization implicated in the sweep. The Good Lawyer carted off behind them.

The son-in-law and his small daughter, who would have only a couple of memories of her mother—of her grandfather—disappeared after the trial, never to be heard from again.

The lawyer's full name was Daniel Nicholas Bell, aka: D. Nicholas Bell.

His son-in-law went by the name of Ethan Young.

Ethan's daughter's name was Kristin.

I drop my phone to the ground and smash it. I smash it in one quick motion, kicking it hard with my foot, as hard as I've ever kicked anything.

And I open the bathroom door. I open the bathroom door to get Bailey and grab our things and get the hell out of Austin. Not in five minutes. Not in five seconds. Now.

"Bailey, we need to get out of here right now," I say. "Just grab what you've already packed. We're going."

But the hotel room is empty. Bailey is no longer there.

She is gone.

"Bailey?"

My heart stars to race as I reach for my phone to call her, to text her. And I remember that I just smashed my phone. I have no phone.

So I run into the hallway, which is empty, save for a housekeeping cart. I run past it and toward the elevator bank, the staircase. She isn't there. No one is there. I take the elevator down to the hotel lobby, hoping she went to the hotel bar to get a snack. I run into the hotel restaurants, each of them, into the Starbucks. Bailey is not there either. Bailey is not anywhere.

You make a hundred decisions. You make decisions all the time. And the one you don't think of twice shouldn't get to determine what happens to her: Go into your hotel room, double bolt the door. You think you're safe. But then you head into the bathroom. You head into the bathroom and trust a sixteen-year-old to stay on the bed, stay in the room, because where is she going to go?

Except she is terrified. Except there is that. Except she told you she didn't want to leave Austin.

So why did you believe she would go without a fight?

Why did you believe she would listen to you?

I race back into the elevator, race back down the hall. I am enraged at myself that my phone is broken on the bathroom floor, that I don't have it to text her. That I don't have it to turn on locations and track her.

"Bailey, please answer me!"

I head into the hotel room and look around again—as though she will be hiding somewhere in those 580 square feet. I search the closet, search under the beds anyway, hoping to find her huddled in a ball, crying. Needing to be alone. Miserable, but safe. How quickly I would take that! Miserable, safe.

The door swings open. I feel temporary relief. It is a relief I have never felt before, thinking Bailey is back, thinking that I just missed her when I did my frantic search in the hotel—that she did, after all, just go down the hall to get a bucket of ice or a soda. That she went to call Bobby. That she found a cigarette and went outside to smoke it. Any of it, all of it.

But Bailey isn't standing there.

Grady Bradford is.

Grady is standing there in his faded jeans and backward baseball cap. His stupid windbreaker.

He drills me with an angry look, his arms crossed over his chest. "So you certainly went and made a mess of everything now," he says.

— Part 3 —

Rotten wood cannot be carved.

—Confucius

When We Were Young

The U.S. Marshals' office in downtown Austin is on a side street, its windows peering in on other buildings, peering in on the parking garage across the street. Most of those buildings are now dark and closed for the night. The parking lot is mostly empty. But Grady's office—and his colleagues' offices—are lit up and bustling.

"Let's walk through this again," Grady says.

He sits on the edge of his desk as I pace back and forth. I can feel his judgment but it's unnecessary. No one is judging me more than I'm judging myself. Bailey is missing. She's missing. She is out there, alone.

"How's this helping to find Bailey?" I say. "Unless you arrest me, I'm going out there to look for her."

I start to walk out of the office, but Grady hops down from his desk and blocks my exit.

"We have eight deputies looking for her," he says. "What you need to do right now is go through it all again. If you want to help us find her, that's the only thing to do."

I hold his gaze but relent, knowing he's right.

I walk back over to the windows and look outside, as though there is something I can do—as though I'll spot Bailey somewhere on the street below. I don't know who I'm looking at—the myriad of people walking through nighttime Austin. The sliver of moon, the only light, makes it feel even more terrifying that Bailey is roaming among them.

"What if he took her?" I say.

"Nicholas?" he says.

I nod, my head starting to spin. I go obsessively over everything I know about him now—how dangerous he is, the heights Owen went to get away from him. To keep his daughter away from Nicholas's world. How I've brought her back.

Protect her.

"That's unlikely," Grady says.

"But not impossible?"

"I guess nothing is impossible, now that you brought her to Austin."

I try to comfort myself, something Grady apparently has no desire to do. "He couldn't have found us so quickly…" I say.

"No, probably not."

"How did you even find us?" I ask.

"Well, your call this morning didn't help. And then I heard from your lawyer, a Jake Anderson, in New York City. He told me you were in Austin and he couldn't reach you. That you went

116

dark and he was worried. So I put a trace on you. Clearly not soon enough..."

I turn and look at him.

"Why on earth would you come to Austin?" he says.

"You showed up at my house, for starters," I say. "I found that suspicious."

"Owen never told me you were a detective."

"Owen never told me about any of this. Period."

It seems unwise to harp on the fact that I wouldn't have come here if Grady had told me what was going on, if anyone had told me the truth about Owen and his past. Grady is too angry to care. Still, I can't stop myself. If we are pointing fingers, they shouldn't be pointed at me.

"In the last seventy-two hours, I've learned that my *husband* isn't the person I thought he was. What was I supposed to do?"

"What I told you to do," he says. "Lay low, get yourself a lawyer. Let me do my job."

"And what is that exactly?"

"Owen made a decision over a decade ago to get his daughter out of a life he couldn't protect her from otherwise. To give her a clean start. I helped him do that."

"But Jake told me... I thought Owen wasn't in the protection program."

"Jake would have been correct that Owen wasn't in witness protection. Not exactly."

I look at him, confused. "What the hell does that mean?"

"Owen was set to join WITSEC after he agreed to testify, but he never felt safe. Thought there were too many holes, too many people he'd have to trust. And, during the trial, there was a small leak."

"What do you mean a small leak?"

"Someone in the New York office compromised the identities we had secured for Owen and Bailey," he says. "Owen didn't want any part of government involvement after that."

"Shocking," I say.

"It wasn't typical, but I did understand why he wanted to go another route. Why he disappeared with Bailey. No one knew where they were going. No one else in the Marshals Service knew. We made sure there wasn't a line that would lead to him."

Grady flew halfway across the country to check on Owen—to check on his family, to help Owen out of this mess.

"Except you, you mean," I say.

"He trusted me," he says. "Maybe because I was new here then. Maybe I earned it. You'll have to ask him why."

"Can't really ask him much of anything at the moment," I say.

Grady walks over to the windows, leans against them. Maybe it's because I'm looking for it, but I see something in his eyes, something like sympathy.

"Owen and I don't talk a whole lot," he says. "For the most part, he's just been living his life. I think the last time he reached out was when he told me he was marrying you."

"What did he say?"

"He told me that you were a game changer," he says. "He said he'd never been in love like that before."

I close my eyes against it, how deeply I feel that, and how deeply I feel the same.

"Truth is, I tried to talk him out of pursuing anything with you," Grady says. "I told him his feelings would pass."

"Well thank you for that."

"He wouldn't listen to me about walking away," he says. "But he did take my advice, apparently, when I told him he couldn't tell you about his past. That it was too dangerous for you. That if he really wanted to be with you, he needed to leave his past out of it."

I think of the two of us in bed, Owen struggling with whether to tell me— Owen wanting to tell me the entire truth of his past. Maybe Grady's warning stopped him. Maybe Grady's warning stopped Owen and me from being in a position to handle this together.

"Is this your way of telling me I should blame you instead of him?" I say. "Because I'm happy to do that."

"This is my way of telling you we all have secrets we don't share," he says. "Kind of like your lawyer friend Jake? He told me that you guys were engaged once upon a time."

"That's not a secret," I say. "Owen knew all about Jake."

"And how do you think he'd feel about you involving him in this?" he says.

I was running out of choices, I want to say. But I know it's a fool's errand to argue with him. Grady is intent on putting me on the defensive, as if that will make it easier for him to pry something out of me—not exactly a secret, more like my will. My will to do anything but listen to what he thinks we should do now.

"Why did Owen run, Grady?" I ask.

"He had to," he says.

"What does that mean?"

"How many photographs have you seen of Avett in the news this week? The media would be all over Owen too. His picture would be everywhere and they'd find him again. Nicholas's employers. Even though he looks different than he did, he doesn't look that different. He couldn't risk that kind of exposure. He had to get out of there before that happened," he says. "Before he blew up Bailey's life."

I take that in. It makes me understand in a different way why there was no time to tell me anything— why there was no time to do anything but go.

"He knew he would have been brought in," he says. "And when he was, he would've been fingerprinted, just like Jordan Maverick was this afternoon. And that would reveal who he actually was, game over."

"So they think Owen's guilty?" I say. "Naomi, the FBI, whoever else?"

"No. They think he has answers they need, that's a different thing," he says. "But if you're asking me if Owen was a willing participant in the fraud? I would say not likely."

"What's more likely?"

"That Avett knew about Owen."

I meet his eyes.

"Not any of the specifics, Owen never would have told him, but he knew he hired someone who came out of nowhere. No references to speak of, no ties to the tech world. Owen said at the time that Avett just wanted the best coder he could find, but I think Avett was looking for an angle. He wanted someone he could control, if it turned out he needed that control. And it turned out he did."

"You think Owen knew what was happening at The Shop but he couldn't stop it?" I say. "That he stayed there hoping he could fix it, get the software operational, before he got caught in the crosshairs."

"I do," he says.

"That's a pretty specific guess," I say.

"I know your husband pretty specifically," he says. "And he's been watching his back for such a long time that he knew if The Shop scandal touched him, he'd have to disappear all over again. Bailey would have to start over. And this time, of course, she'd have to be told the history. Not ideal to say the least..." He pauses. "Let alone what you would've had to give up, assuming you chose to go with them."

"Assuming I chose to go?"

"Well, you couldn't really hide out as a woodturner. Even a furniture designer. Whatever you call yourself. You would have to give up everything. Your job, your livelihood. I'm sure he didn't want that for you."

I flash to it—one of my early dates with Owen. He asked me what I would do if I hadn't become a woodturner.

And I told him that it was probably because of my grandfather—maybe it was because I associated woodturning with the only stability I'd ever had—but it was all I'd ever wanted to do. I had never really imagined doing anything else.

"He didn't think I'd choose to go with them, did he?" I say, more to myself than to him.

"That doesn't matter now. I've managed to tamp it down, to keep your friends at the FBI at bay..." he says. "But I won't be able to pull rank much longer unless you guys are officially being protected."

"Meaning WITSEC?"

"Yes, meaning WITSEC."

I don't say anything, trying to take in the weight of that. I can't begin to fathom being a protected person. What will that look like? My only experience with anything close is what I've seen in the movies—Harrison Ford hanging out with the Amish in *Witness*, Steve Martin sneaking out of town to get the good spaghetti in *My Blue Heaven*. Both of them depressed and lost. Then I think of what Jake said. How in reality it's nowhere near as good as that.

"So Bailey will have to start over?" I say. "New identity? New name? All over again?"

"Yes. And I'd take starting over for her," he says. "I'll take it for her father too as opposed to what's happening now."

I try to process that. Bailey no longer Bailey. Everything she has worked so hard for—her schooling, her grades, her theater, herself—it will be erased.

Will she even be allowed to perform in musicals anymore, or will that be a tell? A way to lead people to Owen. The new student at a random school in Iowa starring in the school musical. Will Grady say that's another way they can track them? That instead of pursuing her old interests, she has to take up fencing or hockey or just completely stay under the radar. Any way you shake it out, it certainly means Bailey will be asked to stop being Bailey—at the exact moment she is becoming singularly, inimitably herself. It feels like a staggering proposition—to give up your life when you're a sixteen-year-old. It's a different position than when you were just a toddler. It's a different proposition when you're forty.

But still. I know she would pay that price to be with her father. We would both gladly pay that price, again and again, if it meant we could all be together.

I try to find comfort in that. Except there is something else gnawing at me—something Grady is skirting around that isn't sitting right—something that I can't hold in my hands just yet.

"Here's what you've got to understand," he says. "Nicholas Bell is a bad man. Even Owen didn't want to accept how bad of a man he was, not for a long time, probably because Kate was loyal to her father. And Owen was loyal to Kate, and to Charlie, who Owen was quite close to, as well. They believed their father was a good man with some questionable clients. And they convinced Owen of that. They convinced him that Nicholas was a defense attorney, doing his job. No illegal activity of his own. They convinced him because they loved their father. They thought he was a good father, a good husband. He was a good father, a good husband. They weren't wrong. He is just other things too."

"Like what?"

"Like complicit in murder. And extortion. And drug trafficking," he says. "Like completely and totally unrepentant for how many lives he helped ruin. Like how many people whose entire fucking world he helped destroy."

I try not to show it on my face, how that gets to me.

"These men that Nicholas worked for are ruthless," he says. "And unforgiving. There's no telling what kind of leverage they would use to get Owen to turn himself in."

"They could go after Bailey?" I say. "That's what you're saying? That they'd go after Bailey to get to Owen?"

"I'm saying, unless we move her quickly, it's a possibility."

That stops me, even in the heat of this. What Grady's insinuating. Bailey being in danger. Bailey, who is wandering the streets of Austin alone, potentially already in danger.

"The point is, Nicholas won't stop them," he says. "He couldn't stop them even if he wanted to. That's why Owen had to get Bailey out. He knew Nick's hands weren't clean in any of this. And he used that information to hurt the organization. Do you understand that?"

"Maybe you should say it slower," I say.

"Nicholas wasn't always dirty, but at some point he started passing messages for leadership, from lieutenants in prison to leadership outside of prison. Messages that couldn't be sent another way except through a lawyer. And these weren't innocent messages. These were messages like who needs to be punished, like who needs to be killed. Can you imagine knowingly passing along a message that would result in a man and his wife being killed and their two kids being left without parents?"

"And where does Owen come in?"

"Owen helped Nicholas set up an encryption system that Nicholas ultimately used to send these messages, to record these messages when they needed to be recorded," he says. "After Kate was killed, Owen hacked into the system and turned everything over to us. All the emails, all the correspondence... Nicholas served more than six years in prison for conspiracy to commit. Which we were able to prove directly from those files. You don't betray Nicholas Bell like that and come back from it."

This is when it hits me—the piece that has been gnawing at me, the piece that Grady hasn't been addressing.

"So why didn't he come to you then?" I say.

"Excuse me?"

"Why didn't Owen come straight to you?" I say. "If the only way this ends well, if the only way to truly keep Bailey safe now is for her to be in witness protection, for Owen to be in witness protection, then when everything in The Shop blew up, why didn't Owen reach out to you? Why didn't he show up at your door and ask you to move us?"

"You'll have to ask Owen that."

"I'm asking you," I say. "What happened with the leak last time, Grady? Did you guys nip it in the bud or was Bailey's life compromised?"

"What does that have to do with what's happening now?"

"Everything. If what happened made my husband think you can't keep Bailey safe now, it has everything to do with what's happening now," I say.

"The bottom line is that WITSEC is the best option that Owen and Bailey have for staying safe," he says. "Period."

He says this without apology, but I can see that my question got to him. Because he can't deny it. If Owen were really certain that Grady could keep Bailey safe, that he could keep all of us safe, he would be here with us now. As opposed to wherever he is.

"Look, let's not get sidetracked here," he says. "What you need to do now is help me figure out why Bailey left the hotel room."

"I don't know why," I say.

"Wager a guess," he says.

"I think she didn't want to leave Austin," I say.

I don't add the details. She probably didn't want to go yet, not when she was so close to finding answers of her own—answers to questions about her past, answers Owen left me ill-equipped to even begin to deal with. It calms me somewhat to believe this is the reason, to believe she is alone somewhere but safe, searching for answers she doesn't trust anyone else to find for her. I should recognize that trait in someone. I have it myself.

"Why do you think she wants to stay in Austin?" he says.

At the moment I tell him the only piece of truth I know. "Sometimes you can sense it," I say.

"Sense what?" he says.

"When it's all up to you."

Grady gets called into a meeting and a different U.S. marshal, Sylvia Hernandez, leads me down the hall and into a conference room, where she says I can make a phone call—as though the call isn't being taped or traced or whatever else they do here to make sure they know everything you do. Before you even do it.

Sylvia sits outside the door and I pick up the phone. I call my best friend.

"I've been trying to reach you for hours," Jules says when she picks up. "Are you guys okay?"

I sit down at the long conference room table, holding my head in my hand, trying not to fall apart. Even though it feels like the moment to fall apart, when I am safe to—Jules there to catch me.

"Where are you?" she says. "I just got a crazy call from Jake, screaming about how your husband is putting you in danger. Can't say I miss that guy."

"Yeah, well, Jake is Jake," I say. "He's just trying to help. In his incredibly unhelpful way."

"What's going on with Owen? He didn't turn himself in, did he?" she says.

"Not exactly."

"What exactly?" she said. But she says it softly. Which is also her way of saying I don't need to explain right now.

"Bailey is missing," I say.

"What?" she says.

"She took off. She left the hotel room. And we can't find her."

"She's sixteen."

"I know that, Jules. Why do you think I'm so scared?"

"No, I'm saying, she's *sixteen*. Sometimes disappearing for a bit is what you need to do. I'm sure she's fine."

"It's not as simple as that," I say. "Have you heard the name Nicholas Bell?"

"Should I have?"

"He's Owen's former father-in-law."

She is silent, something coming to her. "Wait, you don't mean Nicholas Bell... like, *the* Nicholas Bell? The lawyer?"

"Yes, that's him. What do you know about him?"

"Not a lot. I mean... I remember reading in the papers when he was released from prison a couple of years ago. I think he was in there for assault or murder or something. He was Owen's father-in-law?" she says. "I don't believe it."

"Jules, Owen's in big trouble. And I don't think there's anything I can do to stop it."

She is quiet, thoughtful. I can feel her trying to add up some of the pieces that I'm not helping her see.

"We'll stop it," she says. "I promise you. First we'll get you and Bailey home. Then we can figure out how."

My heart clutches in my chest. This is what she has always done—what we have done for each other. And this is why I can't breathe suddenly. Bailey is wandering the streets of this strange city. And even when we find her—and I have to believe they'll find her soon—Grady just informed me that I'm not going home. Not ever.

"Did I lose you?" she says.

"Not yet," I say. "Where did you say you were?"

"I'm home," she says. "And I got it open."

The way she says it is loaded. And I realize she is talking about the safe, the small safe inside the piggy bank.

"You did?"

"Yep," she says. "Max found a safecracker who lives in downtown San Francisco, and we opened it about an hour ago. His name is Marty and he is about ninety-seven years old. It's insane what this guy can do with a safe. He listened to the machine for five minutes and opened it that way. Stupid little piggy bank, made of steel."

"What's inside?"

She pauses. "A will. The final will, for Owen Michaels né Ethan Young. Do you want me to tell you what it says?"

I think about who else is listening. If Jules starts to read, I think of who else will be listening to Owen's will—not the will I pulled up on his laptop computer, but the will that the other will alluded to, as if in a secret message to me.

Owen's real will, his more complete will. Ethan's will.

"Jules, there are probably people listening to this call, so I think we should stick to a few things, okay?"

"Of course."

"What does it say about Bailey's guardians?"

"That you're her primary guardian," she says. "In case of Owen's death, but also in case of his inability to care for her himself."

Owen prepared for this. Maybe not exactly this, but something like this. He prepared for it in a way that Bailey would get to be with me—that he wanted Bailey with me. At what point did he trust me enough to do that? At what point did he decide that being with me was what was best for her? It breaks something wide open in me to know that he got there, that he thought I could do it. Except now she is missing, somewhere in this city. And I allowed that to happen too.

"Does he mention any other names?" I say.

"Yes. There are different rules based on whether you can't care for her or based on Bailey's age," she says.

As she reads, I listen to her carefully, taking notes, writing down the names I recognize. But really, I'm listening for just one name—one person who I am trying to figure out whether to trust, whether Owen trusts, despite any and all evidence that he shouldn't. When I hear it, when she says Charlie Smith, I stop writing. I tell her I need to go.

"Be careful," she says.

This instead of goodbye, instead of her usual "I love you." Considering the circumstances, considering what I need to figure out how to do now, it's the same thing.

I stand up and look out the conference room windows. It has started raining, Austin nightlife active below, despite it. People walk the streets with umbrellas, heading to dinner and shows, debating about a nightcap or a late movie. Or deciding they've had enough, that the rain is getting harder, and they want to go home. Those are the lucky ones.

I turn toward the glass door. U.S. Marshal Sylvia sits on the other side. She is looking at her phone, either disinterested in me or busy with something more important than her babysitting assignment. Perhaps she is busy with the one thing I know about too well. Finding Owen. Finding Bailey.

I'm about to walk into the hall and demand a status update, when I see Grady walking down the hall.

He knocks on the door as he opens it, and smiles at me—a softer Grady, who seems to have thawed somewhat.

"They have her," he says. "They have Bailey. She's safe."

I let out a breath, tears filling my eyes. "Oh, thank goodness. Where is she?"

"Up at campus, they're bringing her back here," he says. "Can we talk for a minute before they do? I just think it's really important that we are on the same page with her about what the plan is going to be."

What the plan is going to be. He means the plan to move her, to move us.

He means that he wants me to help hold it all steady when he tells her that life as she knows it is over.

"And we need to talk about something else," he says. "I didn't want to get into it before, but I haven't been completely transparent with you..."

"I wouldn't have guessed."

"We received a package yesterday with a zip drive of Owen's work emails. I had to verify they were real, and they are. He kept meticulous records of the pressure Avett was applying to push through the IPO, despite Owen's objections. And all the work he did after to try and make it okay..."

"It wasn't just a specific guess then?" I say. "About Owen's culpability in all this?"

"No, I guess not," he says.

"So it's really my husband who tamped it down?" I say.

My voice rises. I try to check it, but I can't. Because Owen is doing everything to protect us, even from wherever he is now. And I just don't trust that Grady knows how to do the same.

"He has certainly helped," he says. "WITSEC can be challenging about who they're willing to help out, and these files plus his history underscore why he didn't blow the whistle until now. Why he felt he had no choice but to stay on board."

I take this in, feeling a weird mix of relief and something else. At first I think it's irritation at Grady for withholding this, withholding that he'd heard from Owen, but then I realize it's something more sinister. Because it's

me—what
g from me.
aring this
say.
e a united
e," he says.
est way for
And I know
ou won't be
."

It means that money Owen left for Bailey? It's legitimate earnings. It's money Owen kept clean," he says. "You'll be entering WITSEC with a nice nest egg. Most people in our program don't have anything close."

"Sounds to me, Grady, that you're saying if we decline, the money goes away..."

"If you decline, all of it goes away," he says. "Being a family again, safely, goes away."

I nod, knowing that's what Grady's trying to convince me of—that I should be on board with Bailey and me entering protection. That I *need* to be on board because everything is set up for Owen to join us in this new life. Everything is set up for our family to be reunited. New names, but reunited. Together.

Except this is what I can't let go of despite Grady's insistence, what I know Owen doesn't want me to let go of. My doubt. My doubt when I think about the leak at WITSEC and when I think about Nicholas Bell. My doubt when I think about Owen's hasty exit and what I know about him, which would explain it. The only thing that would explain it.

Everything I know about Owen is convincing me of something else.

Grady is still talking. "We just need Bailey to understand that this is the best way to keep her as safe as possible," he says.

As safe as possible. That stops me. Because he doesn't just say safe. Because there is no safe. Not anymore.

Bailey isn't wandering the streets, but she is on her way to this office and to a world in which to be *as safe as possible*, Grady is going to tell her she is going to have to become someone else. Bailey, no longer Bailey.

Unless, of course, I manage to stop it. All of it.

Which is when I brace myself against it. What I need to do now.

"Look, we can get into all of this," I say. "The best way to handle Bailey. But I just need to go to the restroom first... splash some water on my face. I haven't slept in twenty-four hours."

He nods. "No problem."

He holds the door open and I start to head out of the conference room, pausing in the doorway, pausing when I'm right next to him. I know this is the most important part, making him believe me.

"I'm so relieved she's safe," I say.

"Me too," he says. "And look, this isn't easy, I get that. But this is the best thing to do, and you'll see, Bailey will get comfortable with it sooner than you think, and it won't all seem so scary. You'll get to be together and we'll get to bring Owen to you as soon as he reemerges. I'm sure that's what Owen's waiting for now, to make sure you're safe, first, make sure you're all set up..."

Then he smiles. And I do the one thing I can. I smile back. I smile like I trust him that he knows why Owen is still gone, like I trust a relocation will be the answer he and his daughter need to be together. To be safe. Like I trust that anyone is capable of keeping Bailey safe—except for me.

Grady's phone rings. "Give me a minute?" he says.

I point toward the restroom. "Can I?"

"Sure thing. Go ahead," he says.

He is already walking toward the windows. He's already focusing on whoever is on the other end of his phone call.

I head down the hall, and in the direction of the restroom, turning back to make sure Grady isn't watching. He isn't. His back is to me, his phone to his ear. He doesn't turn around as I walk past the restroom's door and the elevator, where I press the down button. He keeps staring out the conference room windows, staring at the rain while he talks.

The elevator arrives blessedly fast and I jump in, alone, pushing the close button. I'm in the lobby before Grady gets off his phone call. I'm outside, in the rain, before Sylvia Hernandez is sent into the ladies' room to check on me.

I have turned the corner before she or Grady look on the conference room table and see what I left there for them to find. I left the note on the table, beneath the phone. The note that Owen left me. I left it for Grady.

Protect her.

And I walk at a quick clip down the unfamiliar Austin streets to be there for Bailey now, to be there for her and Owen the best way I know how, even though it's taking me back to the last place I am supposed to go.

Everyone Should Take Inventory

Here's what I know.

At night, before he went to sleep, Owen did two things. He turned on his left side and then he leaned into me, wrapping his arm around my chest. He would fall asleep that way—with his face against my back, his hand on my heart. He was peaceful.

He went for a run every morning to the foot of the Golden Gate Bridge and back home.

He would live on Pad Thai, given the choice.

He never took off his wedding ring even to shower.

He kept the windows open in the car. Ninety degrees or nine degrees.

He talked about going ice fishing on Lake Washington every winter. He never went.

He couldn't turn off a movie, no matter how awful, until he'd made it to the credits.

He thought champagne was overrated.

He thought thunderstorms were underrated.

He was secretly afraid of heights.

He only drove a stick shift. He extolled the virtues of only driving a stick shift. He was ignored.

He loved taking his daughter to the ballet in San Francisco.

He loved taking his daughter on hikes in Sonoma County.

He loved taking his daughter for breakfast. He never ate breakfast.

He could make a ten-layer chocolate cake from scratch.

He could make some mean coconut curry.

He had a ten-year-old La Marzocco espresso machine that was still sitting in its box.

And he was married once before. He was married to a woman whose father defended bad men—even if he thought it was a little simplistic to call them bad men, even if he thought it was incomplete. He accepted his father-in-law's work because he was married to this man's daughter and that's who Owen was. Owen accepted his father-in-law out of need, out of love, and maybe out of fear. Though he wouldn't have named it as fear. He would have named it, incorrectly, as loyalty.

Here's what else I know. When Owen lost his wife, it all changed. Every single thing changed.

Something broke open in him. And he became angry. He became angry with his wife's family, with her father, with himself. He was angry about what he'd allowed himself to turn a blind eye to—in the name of love, in the name of loyalty. Which is part of the reason why he left.

The other reason is that he needed to get Bailey away from that life. It was primal and it was urgent. Keeping Bailey anywhere near his wife's family felt like the greatest risk of all.

Knowing all that, here's what I may never know. If he'll forgive me for what I feel like I have to risk now.

The Never Dry, Part Two

The Never Dry is open now.

There is a mix of the after-work crowd, a few graduate students, and a couple on a date—spiky green hair for him, tattoo sleeve for her—completely focused on each other.

A young, sexy bartender in a vest and a tie holds court behind the bar, pouring the couple matching manhattans. A woman in a jumpsuit eyes him, tries to get his attention for another drink. She tries, simply, to get his attention.

And then there's Charlie. He sits alone in his grandfather's booth, drinking a glass of whisky, the bottle resting beside it.

He runs his finger along the glass, looking lost in thought. Maybe he's playing it back in his head, what happened between us earlier, what he could have done differently when he met this woman he didn't know and his sister's daughter whom he only wanted to know again.

I walk up to his table. He doesn't notice me standing there, at first. When he does, instead of looking at me with anger, he looks at me in disbelief.

"What are you doing here?" he says.

"I need to talk to him," I say.

"Who?" he says.

I don't say anything else, because he doesn't need me to clarify. He knows exactly who I'm talking about. He knows who I'm angling to see.

"Come with me," he says.

Then he stands up and steers me down a dark hallway, past the restrooms and the electrical closet, to the kitchen.

Charlie pulls me into the kitchen, the door swinging closed behind us.

"Do you know how many cops have come in here tonight? They're not asking me anything yet, but they're coming in so I can see them. So I'll know they're here. They're all over the place."

"I don't think they're cops," I say. "I think they're U.S. marshals."

"Do you think this is funny?" he says.

"None of it," I say.

Then I meet his eyes.

"You had to tell him we were here, Charlie," I say. "He's your father. She's your niece. You've both been looking for her since the day he took her away. You couldn't keep that to yourself, even if you wanted to."

Charlie pushes open the emergency door, which leads to a back staircase and the alley below.

"You need to leave," he says.

"I can't do that," I say.

"Why not?"

I shrug. "I have nowhere else to go."

It's true. In a way I'm uncomfortable acknowledging to myself—let alone to him—Charlie is the only shot I have left to make this okay again.

Maybe he senses that because he pauses, and I see him falter in his resolve. He lets the emergency door close.

"I need to talk to your father," I say. "And I'm asking my husband's friend to help make that happen."

"I'm not his friend."

"I don't think that's true," I say. "I had my friend Jules find Ethan's will for me." *Ethan,* using that name. "His real will. And he put you in it. He put you in it as a guardian for Bailey, along with me. He wanted her to have you if anything ever happened to him. He wanted her to have me and he wanted her to have you."

He nods slowly, taking this in, and for a second I think he is going to start crying. His eyes water, his hands move to his forehead, pulling on his eyebrows, as if trying to stop the tears. These tears of relief that there is a window open to his seeing his niece again—and tears of utter sadness that seeing her for the last decade has been an impossibility.

"And what about my father?" he says.

"I don't think he wants her to have anything to do with Nicholas," I say. "But the fact that Ethan put you in there lets me know that my husband trusted you, even if you seem pretty conflicted about that."

He shakes his head, like he can't believe this is his reality. It's a feeling I can relate to.

"This is an old battle," he says. "And Ethan isn't innocent. You think he is. But you don't know the whole story."

"I know I don't."

"So what do you think? That you're going to talk to my father and broker some peace between him and Ethan? It doesn't matter, nothing you say matters. Ethan betrayed my father. He destroyed his life and ended my mother's life in the process. And if there's nothing I can do to mend this, then there's nothing you can do either."

Charlie is struggling. I see it. I see him struggling with what to tell me about his father, what to tell me about Owen. If he offers up too little, I won't walk away from him. Maybe I won't walk away if he says too much either. And he wants me to walk away. He thinks it's better for everybody if I do. But I am playing past that. Because I know there is only one way to make things better now.

"How long have you been married to him?" he says. "To Ethan?"

"Why does that matter?"

"He's not who you think he is."

"So I keep hearing," I say.

"What has Ethan told you?" he says. "About my sister?"

Nothing, I want to say. *Nothing I know to be true.* She doesn't, after all, have fierce red hair or love science. She didn't go to college in New Jersey. She may very well not know how to swim across a pool. I know now why he told us all those things—why he made up such an elaborate backstory. It was so, on the off chance the wrong person ever approached Bailey, if the wrong person ever suspected Bailey of being who she actually was, she'd be able to look that person in the eye and honestly deny it. *My mother is a redheaded swimmer. My mother is nothing like the person you think I belong to.*

I meet Charlie's eyes, answer honestly. "He hasn't told me much. But he once told me how much I would have liked her," I say. "He told me we would have liked each other."

Charlie nods, but he stays quiet. And I can feel all the questions he has about my life with Owen, all the questions about Bailey: about who she is now and what she likes now and how she may still be a little like his lost sister, who he clearly loved. But he can't ask any of those questions, not without fielding questions of his own, questions for which he doesn't want to provide answers.

"Look," he says, "if you want someone to tell you that there's enough goodwill because of Kristin that my father can get over what happened between him and Ethan, that they can reach some kind of truth, they can't. He won't. It doesn't work like that. My father isn't over it."

"I know that too," I say.

And I do know that. But I'm banking on the fact that Charlie wants to help me anyway. Or we wouldn't be having this conversation. We'd be having a different conversation—a conversation neither of us wants to have about what Owen has done to this family. And to me. We'd be having a conversation that would break my heart wide open.

He looks at me more gently. "Did I scare you earlier?" he says.

"I should be asking you that."

"I didn't mean to come at you the way I did. It was just that you surprised the hell out of me," he says. "You wouldn't believe how many people come here, stirring up trouble for my father. All these crime junkies who saw the trial coverage on Court TV, who think they know my father, who want autographs. Even all these years later. I think we're on some criminal enterprise tour of Austin. Us and the Newton Gang..."

"That sounds awful," I say.

"It is," he says. "It's all awful."

Charlie looks at me, taking me in. "I don't think you know what you're doing. I think you're still hoping for a happy ending. But this story doesn't end well," he says. "It can't."

"I know it can't. I'm just hoping for something else."

"What's that?"

I pause. "That it doesn't end here."

On the Lake

Charlie drives.

We head northwest of the city past Mount Bonnell and into Texas Hill Country. Suddenly I'm surrounded by rolling hills, trees and foliage everywhere, the lake muted outside the car windows, tepid. Unmoving.

The rain abates as we turn down Ranch Road. Charlie doesn't say much, but he tells me that his parents bought their Mediterranean estate nestled on the shores of the lake a couple of years ago—the year Nicholas got out of prison, the year before his mother died. This was his mother's dream house, he says, this private retreat, but Nicholas has stayed there since her death, on his own. I learn later that it cost them a cool ten million dollars—this estate which, as I see on a plaque at the foot of the driveway, Charlie's mother, Meredith, named THE SANCTUARY.

It is easy to see why she has chosen this name. The estate is enormous, wildly beautiful, and private. Entirely private.

Charlie enters a code and the metal gates open to reveal a cobblestone driveway, at least a quarter of a mile long, that slowly winds its way to a small guardhouse. The guardhouse is covered in vines, making it inconspicuous.

The main house is less inconspicuous. It looks like it belongs on the French Riviera—complete with cascading balconies, an antique-tile roof, a stone facade. Most notable are the gorgeous bay windows running at least eight feet tall, welcoming you, inviting you in.

We pull up to the guardhouse and a bodyguard emerges. He is pro-linebacker huge, dressed in a tight suit.

Charlie unrolls the window as the bodyguard bends down, leans against the driver's-side window. "Hiya, Charlie," he says.

"Ned. How you doing tonight?"

Ned's eyes move in my direction and he gives me a small nod. Then he turns back to Charlie. "He's expecting you," he says.

He taps on the car's hood and then goes back into the guardhouse to open a second gate.

We pull through it, drive onto the circular driveway, and stop by the front door.

Charlie puts the car in park and shuts off the ignition. But he doesn't move to get out of the car. It seems he wants to say something. He must change his mind though—or think better of it—because, without a word, he opens the driver's-side door and gets out.

I follow his lead and step out of the car into the cool night, the ground slick from the rain.

I start walking toward the front door, but Charlie points to a side gate.

"This way," he says.

He holds the gate open for me and I walk through it. I wait as he locks the gate behind himself and we start heading down a pathway that runs along the side of the house, succulents and plants lining the path's edges.

We walk side by side, Charlie on the path's outer edge. I look into the house—look through those long, French windows—to see room after room, every one of them lit up.

I wonder if it's all lit up for my benefit—so I can see how impressive the design is, how every detail has been considered. The long, winding hallway is lined with expensive art, with black-and-white photographs. The grand room has cathedral ceilings and deep wooden couches. And the farmhouse kitchen, which wraps around the back of the house, is accented with a terra-cotta floor and an enormous stone fireplace.

I keep thinking how Nicholas lives here alone. What is it like to live in a house like this alone?

The pathway winds around to a checkered veranda, which displays antique pillars and a breathtaking view of the lake—small boats twinkling in the distance, a canopy of oak trees, the cooling calm of the water itself.

And a moat.

This house, Nicholas Bell's house, has its own moat. It's a stark reminder that there is no getting in or out of here without explicit permission.

Charlie points at a row of chaise lounges, sitting down in one himself, the lake glistening in the distance.

I avoid meeting his eyes, staring out at the small boats instead. I know why I needed to come here. But now that I'm actually here, it feels like an error. Like I should have heeded Charlie's warning, like nothing good is waiting inside.

"Take a seat anywhere," Charlie says.

"I'm fine," I say.

"He could be a little while," Charlie says.

I lean against one of the pillars.

"I'm okay standing," I say.

"Maybe it's not you that you should be worrying about..."

I turn at the sound of a male's voice, startled to find Nicholas standing in the back doorway. He has two dogs by his side, two large chocolate Labradors. Their eyes hold tightly on Nicholas.

"Those pillars aren't as strong as they look," he says.

I step away from the pillar. "Sorry about that," I say.

"No, no. I kid, I just kid with you," he says.

He waves his hand as he walks toward me, his fingers slightly crooked. This thin man with a struggling goatee—frail-looking with those arthritic fingers, his loose-fitting jeans, his cardigan sweater.

I bite on my lip, trying to hold my surprise in check. This isn't the way I expected Nicholas to look—soft, gentle. He looks like someone's loving grandfather. The way he talks so softly—with the slow cadence, the dry humor—he reminds me of my own loving grandfather.

"My wife bought those pillars from a monastery in France and had them shipped here in two pieces. A local artisan put them back together, returning them to their original presentation. They're plenty sturdy."

"They're also beautiful," I say.

"They are beautiful, aren't they?" he says. "My wife had a real flair for design. She picked everything that went into this house. Every last thing."

He looks pained, even speaking of his wife.

"I don't make it a habit of talking about the workmanship of my home, but I thought you'd appreciate a little history..." he says.

This stops me. Is Nicholas trying to suggest he knows what I do for a living? Could he know? Could there be a leak already? Or maybe I'm the leak. Maybe I said something to Charlie without realizing it. Something that has given us all away.

Either way, Nicholas is in charge now. Ten hours ago, that might not have been the case. But I changed all of that when I arrived in Austin. And now it's Nicholas's world. Austin is Nicholas's world, and I've walked us back into it. As if cementing the point, two bodyguards walk outside—Ned and another guy. Both of them are large and unsmiling. Both of them stand right behind Nicholas.

Nicholas doesn't acknowledge them. Instead he reaches out his hands to take mine. Like we are old friends. What choice do I have? I put my hand out, let him wrap his palms around mine.

"It's a pleasure to meet you..." he says.

"Hannah," I say. "You can call me Hannah."

"Hannah," he says.

He smiles—genuine and generous. And suddenly I'm more disturbed by that than I am by the idea of him presenting as the opposite. At what point was Owen standing in front of him thinking, *Nicholas has to be good*? How could he have a smile like that if he wasn't? How could he have raised the woman who Owen loved?

It's hard to look at him so I look down, toward the ground, toward the dogs.

Nicholas follows my eyes. Then he bends down, pets his dogs on the back of their heads.

"This is Casper and this is Leon," he says.

"They're gorgeous dogs."

"They certainly are. Thank you. I brought them here from Germany. We are in the middle of their *Schutzhund* training."

"Meaning what?" I say.

"The official translation is 'protection dog.' They're supposed to keep their owners safe. I just think they're good company." He pauses. "Did you want to pet them?"

I don't think it's a threat, but it also doesn't feel like an invitation, at least not one I'm interested in accepting.

I look over at Charlie, who is still lying down on his chaise lounge, his elbow covering his eyes. His casual pose seems forced, almost like he is as uncomfortable being at his father's as I am. But then Nicholas reaches out, puts his hand on his son's shoulder. And Charlie holds his father's hand there.

"Hey, Pop."

"Long night, kid?" Nicholas says.

"You could say that."

"Let's get you a drink then," he says. "You want a scotch?"

"That sounds great," he says. "That sounds perfect."

Charlie looks up at his father, sincere and open. And I understand that I misread his anxiety. Whatever he's feeling badly about, it doesn't seem to be about his father, whose hand he still holds.

Grady was apparently correct about that much—whoever Nicholas might have been in his professional life, however ugly or dangerous, he's also the man that puts his hand on his grown son's shoulder and offers him a

nightcap after a hard night at work. That's who Charlie sees.

It makes me wonder if Grady is right about the rest. Or, I should say, how right Grady is about the rest. That to stay safe—to keep Bailey safe—I should be anywhere but here.

Nicholas nods toward Ned, who walks over to me. I flinch and move backward, putting my hands up.

"What are you doing?" I say.

"He's just going to make sure you're not wearing a wire," Nicholas says.

"You can take my word for it," I say. "What would I have to gain by wearing a wire?"

Nicholas smiles. "Those are the type of questions I don't get involved in anymore," he says. "But if you wouldn't mind..."

"Raise your arms, please," Ned says.

I look toward Charlie to back me up—to say this is unnecessary. He doesn't.

I do what Ned asks, telling myself that this is like a pat down at the airport, someone checking me out for the TSA. Nothing to think about. But his hands feel cold, and the entire time he moves them down my sides, I can see his gun on his hip. Ready to be used. And I can see Nicholas watching. The protection dogs by his side, apparently ready to be used too.

I feel my breath catch in my throat, trying not to show it. If one of these men were to see my husband, they would hurt him. They would hurt him so badly that nothing I do now would matter. Grady's voice runs through my head. *Nicholas is a bad man. These men are ruthless.*

Ned steps away from me and motions to Nicholas, which I assume means I'm all clear.

I meet Nicholas's eyes, still feeling the bodyguard's hands on my body. "Is this how you welcome all your guests?" I say.

"I don't tend to have many guests these days," he says.

I nod, straightening out my sweater, wrapping my arms around myself. Then Nicholas turns to Charlie.

"You know what, Charlie? I'd like some time alone with Hannah. Why don't you enjoy a drink by the pool? And head home."

"I'm Hannah's ride," he says.

"Marcus will take her where she needs to go. We'll talk tomorrow. Yeah?"

Nicholas gives his son a final pat. Then before Charlie can say anything, as if there is anything to say, Nicholas opens the doors to his house and walks inside.

He pauses in the doorway though. He pauses in the doorway, leaving me with a choice to make. I can leave now and go home with Charlie or I can stay here alone with him.

These are my choices—stay with Nicholas and help my family or leave my family and help myself. It feels like a weird test, as if I need to be tested, as if I haven't already gotten to the place where helping my family and helping myself have become the same thing.

"Shall we?" Nicholas says.

I can still leave here. I can still leave him. Owen's face is in my mind. He wouldn't want me here. Grady's face. *Go. Go. Go.* My heart races in my chest so loudly that I'm sure Nicholas can hear it. Even if he can't, I'm sure he can feel it— the tension coming off me.

There is a moment when you realize you are out of your depth. This is mine.

The dogs stare up at Nicholas. Everyone stares at Nicholas, including me.

Until I move in the only direction I can. Toward him.

"After you," I say.

Two Years Ago

"Bailey, I love your dress," I said.

We were in Los Angeles, having dinner at Felix, in Venice. I was working with a client on her house in the Venice Canals and Owen thought it would be a perfect opportunity for Bailey and me to spend some time together. This was probably the eighth time we'd met, but usually she tried to get out of doing more than just having a meal together. Usually, it wasn't the three of us for a whole weekend. We took her to see Dudamel at The Hollywood Bowl, which she loved. And now we were having dinner at the best Italian restaurant in Los Angeles, which she also loved. The only thing she didn't love? Doing it all with me there.

"That shade of blue looks so pretty on you," I said.

134

She didn't answer, didn't even offer a rote head shrug. She ignored me, downing some of her Italian soda.

"I have to go to the bathroom," she said.

And she was up, and gone, before Owen could answer.

Owen watched her go. When she disappeared around the corner, he turned toward me.

"I was going to surprise you," he said. "But maybe this is a good time to tell you that I'm taking you to Big Sur next weekend."

I was staying in Los Angeles for the week to finish work on my project in the Canals and then I was planning on flying up to Sausalito on Friday. We had talked about taking a ride down the coast to visit cousins of Owen's. The cousins, he said, lived in Carmel-by-the-Sea—a small, touristy town on the end of the Peninsula.

"There aren't actually cousins in Carmel-by-the-Sea?" I said.

"Someone's cousins, probably," he said.

I laughed.

"That's a benefit of me," he said. "I don't really have any cousins anywhere. I don't come with family at all, except Bailey."

"And she's a boon," I said.

He smiled at me. "You really feel that way, don't you?"

"Of course." I paused. "Not that the feeling is mutual."

"It will be."

He took a sip of his drink and moved it across the table toward me.

"Have you ever tried a bourbon Good Luck Charm?" he said. "I only drink it on special occasions. It's a mix of bourbon and lemon and spearmint. And it works. It brings luck."

"What do you need luck for?"

"I'm going to ask you something that you're going to say is too soon to ask you," he said. "Is that okay?"

"Is that the question?" I said.

"The question's coming," he said. "But not like this, not when my kid's in the bathroom, so you can start breathing again..."

He wasn't wrong. I hadn't taken a breath at all, worrying he was actually going to pop the question. I was terrified if he did that I wouldn't be able to say yes. And I wouldn't be able to say no.

"Maybe I'll ask you in Big Sur. We're staying on top of these cliffs, surrounded by oak trees, prettiest trees you've ever seen in your life. And you get to sleep beneath them, you sleep in yurts, which look up at all those trees, which look out on the ocean. One of them has our name on it."

"I've never slept in a yurt," I said.

"Well, you won't be able to say that next week."

He took his drink back, took a long sip.

"And I know I'm getting ahead of myself, but you should probably know, I can't wait to be your husband," he said. "Just for the record."

"Well, I'm not going on the record," I said. "But I feel the same."

This is when Bailey came back to the table. She sat down and dug into her pasta, a delicious southern Italian rendition of Cacio e Pepe. It was a decadent mix of cheese and spicy pepper and salty olive oil.

Owen leaned in and took a huge bite, right off her plate.

"Dad!" She laughed.

"Sharing is caring," he said, his mouth full. "Wanna hear something cool?"

"Sure," she said. And she smiled at him.

"Hannah got us all tickets to see the revival of *Barefoot in the Park* tomorrow night at the Geffen," he said. "Neil Simon is one of her favorites too. Doesn't that sound great?"

"We're seeing Hannah again tomorrow?" she said. The words were out of her mouth before she could stop herself.

"Bailey..." Owen shook his head.

Then he gave me an apologetic look: *I'm sorry she's being like this.*

I shrugged: *It's really okay, however she wants to be.*

I meant it. It was okay with me. She was a teenager who hadn't had a mother for most of her life. All she had was her father. I didn't expect her to be good with the prospect of sharing him with someone else. I didn't think anyone else should expect that of her either.

She looked down, embarrassed. "Sorry I just... have a lot of homework to do," she said.

"No, please, it's fine," I said. "I have a ton of work to do too. Why don't you two go to the play? Just you and your dad. And maybe we'll meet up back at the hotel, if you end up getting your work done?"

She looked at me, waiting for the catch. There was none. I wanted her to understand that. Regardless of what I was going to do right in terms of her, and what I was going to do wrong (and based on how things were starting, I knew I was going to do a lot that she considered wrong), there was never going to be a catch. That was a promise I could make her. As far as I was concerned, she didn't have to be nice. She didn't have to pretend. She only had to be herself.

"Honestly, Bailey. No pressure either way..." I said.

Owen reached over and took my hand. "I'd really like us to all go together," he said.

"Next time," I said. "We'll do it next time."

Bailey looked up. And I saw it there before she could hide it. I saw it in her eyes, like a secret she didn't mean to let me in on—her gratitude that I had understood her. I saw how much she needed someone to understand her, someone besides her father. How she thought it for just a second—that just maybe that someone might turn out to be me.

"Yeah," she said. "Next time."

And, for the first time, she smiled at me.

You Have to Do Some Things on Your Own

We walk down the long hallway lined with those art photographs, passing by one of the California Coast. The gorgeous coast near Big Sur. The photograph is at least seven feet long, a bird's-eye view of that almost impossible stretch of road carved into the divide of steep mountain, rock, and ocean. I'm so focused on it, taking some comfort in the familiar landscape, that I almost miss it when we pass the dining room. I almost miss the dining room table inside. My dining room table—the one that was featured in *Architectural Digest.* The table that helped launch my career.

It's my most reproduced piece. A big box store even started replicating the table after the *AD* feature came out.

It stops me. Nicholas said his wife carefully picked every piece of furniture in this house. What if she came across the feature in *Architectural Digest*? What if that was what led her to the table? It was possible. The feature was still on their website. Enough clicks in recent years could have led her to her lost granddaughter, if she had been searching closely enough, if she had only known what to be searching for.

Enough moves, after all, led me here, to this house I don't want to be in—a piece of my past finding me here, as if I need another reminder that everything that matters in my life is at the mercy of what happens now.

Nicholas pulls open a thick, oak door and holds it for me.

I avoid looking back at Ned, who is a couple of feet behind us. I avoid looking at the drooling dogs, who stroll by his side.

I follow Nicholas into his home office and take it in—the dark leather chairs and reading lamps, the mahogany bookshelves. Encyclopedias and classic books line the shelves. Nicholas Bell's diplomas and accolades hang on the walls. Summa cum laude. Phi Beta Kappa. *Law Review.* They are framed, proudly.

His office feels different from the rest of the house. It feels more personal. The room is filled with photographs of his family—on the walls, on the credenza, on the bookshelves. The desk is devoted entirely to photographs of Bailey, though. Photographs that are framed in sterling silver, photographs that are blown up into twice their normal sizes. They are all of small Bailey with her dark eyes, wide like saucers. And her tender curls—none of them yet purple.

Then there is her mother, Kate. She holds Bailey in nearly every photograph displayed: Bailey and Kate eating ice cream; Bailey and Kate cuddling on a park bench. I focus on one of Bailey at a few days old, in a little blue beanie. Kate lies in bed with her, her lips to Bailey's lips, her forehead against her forehead. It just about breaks my heart. And I assume that is why Nicholas keeps it in his view—why he keeps all of them in view—so every day they will just about break his.

This is the thing about good and evil. They aren't so far apart—and they often start from the same valiant place of wanting something to be different.

Ned remains in the hallway. Nicholas nods in his direction, and he closes the door. The thick, oak door. The bodyguard is in the hallway, the dogs in the hallway.

And the two of us are inside the office, alone.

Nicholas walks over to the bar and pours us each a drink. Then he hands mine over and takes a seat behind his desk, leaving me the chair in front of it—a deep, leather chair with gold etchings.

"Make yourself comfortable," he says.

I sit down with my drink in my hand. But I'm not happy about having my back to the door. I have the thought, for a second, that it isn't impossible someone could walk in and shoot me. One of the bodyguards could surprise me, the dogs could spring to action. Charlie himself could storm in. Maybe I have misunderstood what Owen put in his will. Maybe in this attempt to get Bailey and Owen out of what I have gotten them deeper into, I have left myself alone in the lion's den. A sacrifice. In the name of Kate. Or Owen. Or Bailey.

I remind myself that's okay. If I do what I came here to do, I'll accept that.

I put my drink down. And my eyes travel back to the photographs of baby Bailey. I notice one of her in a party dress, a bow wrapped around her head.

It provides me some comfort, which Nicholas seems to notice. He picks it up and hands it to me.

"That was Kristin's second birthday. She was already talking in full sentences. It was amazing. I took her to

the park, maybe the week after that, and we ran into her pediatrician. He asked her how she was doing and she gave him a two-paragraph answer," he says. "He couldn't believe it."

I hold the photograph in my hands. Bailey stares back at me, those curls a prelude to her whole personality.

"I believe it," I say.

Nicholas clears his throat. "I take it she's still like that?"

"No," I say. "Monosyllables are more her speed these days, at least when it comes to me. But, in general, yes. In general, she is a star."

I look up and see Nicholas's face. He looks angry. I'm not sure why. Is he mad that I have done something to make Bailey not like me the way I wish she would? Or is he mad he has never been given the chance himself?

I hand him back his photograph. He places it back on his desk, moving it obsessively to the place where it was before, keeping each piece of her that he has exactly where he can find it. It feels like a bit of magical thinking, like if he holds on to her just so, that will help him find her again.

"So, Hannah, what can I do for you, exactly?"

"Well, I am hoping we can come to an agreement, Mr. Bell."

"Nicholas, please," he says.

"Nicholas," I say.

"And no."

I take a breath, moving forward in my seat. "You didn't even hear what I have to say yet."

"What I mean is no, that's not why you're here, to come to an agreement," he says. "We both know that. You're here in the hopes that I'm not who everyone is telling you I am."

"That's not true," I say. "I'm not interested in who was right or who was wrong here."

"That's good," he says, "because I don't think you'd like the real answer. People don't tend to work that way. We have our opinion and we filter information into a paradigm that supports it."

"Not a big believer that people can change their minds?" I say.

"Does that surprise you?"

"Not usually, but you're a lawyer," I say. "Isn't convincing people a large part of the job?"

He smiles. "I think that you're confusing me with a prosecutor," he says. "A defense attorney, at least a good defense attorney, never tries to convince anyone of anything. We do the opposite. We remind everyone you can't know anything for sure."

Nicholas reaches for the brown box on his desk, a smoke box. He opens the lid and takes out a cigarette.

"I won't ask if you want one. Disgusting habit, I know. But I started smoking when I was a teenager, there wasn't much else to do in the town I came from. And I started smoking again in prison, same issue," he says. "Haven't been able to kick it since. When my wife was still with us, I'd try. Got those nicotine patches. Have you seen those? They help if you have the discipline, but I don't pretend to anymore. Not since I lost my wife... What's the point? Charlie gives me grief about it, but there isn't

much he can do. I figure I'm an old man. Something else will get me first."

He puts the cigarette to his mouth, silver lighter in hand.

"I'd like to tell you a little story, if you'll indulge me," he says. "Have you heard of Harris Gray?"

"I don't think so," I say.

He lights up, takes a long inhale.

"No, of course not. Why would you have? He introduced me to my former employers," he says. "He was twenty-one when I first met him and very low on the totem pole. If he had been any more senior, the gentlemen at the head of the organization would have called in one of their in-house lawyers to help him out and I wouldn't be sitting across from you now. But he wasn't. And so I was called in to defend him by the city of Austin. Random assignment sent to the public defender's office on a night I was working late. Harris was caught with some OxyContin. Not a ton, but enough. He was charged with intent to distribute. Which, needless to say, was his intent." He takes another drag. "My point is, I did my job, maybe a little too well. Usually Harris gets locked up for a period of time, thirty-six months, maybe seventy-two in front of the wrong judge. But I got him off."

"How did you do that?" I ask.

"The way you do anything well," he says. "I paid attention. And the prosecutor didn't expect that. He was sloppy. He didn't disclose some of the exculpatory evidence, so I got the case dismissed. And Harris went free. After that, his employers asked to meet me. They were impressed. They wanted to tell me so. And they wanted me to do it again for other members of their organization who found themselves in trouble."

I don't know what he expects me to say, but he looks at me, perhaps just to make sure I'm listening.

"These gentlemen at the head of Harris's organization decided I showed the kind of prowess that was integral to keeping their workforce... working. So they flew me and my wife to South Florida on a private plane. I had never flown first class before, let alone on a private plane. But they flew me there on their plane and put us up in a waterfront hotel suite with our own butler and made me a business proposition, one that felt difficult to say no to." He pauses. "I'm not quite sure why I mention the plane or the oceanfront butler. Maybe to suggest to you I was more than slightly out of my depth with my employers. Not that I'm saying that I didn't have a choice in working for them. I believe you always have a choice. And the choice I made was to defend people who, by law, deserve a proper defense. There's honor in that. I never lied to my family about it. I spared them some of the details, but they knew the general picture and they knew I didn't cross any lines. I did my job. I took care of my family. At the end of the day, it's not all that different from working for a tobacco company," he says. "The same moral calculation needs to be made."

"Except I wouldn't work for a tobacco company either," I say.

"Well, we don't all have the luxury of your strict moral code," he says.

There's an edge to how he says this. I'm taking a chance, arguing with him, except it occurs to me that this may be precisely why he is walking me through his history, the version of it he wants me to see. To test me. To test whether I'm going to do exactly that—argue, engage. This has to be why he presented his story this way—this is the first test. He wants to see whether I'll blindly let him spin in order to ingratiate myself to him or whether I'll be human.

"It's not that my moral code is so strict, but it seems to me that your employers are causing all sorts of harm and you knew that," I say. "And you still chose to help them."

"Oh, is that the distinction?" he says. "Do no harm? What about the harm you do when you rip a child from her family right after she loses her mother? What about the harm you do when you deprive that child of knowing everyone who could have reminded her of her mother? Everyone who loved her?"

That stops me. And I understand it now. Nicholas didn't run me through his story to present himself in a better light or to see if I'd engage with him. He told me so I'd lead him here, exactly to this place, where he could put his fury out there. He wanted to wound me with it. He wanted to wound me with the harm Owen caused—with the price of what he chose to do.

"I think it's his hypocrisy that I find the most staggering," he says. "Considering that Ethan knew exactly what I was doing and what I wasn't doing for my employers. He knew more than my own children. In part because he knew about encryption and computers. In part because he and I became close and I let him in. Let's just say he helped me do certain things. That's how he was able to cause the trouble that he did."

I don't know how to argue with that. I don't know how to argue with Nicholas about any of this. This is how he sees himself, as a family man, as a wronged man. And he sees Owen as the man who wronged him, which makes Owen just as guilty as he is. I can't argue with something so intrinsic to his understanding of himself. So I decide not to. I decide to go another way.

"I don't think you're wrong about that," I say.

"No?" he says.

"The one thing I know about my husband is that he would do anything for his family. And that's who you were to him, so I imagine he was quite involved with whatever you asked him to be involved with." I pause. "Until he decided he couldn't be anymore."

"I'd already been working for my employer for a long time when Ethan came into my daughter's life," he says. "For other clients too, mind you. I continued to fight for people you'd approve of, I still work for those clients, though I'm sure you're less interested in my good deeds."

I don't say anything. He isn't looking for me to say anything. He is looking to make his point, which is when he starts to get there.

"Ethan blamed me for what happened to Kate. He blamed the men I worked for when they had nothing to do with it. She was working for a Texas Supreme Court judge, a very influential Texas Supreme Court judge? Did you know that?"

I nod. "I did."

"Did you know this judge had shifted the Texas court sharply to the left and was imminently set to cast the deciding vote against a large energy corporation, the second largest in the country? If you want to talk about real criminals, these gentlemen were dispelling highly toxic chemicals into the atmosphere at a clip that could make your eyes swell shut."

He watches me.

"My point is that this judge, Kate's boss, was writing a majority opinion against the corporation. It would lead to sweeping reform and cost the energy corporation close to six billion dollars in improved conservation efforts. And the day after my daughter was killed, the judge came home to a bullet in his mailbox. What does that sound like to you? A coincidence? Or a warning shot?"

"I don't know enough," I say.

"Well, Ethan decided he knew enough. He couldn't be reasoned with that the men I had spent two decades protecting wouldn't do that to my daughter. That I knew these men and they had their own code of honor. That wasn't how they did things. Even their most nefarious colleagues didn't do things like that unprompted. But Ethan didn't want to believe it. He just wanted to blame me. And he wanted to punish me. As if I wasn't punished enough." He pauses. "There is nothing worse than losing your child. Nothing. Especially when you are someone who lives his life for his family."

"I understand that," I say.

"Your husband didn't. That was the part he could never understand about me," he says. "After his testimony, I spent six and a half years in prison as opposed to putting my family at risk by sharing my employer's secrets. Which they also view as service. So my employers continue to be generous with me now. Even though I'm retired, they consider me family."

"Even though your son-in-law caused many of them to go to prison?" I say.

"The people in the organization that were sent to jail along with me were mostly lower level," Nicholas says. "I took the hit for the upper management. They haven't forgotten that. They won't."

"So you could ask them to spare Ethan? Theoretically? If you wanted to?"

"Haven't you been listening to what I've been telling you?" he says. "I have no desire to do that. Besides, I can't pay off his debt. No one can."

"You just said they'd do anything for you."

"Maybe that's what you wanted to hear," he says. "What I said was they are generous with me about certain things. Not everything. Even families don't let everything go."

"No," I say. "I guess they don't."

This is when I realize something else that is going on. I figure it out in what Nicholas isn't owning—not yet, at least.

"You never liked Ethan, did you?" I say.

"Excuse me?" he says.

"Even before all of this, when you first met him, he wasn't your choice. For your daughter. This poor kid from South Texas, wanting to marry your only daughter. That couldn't have been what you wanted for her. He could have been you. He grew up in a town like the one you came from. He was a little too much like what you had organized your life to be better than."

"Are you a therapist?"

"Not at all," I say. "I just pay attention."

He looks at me amused. Apparently he likes this. He likes me throwing his words back at him.

"So what are you asking me?" he says.

"Everything you did, you did so your children would have different choices than you did. Kate. Charlie. Easier choices. So they'd have a promising childhood. The best schools, the greatest possibilities. So they wouldn't have to struggle so hard. And yet, one of your children drops out of architecture school and decides to take over your wife's family bar. Gets divorced."

"Careful," he says.

"And the other one chooses someone who was the last person you'd want for her."

"As my wife used to say, we don't get to pick who our children love. I made my peace that she chose Ethan. I just wanted her to be happy."

"But you had a feeling, didn't you? He wasn't the best person for Kate, he wasn't going to make her happy."

Nicholas leans forward, his smile gone.

"Did you know when Kate and Ethan started dating she didn't speak to me for a year?"

"I didn't even know Kate existed yesterday," I say. "So the details as to how that relationship played out aren't something I'm familiar with."

"She was a freshman in college and she decided she didn't want to have anything to do with us. With me, rather... her mother she never stopped talking to," he says. "That was Ethan's influence on her. We came through it though. Kate came home again and we made peace. That's what daughters do. They love their fathers. And Ethan and I..."

"You came to trust him?" I say.

"I did. I clearly shouldn't have," he says. "But I did. I could tell you one story about your husband and you'd never see him the same way again."

I stay quiet. Because I know Nicholas is telling the truth, at least the way he sees it. Owen, in his eyes, is bad. He has done bad things to Nicholas. He betrayed his trust. He stole his granddaughter. He disappeared.

Nicholas isn't wrong about any of that. He may not even be wrong about me. If I choose to wade into the chasm of doubt Nicholas wants to create about Owen, it won't be hard to go there. Owen isn't who I thought he was, at least not in the details. There are parts I wish didn't exist, parts I can't look away

from now. In one way or another, this is the deal we all sign when we love someone. For better or worse. It's the deal we have to sign again and again to keep that love. We don't turn away from the parts of someone we don't want to see. However quickly or long it takes to see them. We accept them if we are strong enough. Or we accept them enough to not let the bad parts become the entire story.

Because there is this too. The details are not the whole story. The whole story still includes this: I love Owen. I love him, and Nicholas isn't going to sway me that I shouldn't. He isn't going to sway me that I've been fooled. Despite everything, despite any evidence to the contrary, I believe I haven't. I believe I know my husband, the pieces and parts that matter most. It's why I'm sitting here. It's why I say what I say next.

"Regardless of that," I say, "I think you know how much my husband loves your granddaughter."

"What's your point?" he says.

"I want to make you a deal."

He starts to laugh. "We're back to this? Darling, you don't know what you're saying. It's not your deal to make."

"I think it is."

"How do you figure?"

I take a deep breath, knowing this is the moment of truth with Nicholas. It all comes down to how I sell him this. He'll hear me now or he won't. And the only thing that hangs in the balance is my family's future. My identity. Bailey's identity. Owen's life.

"I think that my husband would rather be killed than let you near your granddaughter. That's what I think. He proved that by uprooting everything and moving her away from here. As angry as you are about that, you respect him for being that kind of father. You didn't think he had that in him."

Nicholas doesn't say anything, but he doesn't look away either. He holds my eyes with his. I sense he's getting angry, a little too angry, but I keep going.

"And I assume you would like to have a relationship with your granddaughter? I think you want a relationship with her more than almost anything. That you'd be willing to make arrangements with your former colleagues to allow that to happen. From what you're saying, you can insist they leave us alone, let us keep living our lives," I say. "If you want to know your granddaughter, I think you know it's your only play. Either that or letting her disappear again. Because that is the other option, that is what I'm being told is the option I should be considering. WITSEC, starting over. Your granddaughter no longer allowed to be your granddaughter. Again."

And, like that. It happens. Like a flip has been switched, Nicholas's eyes going dark, going empty. His face pulsing red.

"What did you just say?" he says.

He stands up. I push back my chair, almost before I know I'm doing it. I push back closer to the door, as if it's possible he's going to lunge for me. It feels possible. Anything feels possible suddenly unless I get out of this room. Until I get away from him.

"I don't like to be threatened," Nicholas says.

"I'm not threatening you," I say, trying to hold my voice steady. "That wasn't my intention."

"So what is your intention?"

"I'm asking you to help me keep your granddaughter safe," I say. "I'm asking you to put me in a position where she can know her family. Where she can know you."

He doesn't sit back down. He stares at me. For a long time. For what feels like a long time.

"These other gentlemen," he says, "my former employers... I could potentially work something out with them. It would cost me quite a bit of capital. And they certainly would wonder who I am becoming in my old age. But... I think we could make sure they leave you and my granddaughter alone."

I nod, my throat catching as I start to ask the question, the next question I need to ask.

"And Ethan?" I say.

"No, not Ethan," he says.

He says it without equivocation. He says it with finality.

"If Ethan were to return, I couldn't assure you of his safety," he says. "His debt is too large. As I said, I can't protect Ethan, even if I were inclined to. Which, to be clear with you, I'm not."

I was prepared for this, for this intractable position. I was as prepared as I could get—a tiny part of me believing I wasn't going to have to acquiesce to it. To do what I came here to do. A tiny part of me in disbelief even as I start to do it.

"But your granddaughter," I say. "You could keep her safe? That's what you're saying?"

"Potentially, yes."

I stay quiet for a moment. I stay quiet until I trust myself to speak. "Okay then," I say.

"Okay then?" he says. "Okay then, what?"

"I'd like you to speak with your former employers about doing that," I say.

He doesn't even try to hide just how confused he is. He is confused because he thought he knew what I was doing here. He thought I was going to beg for Owen's life, for his safety. He doesn't understand that this is exactly what I'm doing, even if it doesn't look like it.

"Do you understand what you're considering here?" he says.

I'm considering an Owen-less life. That's what. A life that isn't anything like what I'd imagined for myself, but a life where Bailey gets to stay Bailey. She gets to stay the young woman she's become under Owen's watchful eye, the one he is so proud of. She'll continue to live her life, heading to college in two years, heading to whatever life she wants, not as someone else—not as someone she has to pretend to be—but as herself.

Bailey and I will go on—but without Owen, without Ethan. Owen, Ethan: the two of them start melding themselves together in my mind—the husband I thought I knew, the husband I didn't.

The husband I don't get to have. This is what I'm considering.

This is the deal I'm willing to make if Nicholas is. Which is when I tell him why.

"It's what Ethan wants," I say.

"To live his life without her?" he says. "I don't believe that."

I shrug. "It doesn't make it any less true," I say.

Nicholas closes his eyes. He looks tired suddenly. And I know it's partially because he is thinking of himself—of the daughter (and granddaughter) he's had to live his life without. But also because he is feeling sympathy for Owen, sympathy he doesn't want to feel, but he is feeling it all the same.

And there it is, what Nicholas least expects to show me. His humanity.

So I decide to tell him the truth, to say out loud the one thing I've been thinking all week, but haven't said out loud—not to anyone.

"I never really had a mother," I say. "She left when I was little, not much older than when you last saw your granddaughter. And she hasn't been involved in my life in any meaningful way. An occasional card or a phone call."

"And why are you telling me this?" he says. "For my compassion?"

"No, I'm not doing it for that," I say. "I had my grandfather, who was completely amazing. Inspiring. And loving. I had more than most people."

"So why?"

"I'm hoping it helps you understand that even in the face of what else I may lose here, my priority is your granddaughter. Doing what's right for her, whatever the cost, is worth it," I say. "You know that better than I do."

"What makes you say that?" he says.

"You were there first."

He doesn't say anything. He doesn't have to. Because he understands what I'm telling him. My mother never tried to fight for her family—she never tried to fight for me. That defines her. Apparently, I'm willing to give up everything to do the opposite for Bailey. One way or another, that will define me.

And if Nicholas agrees to what I'm asking him, it will define him too. We will have that in common. We'll have Bailey in common. We'll be the two people doing whatever is needed for her.

Nicholas crosses his arms over his chest, almost like in a hug, almost as if bracing himself against what he doesn't know if he should do.

"If a part of you thinks that it will change one day," he says. "That one day this will go away and Ethan can come back to you, slip back into your lives and they'll let it slide... it won't. That's untenable. These men, they don't forget. That can never happen."

I summon up the strength to say what I honestly believe. "I don't."

Nicholas is watching me, taking me in. And I think I have him. Or, at least, we are moving closer toward each other. For better or worse.

But there is a knock on the door. And Charlie walks in. Charlie who apparently stayed, despite Nicholas's instructions. Nicholas doesn't look

happy with him for that. But he's about to get less happy.

"Grady Bradford is at the front gate," he says. "And there are a dozen other U.S. marshals standing behind him."

"It took him long enough," Nicholas says.

"What do you want me to do?" Charlie says.

"Let him in," he says.

Then Nicholas turns and meets my eyes, the moment between us apparently over. "If Ethan comes home, they'll know," he says. "They'll always be watching for him."

"I understand that."

"They may find him even if he doesn't come home," he says.

"Well," I say. "They haven't found him yet."

He tilts his head, takes me in. "I think you're wrong," he says. "I think it's the last thing Ethan would want, to spend his life away from his daughter..."

"I don't think it's the last. No."

"What is?" he says.

Something happening to Bailey, I want to say. *Something happening because of Owen, because of his ties to all of this, that ends with Bailey getting hurt. That ends with her getting killed.*

"Something else," I say.

Protect her.

Charlie touches my shoulder. "Your ride is here," he said. "You need to go."

I get up to leave. Nicholas had seemed to hear me but then doesn't seem to want to hear anything at all. And it's over.

There is nothing else to do. So I follow Charlie. I walk toward the door.

146

Then Nicholas calls out after us.

"Kristin..." he says. "Do you think she'll be open to meeting me?"

I turn around and meet his eyes. "I think so," I say. "Yes."

"What will that look like?"

"She's going to be the one to decide how much and how often she sees you. But I will make sure that the well isn't poisoned. I'll make sure she understands that a lot of what happened here has nothing to do with how you feel about her. And that she should know you."

"And she'll listen to you?"

A week before the answer would have been no. Earlier today, wasn't it no too? She walked out of the hotel room, knowing I wanted her to stay put. And yet, I need him to believe the answer is yes. I need him to believe it and I need to believe it too, in order to pull this off. I know everything comes down to this.

I nod. "She will."

Nicholas pauses for a moment. "Go home," he says. "You'll be safe. Both of you. You have my word."

I take a deep breath in. I start to cry, right in front of him, covering my eyes quickly.

"Thank you," I say.

He walks up to me, hands me a tissue. "Don't thank me," he says. "I'm not doing it for you."

I believe him. I take his tissue anyway. Then I get out of there as quickly as I can.

The Devil Is in the Details

Grady says one thing in the car that will stay with me forever.

He says one thing to me on the way back to the U.S. Marshals' office where Bailey is waiting.

The sun comes up over Lady Bird Lake as we drive, Austin stirring in the early morning. When we merge onto the highway, Grady turns from the road to look at me—as if I would miss it otherwise, how unhappy he is with what I've decided to do.

Then he says it.

"They're going to get their revenge against Owen, one way or another," he says. "You should know that."

I hold his eyes, because it's the least I can do. Because I'm not going to let him scare me.

"Nicholas just doesn't let things go," he says. "You're being played."

"I don't think so," I say.

"And what if you're wrong?" he says. "What's the plan? To get on a plane, go back to your life and just hope you guys are safe? You're not safe. It doesn't work that way."

"How do you know?"

"Fifteen years' experience for one thing."

"Nicholas has no problem with me," I say. "I walked into this without knowing anything."

"I know that, you know that. But Nicholas doesn't, not beyond a doubt. And that's not the kind of wager he makes."

"I think this is an exceptional circumstance."

"Why?"

"I think he wants to know his granddaughter," I say. "More than he wants to punish Owen."

That stops him. And I can see him considering it. And I see him coming to the conclusion I came to—that, just maybe, that's true.

"Even if you're right about that, if you do this, you'll never see Owen again."

There it is, the buzzing in my ear, in my heart. Nicholas saying it, now Grady saying it. As though I don't know it. I do know, the gravity of it running through me, through my blood.

I'm giving up Owen. I'm giving up the chance that on the other side of all this, if there is another side, things will get to go back to Owen and me, together. That it will ever go back to the two of us. I can doubt that Owen is coming home. I can doubt it, but this way I know it.

Grady pulls over, on the side of the highway, trucks racing past, the wind shaking the car.

"It's not too late. Fuck Nicholas. Fuck whatever deal that Nicholas thinks you just made him," he says. "It wasn't your deal to make. You need to think of Bailey."

"Bailey is *all* I'm thinking about," I say. "What is best for her. What Owen would want me to do for her."

"You honestly think he'd want you to pick a path where he never gets to see her again? Never gets to have a relationship with her?"

"You tell me, then, Grady," I say. "You've known Owen a lot longer than I have. What do you think he wanted me to do when he disappeared?"

"I think he wanted you to lie low until I could help resolve this. Hopefully without his face ending up on the news. Hopefully with a way for you all to keep your identities intact. And, if necessary, with me finding a way to move you all so you could stay together."

"That's where you lose me," I say. "Every time."

"What are you talking about?" he says.

"What are the chances, Grady? If you moved us, what are the chances they find us anyway?"

"Slim."

"Meaning what? Five percent chance? Ten percent chance?" I say. "How about the leak last time? Was there a slim chance of that happening too? Because it did happen. Owen and Bailey were put in jeopardy under your watch. Owen wouldn't want to risk that. He wouldn't roll the dice on something happening to Bailey."

"I won't let anything happen to Bailey—"

"If these men did find us, they would get to Owen however they could, wouldn't they? They wouldn't stand on ceremony or particularly care if Bailey got caught in the crosshairs. That's correct, is it not?"

He doesn't answer me. He can't.

"Bottom line is that you can't guarantee that won't happen. You can't guarantee me and you couldn't guarantee Owen," I say. "Which is why he left her with me. Which is why he disappeared and didn't come directly to you."

"I think you're wrong about that."

"And I think my husband knows who he married," I say.

Grady laughs. "I would think if this taught you anything it's that no one knows who they marry," he says.

"I disagree," I say. "If Owen wanted me to sit still and let you run this, he would have said so."

"So how do you explain the email correspondence he sent me? The detailed files he kept? They're going to help ensure that Avett is punished for his crimes. The FBI is already into a plea deal that is going to put Avett away for the next twenty years..." he says. "How do you explain your husband doing that? How do you explain away his setting everything up so he could enter witness protection?"

"I think he did that for another reason."

"What's that?" he says. "His legacy?"

"No," I say. "Bailey's."

He smirks, and I can hear all the things he wants to tell me but feels like he can't tell me. I can hear all the things he knows about Owen—the same things Nicholas knows, but with a different sheen on them. Maybe he thinks telling me something closer to the truth will move me closer to his side. I've already picked a side though. Bailey's. And mine.

"I'm going to say this as simply as I can," he says. "Nicholas is a bad fucking man. He is going to punish you one day. Bailey may be safe, but if he can't get to Owen, he'll punish you in order to hurt him. You're completely expendable to him. He doesn't care about you."

"I don't think he does," I say.

"So then you have to know how risky this is for you to just try and go back to your life?" he says. "I can only protect you if you let me."

I don't answer him, because he wants me to say yes—yes, I'll let him protect me. Yes, I'll let him protect us. And I'm not going to say that. I'm not going to say it because I know this much is true: he can't.

Nicholas can probably get to us anyway, if that's what he wants to do. That's what this all has taught me. One way or another, things come back. Things *just* came back. So I may as well take a shot at doing the best thing for Bailey. And, by doing it this way, Bailey gets to stay Bailey.

No one gave her that choice before. She is already losing so much. The least I can do is give it to her now.

Grady starts the car up again, heads back into traffic. "You can't trust him. It's crazy for you to think you can. You cannot make a deal with the devil and expect it to turn out okay."

I turn away from him, look out the window. "Except I just did."

Finding My Way Back to Her

Bailey sits in the conference room. She is crying hard.

And before I even reach for her, she jumps up and races toward me. She holds tightly to me, her head in the crook of my neck.

I hold her like that, ignoring Grady, ignoring everything but her. She pulls away, and I take in her face, her eyes swollen from crying, her hair sticking to her head. She looks like the little girl version of herself, needing more than anything for someone to tell her that she is safe now.

"I shouldn't have left the room," she says.

I push her hair off her face. "Where did you go?"

"I shouldn't have gone anywhere," she says. "I'm sorry. But I thought I heard a knock on the door, which completely freaked me out. And then my cell phone rang and I picked it up. And there was all this static. I kept saying hello and getting that static. And so I went into the hall to see if I could hear any better, and I don't know…"

"You kept going?" I say.

She nods.

Grady shoots me a look, like I'm out of bounds to comfort her. Like I'm simply out of bounds. This is how he sees things now. His plan for Owen and Bailey is on one side of a line and I'm on the other. This is the only way he sees me now—as the main impetus toward his imagined solution.

"I thought it was my father on the phone. I don't know why. Maybe it was the static, or the blocked number. I just felt it strongly that he was trying to reach me and so I thought I'd walk for a minute, see if he tried me again. And when he didn't, I just… kept going. I didn't think too much about it."

I don't ask her why she didn't at least let me know before she left that she was okay. Maybe she didn't trust that I would let her do what she needed to do. That was probably a part of it. But I knew the other part wasn't about me, so I decide not to make it about me now. It's never about someone else the moment you realize it is up to you to get yourself to a better place. It's only about figuring out how to get there.

"I went back to the library," she says. "I went back to campus. I had Professor Cookman's roster with me and I just started going through the yearbook archive again. We ran out of there so fast after seeing the photograph of… Kate. And I just thought… I thought I needed to know. Before I left Austin."

"And did you find him?"

She nods. "Ethan Young," she says. "The last guy on that list…"

I don't say anything, waiting for her to finish.

"And then he did call," she says.

That stops me. "What are you talking about?" I say.

I almost faint. She spoke to Owen. She got to speak to Owen.

"You spoke to your father?" Grady says.

She looks up at him, offers a small nod.

"Can I talk to Hannah alone?" she asks.

He kneels down in front of her, not leaving the room. Which apparently is his way of saying no.

"Bailey," he says, "you've got to tell me what Owen said. It will help me help him."

She shakes her head, like she can't believe she has to have this conversation in front of him. Like she has to have it, at all.

I motion for her to tell me, to tell us. "It's okay," I say.

She nods, keeps her eyes on me. Then she starts talking.

"I had just found this photograph of Dad, he looked heavy and his hair was so long, like shoulder length... like basically a mullet. And I just... I almost laughed, he looked so ridiculous. So different. But it was him," she says. "It was definitely him. And I turned my phone on to call you, to tell you. And then I was getting an incoming call on Signal."

Signal. Why does that sound familiar? It comes back to me: the three of us eating dumplings at the Ferry Building a few months back, Owen taking Bailey's phone and telling her he was putting an app on it. An encryption app called Signal. He told her nothing on the internet ever goes away. He made some terrible joke about if she ever sends *sexy messages* (he actually said *sexy*), she should use the app. And she pretended to throw up her dumplings.

And then Owen got serious. He said if there were a phone call or a text she wanted to disappear, this was the app she should use. He said it twice so she took it in. *I'll keep it on there forever, if you never use the word* sexy *around me again,* she said. *Deal,* he said.

Now, Bailey is talking fast. "When I said hello, he was already talking. He didn't say where he was calling from. He didn't ask if I was okay. He said he had twenty-two seconds. I remember that. Twenty-two. And then he said that

he was sorry, sorrier than he could tell me, that he'd organized his life so he would never have to make this phone call."

I eye her as she fights back tears again. She doesn't look at Grady. She only looks at me.

"What did he say?" I ask gently.

I see it weigh on her. I see it weigh deeper than anything should weigh on such young shoulders.

"He said it's going to be a long time before he can call again. He said..." She shakes her head.

"What, Bailey?" I say.

"He said... he can't really come home."

I watch her face as she tries to process that—this terrible, impossible thing. The terrible, impossible thing he never wanted to say to her. The terrible, impossible thing I've been suspecting myself. The terrible, impossible thing I've *known*.

He is gone. He isn't coming back.

"Does he mean... ever?" she asks.

Before I even answer her, Bailey moans, quick and guttural, her voice catching against that knowledge. Against what she knows too.

I put my hand on her hand, her wrist, and hold her tight.

"I really don't think that..." Grady jumps in. "I just... really don't think you know that's what he meant."

I drill him with a look.

"And as upsetting as the phone call was," he says, "what we need to be talking about right now is next steps."

She keeps her eyes on me. "Next steps?" she says. "What does that mean?"

I hold her gaze so it's just the two of us. I move in close so she'll believe me when I tell her she is the one who gets to decide.

"Grady means where the two of us go now," I say. "Whether we go home…"

"Or whether we help you create a new home," Grady says. "Like I was talking to you about. I can find you and Hannah a good place to stay where you'll get to start over fresh. And your father will join you when he thinks it's safe to come back. Maybe he thinks that can't happen tomorrow, maybe that's what he was trying to say in the phone call, but—"

"Why not?" she interrupts him.

"Excuse me?"

She meets his eyes.

"Why not tomorrow?" she says. "Forget tomorrow. Why not today? If my father truly knows you're the best option, then why isn't he here with us now? Why's he still running?"

Before he can stop himself, Grady lets out a small laugh, an angry laugh, as though I coached Bailey to ask that question—as though it isn't the only question someone who knows and loves Owen would be asking. Owen avoided being fingerprinted. He avoided having his face plastered all over the news. He did what he needed to do to avoid outside forces blowing up Bailey's life. Her true identity. So where is he? There's nothing else to play out. There's no other move to make. If he were going to be coming back, if he thought it was safe to start over together, he'd be here now. He'd be here beside us.

"Bailey, I don't think I'm going to give you an answer right now that will satisfy you," he says. "What I can do is tell you that you should let me help you anyway. That's the best way to keep you safe. That's the only way to keep you safe. You and Hannah."

She looks down at her hand, my hand on top of it.

"So… that is what he meant then? My father?" she says. "He's not coming back?"

She is asking me. She is asking me to confirm what she already knows. I don't hesitate.

"No, I don't think he can," I say.

I see it in her eyes—her sadness moving into anger. It will move back again and from there into grief. A fierce, lonely, necessary circle as she starts to grapple with this. How do you begin to grapple with this? You just do. You surrender. You surrender to how you feel. To the unfairness. But not to despair. I won't let her despair, if it's the only thing I manage to do.

"Bailey…" Grady shakes his head. "We just don't know that's true. I know your father—"

She snaps her head up. "What did you say?"

"I said, I know your father—"

"No. I know my father," she says.

Her skin is reddening, her eyes fierce and firm. And I see it—her decision forming, her need cementing, into something no one can take from her.

Grady keeps talking but she is done trying to hear him. She is looking at me when she says the thing I thought she would say—the thing I thought she would come to all along. The reason I went to Nicholas, the reason I did what I did. She says it to me alone. She has given up on the rest of it. With time, I'm going to have to build that back. I'm going to have to do whatever I can to help her build that back.

"I just want to go home," she says.

I look at Grady, as if to say, *you heard her*. Then I wait for the thing he has no choice but to do.

To let us go.

Two Years and Four Months Ago

"Show me how to do it," he said.

We turned on the lights in my workshop. We had just left the theater, after our non-date, and Owen asked if he could come back to the workshop with me. *No funny business,* he said. He just wanted to learn how to use a lathe. He just wanted to learn how I do what I do.

He looked around and rubbed his hands together. "So… where do we start?" he said.

"Gotta pick a piece of wood," I said. "It all starts with picking a good piece of wood. If that's no good, you have nowhere good to go."

"How do you woodturners pick?" he said.

"*We* woodturners go about it in different ways," I said. "My grandfather worked with maple primarily. He loved the coloring, loved how the grains would turn themselves out. But I use a variety of woods. Oak, pine, maple."

"What's your favorite kind of wood to work with?" he asked.

"I don't play favorites," I said.

"Oh, good to know."

I shook my head, biting back a smile. "If you're going to make fun of me…" I said.

He put his hands up in surrender. "I'm not making fun of you," he said. "I'm fascinated."

"Okay, well then, without sounding corny, I think different pieces of wood appeal to you for different reasons," I said.

He moved over to my work area, bent down so he was eye to eye with my largest lathe.

"Is that my first lesson?"

"No, the first lesson is that to pick an interesting piece of wood to work with, you need to understand that good wood is defined by one thing," I said. "My grandfather used to say that. And I think that is definitely true."

He rubbed his hand along the piece of the pine I was working with. It was a distressed pine—dark in color, rich for a pine.

"What defines this guy?" he said.

I placed my hand over a spot in the middle, blanched to almost a blond, totally washed out.

"I think this part, right here, I think it could turn out interesting," I said.

He put his hand there too, not touching my hand, not trying—only trying to understand what I was showing him.

"I like that, I like that philosophy, is what I mean…" he says. "I kind of think you could probably say the same thing about people. At the end of the day, one thing defines them."

"What defines you?" I said.

"What defines you?" he said.

I smiled. "I asked you first."

He smiled back at me. He smiled, that smile.

"Okay, fine," he said. Then he didn't hesitate, not for a second. "There is nothing I wouldn't do for my daughter."

Sometimes You Can Go Home Again

We sit on the tarmac, waiting for the plane to take off. Bailey stares out the window. She looks exhausted—her eyes dark and puffy, her skin a splotchy red. She looks exhausted and she looks scared.

I haven't told her everything yet. But she understands enough. She understands enough that I'm not surprised she is scared. I'd be surprised if she weren't.

"They'll come visit," I say. "Nicholas and Charlie. They can bring your cousins if you want. I think that would be a nice thing. I think your cousins really want to meet you."

"They won't stay with us or anything?" she says.

"No. Nothing like that. We'll have a meal or two together. Start there."

"And you'll be there?"

"For all of it," I say.

She nods, taking this in.

"Do I have to decide about my cousins right now?" she says.

"You don't have to decide about anything right now."

She doesn't say anything else. She understands—as well as she is allowing herself to integrate it—that her father isn't coming home. But she doesn't want to talk about it, not yet. She doesn't want to navigate with me what things will look like without him, what they'll feel like. That too doesn't need to happen right now.

I take a deep breath in and try not to think about all the things that do have to happen—if not right now, then soon. The steps we'll have to take, one after another, to move through our lives now. Jules and Max will pick us up at the airport, our refrigerator stocked with food for today, dinner waiting on the table. But those things will have to keep happening, day in and day out, until they start to feel normal again.

And there are things I can't avoid happening, like the fallout coming several weeks from now (or several months from now), when Bailey is on her way to something like recovery, and I'll have my first still moment to think about myself. To think about what I've lost, what I'll never have back. To think only of myself. And of Owen. Of what I've lost—what I'm still losing—without him.

When the world gets quiet again, it will take everything I am not to allow the grief of his loss to level me.

The strangest thing will stop it from leveling me. I'll have an answer to the question that I'm only now starting to consider: If I had known, would I be here? If Owen told me, out of the gate, that he had this past, if he had warned me about what I would be walking into, would I have chosen him anyway? Would I have chosen to end up where I am now? It will remind me briefly of that moment of grace my grandfather provided shortly after my mother's departure when I realized I belonged exactly where I was. And I'll feel the answer move through me, like a blinding heat. Yes. Without hesitation. Even if Owen had told me, even if I had known every last bit. Yes, I would choose this. It will keep me going.

"What is taking so long?" Bailey says. "Why aren't we taking off yet?"

"I don't know. I think the flight attendant said something about a backup on the runway," I say.

She nods and wraps her arms around herself, cold and unhappy, her T-shirt unable to compete against the frosty airplane air. Her arms covered with goose bumps. Again.

Except this time I'm prepared. Two years ago—two days ago—I wasn't. But now, apparently, is a different story. I reach into my bag and pull out Bailey's favorite wool hoodie. I slipped the hoodie into my carry-on bag to have it ready for this moment.

I know, for the first time, how to give her what she needs.

It isn't everything, of course. It isn't even close. But she takes her sweater, putting it on, warming her elbows with her palms.

"Thanks," she says.

"Sure," I say.

The plane jerks forward a few feet, and then back. Then, slowly, it starts easing down the runway.

"There we go," Bailey says. "Finally."

She sits back in her seat, relieved to be on the way. She closes her eyes and puts her elbow on our shared armrest.

Her elbow is there, the plane is picking up speed. I put my elbow there too, and I feel her do it, I feel us both do it. We move a little closer to each other as opposed to doing the opposite.

It feels like what it is.

A start.

Five Years Later. Or Eight. Or Ten.

I'm at the Pacific Design Center in Los Angeles, participating in a First Look exhibition, with twenty-one other artisans and producers. I'm debuting a new collection of white oak pieces (mostly furniture, a few bowls and larger pieces) in the showroom they've provided.

These exhibitions are great for exposure to potential clients, but they are also like a reunion of sorts—and, like most reunions, somewhat of a grind. Several architects and colleagues stop by to say hello, catch up. I have done my best with the small talk, but I'm starting to feel tired. And, as the clock winds toward 6 P.M., I feel myself looking past people as opposed to at them.

Bailey is supposed to meet me for dinner, so I'm mostly on the lookout for her, excited to have the excuse to shut it all down for the day. She's bringing a guy she recently started dating, a hedge funder named Shep (two points against him), but she swears I'll like him. *He's not like that,* she says.

I'm not sure if she is referring to him working in finance or having the name Shep. Either way, he seems like a reaction to her last boyfriend, who had a less irritating name (John) and was unemployed. So it is, dating in your twenties, and I'm grateful that these are the things she's thinking about.

She lives in Los Angeles now. I live here too, not too far from the ocean—and not too far from her.

I sold the floating house as soon as Bailey graduated high school. I don't harbor any illusions that this means I've avoided them keeping tabs on us— the shadowy figures waiting to pounce should Owen ever return. I'm sure they are still watching on the off chance he risks it and comes back to see us. I operate as if they are always watching, whether or not he does.

Sometimes I think I see them, in an airport lounge or outside a restaurant, but of course I don't know who they are. I profile anyone who looks at me a second too long. It stops me from letting too many people get close to me, which isn't a bad thing. I have who I need.

Minus one.

He walks into the showroom, casually, a backpack over his shoulders. His shaggy hair is buzz cut short and darker, and his nose is crooked, like it's been broken. He wears a button-down shirt, rolled up, revealing a sleeve of tattoos, crawling out to his hand, to his fingers, like a spider.

This is when I clock his wedding ring, which he is still wearing. The ring I made for him. Its slim oak finish is perhaps unnoticeable to anyone else. I know it cold though. He couldn't look less like himself. There is that too. But maybe this is what you do when you need to hide from people in plain sight. I wonder. Then I wonder if it isn't him, after all.

It isn't the first time I think I see him. I think I see him everywhere.

I'm so flustered that I drop the papers I'm holding, everything falling to the floor.

He bends over to help me. He doesn't smile, which would give him away. He doesn't so much as touch my hand. It would be too much, probably, for both of us.

He hands me the papers.

I try and thank him. Do I say it out loud? I don't know.

Maybe. Because he nods.

Then he stands up and starts to head out, the way he came. And it's then that he says the one thing that only he would say to me.

"The could-have-been boys still love you," Owen says. He isn't looking at me when he says it, his voice low.

The way you say hello.

The way you say goodbye.

My skin starts burning, my cheeks flaring red. But I don't say anything. There's no time to say anything. He shrugs and shifts his backpack higher on his shoulder. Then he disappears into the crowd. And that's that. He is just another design junkie, on his way to another booth.

I don't dare watch him go. I don't dare look in his direction.

I keep my eyes down, pretending to organize the papers, but the heat coming off me is tangible—that fierce red lingering on my skin, on my face, if anyone is paying close enough attention in that moment. I pray they are not.

I make myself count to a hundred, then to a hundred and fifty.

When I finally allow myself to look up, it's Bailey that I see. It cools me out, immediately, centers me. She is walking toward me from the same direction Owen has gone. She's in her gray sweater dress and high-top Converse, her long, brown hair running halfway down her back. Did Owen pass her? Did he get to see for himself how beautiful she has become? How sure of herself? I hope so. I hope so at the same time I hope not. Which way, after all, spares him?

I take a deep breath and take her in. She walks hand in hand with Shep, the new boyfriend. He gives me a salute, which I'm sure he thinks is cute. It isn't.

But I smile as they walk up. How can I not? Bailey is smiling too. She is smiling at me.

"Mom," she says.

Acknowledgments

I started working on this book in 2012. There were many times I put it aside, but I couldn't seem to let it go. I am so grateful to Suzanne Gluck, whose astute guidance on each iteration helped me to find the story that I was hoping to tell.

Marysue Rucci, your thoughtful edits and sage comments have elevated this novel in every way. Thank you for being the best partner a writer could hope for, my dream editor, and a dear friend.

My gratitude to the amazing team at Simon & Schuster: Dana Canedy, Jonathan Karp, Hana Park, Navorn Johnson, Richard Rhorer, Elizabeth Breeden, Zachary Knoll, Jackie Seow, Wendy Sheanin, Maggie Southard, and Julia Prosser; and to Andrea Blatt, Laura Bonner, Anna Dixon, and Gabby Fetters at WME.

Sylvie Rabineau, we've been in this thing together since book one, day one. Thank you for being my most trusted advisor, Jacob's "Sylv," and one of my favorite people on the planet. I love you.

I am indebted to Katherine Eskovitz and Greg Andres for their legal expertise, to Simone Puglia for being a great Austin guide, and to Niko Canner and Uyen Tieu for the gorgeous woodturned bowl that sits on my desk, and that inspired so much of Hannah.

For reading many drafts (over the last eight years!) and providing other invaluable help and insight, thank you: Allison Winn Scotch, Wendy Merry, Tom McCarthy, Emily Usher, Stephen Usher, Johanna Shargel, Jonathan Tropper, Stephanie Abram, Olivia Hamilton, Damien Chazelle, Shauna Seliy, Dusty Thomason, Heather Thomason, Amanda Brown, Erin Fitchie, Lynsey Rubin, Liz Squadron, Lawrence O'Donnell Jr., Kira Goldberg, Erica Tavera, Lexi Eskovitz, Sasha Forman, Kate Capshaw, James Feldman, Jude Hebert, Kristie Macosko Krieger, Marisa Yeres Gill, Dana Forman, and Allegra Caldera. And a special thank you to Lauren Levy Neustadter, Reese Witherspoon, Sarah Harden, and the incredible team at Hello Sunshine— your belief in this book is nothing short of a dream come true.

My heartfelt gratitude also to the Dave and Singer families and to my wonderful friends for their unwavering love and support. And to the readers, book groups, booksellers, and book lovers whose company I am so grateful to keep.

Finally, my guys.

Josh, I'm not quite sure what to thank you for first. It probably should be something about how this novel wouldn't exist without you and your faith in me (it wouldn't), or how I can't quite believe I get to have a partner who, after thirteen years, I'm still so crazy about. But is it okay if I start with the coffee? I so love the coffee. And I love you beyond all measure.

Jacob, my inimitable, big-hearted, wise, hilarious little man. I was reborn when you entered this world. And now I walk through it grateful and humbled by everything you teach me. What can I say, kid, that I don't tell you every day? The great blessing of my life is being your mama.

CPSIA information can be obtained
at www.ICGtesting.com
Printed in the USA
BVHW061405151221
624023BV00008B/542